THE NIGHT
MARA

ANDREW
McCUTCHEON

Novel by Andrew McCutcheon. Illustrations by Martin Masi.

ISBN 978-1-7324876-1-1
ISBN 978-1-7324876-0-4 (ebook)

About the Author

Debut author, Andrew McCutcheon draws inspiration from both fiction and non-fiction. Raised in Southern California, and later settling in New England, his diverse upbringing and influences are the foundation of his imagination and creative drive. The Night Mara is the first novel of many more to come, including a collection of short stories. Andrew's writing also extends beyond print to music with his, soon to be released, experimental blues album, "Desert Highway."

Andrew has served the public and peered through a unique lens into the human condition as a Paramedic for the city of Bridgeport, Connecticut. He does this while finishing his undergraduate in Health Science at Quinnipiac University, with intention to pursue a Physician Assistant master's program. Andrew finds solace in travel, nature photography, hiking, and camping in the deep woods of the Appalachians and Adirondacks, where the dark beyond the campfire beckons his imagination.

Dedicated to my family and friends who have supported my crazy passions. To everyone who has a dream, follow it to the horizon and work the midnight oil to achieve it. Learn, read, write, love, rest, and be happy along the way. Thank you to my readers and enjoy my story into the unknown…

"The slow transition from warmth to cold. Leaves green, turning bright red, and brilliant gold.

Before the unforgiving winter, in a world lost within an age of gilded wonder.

We scramble to harvest and gather, while some choose, to pillage and plunder.

Life endures the surrender. Only to hope one day, for its own revival.

As it desperately clings on for survival"

-Andrew McCutcheon

"Whenever a mortal falls in sin.

Tears fall from angels' eyes.

And that is why at times there fall bright

stars, from out the skies"

-William Shakespeare

"Once Pandora's box is opened, it cannot be

undone. Let the fire of our passions burn on

for eternity."

-Andrew McCutcheon

PART I

THE VISIONS

CHAPTER ONE

Lost deep within her thoughts, Beverly Hollinger paced near a large window overlooking Manhattan's cityscape, wishing for a way out. From across the room, an older gentleman observed her restless, yet poised gait as he twirled a pen between his fingers. The well-tailored man repositioned his pressed vintage-suede sweater vest. Readjusted his matching black tie, then rested a notepad over his armrest. He methodically studied her graceful movements for a moment, then leaned forward with concern. Before she turned away, he caught a glimpse of bewilderment and a sorrow-stricken face. Beverly stopped short near the window as the man spoke, interrupting her chaotic mind.

"It's been quite some time since I last saw you. How've you been?" She gave no response. "Your message seemed urgent. What's been troubling you, Beverly?" He asked in a deep monotone voice, followed again by silence as she collected her thoughts. Without turning to him, she placed her hand against the window and leaned toward her reflection. Her breath left a fog of words waiting to be said against the glass.

Beverly paused for a moment, "Well, it's hard to explain. I've been experiencing these horrible nightmares for the past several months now. You may recall from before, the visions I had from my childhood. Well, they're back again. More frequent and intense than ever before. I don't know what else to do or who to turn to for answers," Beverly muttered as she stared out toward Central Park.

The once plentiful leaves made their final transitions from green to vibrant shades of red, orange, and yellow. Most took on a rusty reddish-brown hue that encapsulated the sparse tree canopies below. The lifeless, wilted leaves were discarded from their origins and left littered across the landscape. Beverly observed the park from fourteen-stories with her hand leaned against the glass, as if to brace herself from falling through. From the high-rise, she watched several children kick away the fallen leaves along the trails. Locals, tourists, joggers, and families made their way through the park—during an unusual mild mid-October weekend—to bask in the warmth before the coming of winter.

Beverly's reflection showed a young woman in her mid-twenties with long flowing chestnut brown hair. She wore a light blue blouse and a beige knee-length skirt, which was snug against her petite malnourished frame. Her weary light bluish-grey eyes stared back at her with an innocent and youthful soul as she continued to look down toward Central Park. Second-guessing, *why can't I enjoy life like everybody else?* Instead..., she was here. Enclosed in a psychiatrist's office and isolated from the rest of the world.

"What do you think caused all this, Beverly?" The psychiatrist inquired from his Irving brown leather armchair. Beverly's reflection in the window shifted a quick disconcerting glare back at him. The doctor coughed as he readjusted himself in his chair. He fidgeted with his pen before placing it on his notepad, which now rested over his lap. Beverly continued to stare out the window as he waited for a response during the awkward silence.

Despite her age, Beverly showed no signs of her physical or mental youth. Her lifeless smile, pale complexion and dark circles under her eyes told another story. Someone who was in constant tidal lock with the epic battle and struggles deep within their mind. In consequence, her youth and innocence were slowly stripped away, day by day. Beverly broke her trance-like stare from the window and lifted her hand away, leaving behind a fleeting handprint that slowly vanished like a ghostly apparition. Without showing any expression, she turned toward the man sitting across the room.

Doctor Spitzer stared down at his notepad to avoid direct eye contact with his patient. He was an older reputable man of short stature and enormous ego, who also fought with his diminished, nearly forgotten youth. Many certifications, awards, and news articles laid scattered across his office walls like trophies from his academic and professional career. New York City's top ten psychiatrists—one front page cover reads with his name listed as number eighth—as it hung in a plaque against the wall. Even though the list was in alphabetical order, he still took offense to the ranking and saw himself as number one. Doctor Jeffrey W. Spitzer prided himself on knowing he had treated them all, no matter how difficult the case. Now he had to prove that fact to himself once again.

He made his start at a psychiatric ward on Riker's Island prison during his fellowship, followed by a career of collaborating with New York's finest. His experience and knowledge made him an invaluable asset to the police department, as he interrogated and discovered the motives of the city's most notorious, violent criminals. His thirty-five-year service with NYPD involved assessing and treating every special-victims case. Year after year, he had to delve deep inside the minds of the deranged as well as the innocent.

These long-term stresses left him jaded and case-hardened, yet still highly competent and professional. In his later years, he chose to expand his expertise in this comfortable out-patient private practice to solve people's ordinary and mundane life struggles.

Despite every patient he had treated before, he knew with intuitive certainty that Beverly's case was similar, however still unique in its own right. He knew she was a victim, and her struggles were real. He had to figure out a way to help her but needed more time. Time was a crucial part of his assessment process, which he could always rely on. He saw the fear and anguish in Beverly's eyes, now manifested in her mind as a result of post-traumatic stress from her early childhood. He tried to envision the terror in his mind as he reminisced back to his early career.

Day after day, night after long night, he had to interrogate the undertow of a narcissistic society. Their calculated movements and expressions designed to manipulate and misconceive others tested his patience to the breaking point. He wondered how much of their actions were genetic or from environmental upbringing, as he spent his entire career trying to find the answers. He thought how could someone with obvious intelligence to do good and benefit others, just let it all slip away and turn toward evil. He understood that emotions, on a rare occasion, could sometimes drive someone to madness, but when a person lacks all empathy, what is it that draws them to chaos. He concluded that apathy would always eventually lead to entropy.

During another awkward silence, he recalled the diminishing mental health of his former patients and how Beverly's case wasn't an exception to that fact. Doctor Spitzer knew something deep down troubled her and himself, but couldn't articulate it in his head or opinions at the moment. Because of this, he didn't want to look straight into her eyes; he didn't want to see in. He didn't want to feel nor want to remember his own past. He remained silent and stared right through her as she walked back toward the designated therapeutic couch.

"Well, Doc. Not to be rude, but isn't this why I'm here? For you to figure out why I'm struggling with all of this." Beverly said to him in a calm but concerned demeanor as she settled herself onto the couch. "I haven't had a good night's rest in…well, I can't remember when," she said, trying to find a position of comfort, which appeared near impossible.

The doctor regained his composure, "I understand this, Beverly. However, I need to know more about what you are experiencing. Many sleep disorders are caused by underlying problems in our subconscious. This is why you're still having nightmares after all these years," he explained, as he glanced over at her, before turning away again.

"Doctor, like I've mentioned in the past. These aren't just some silly reoccurring dreams. I'm wide awake and cannot move when I have these encounters. It's like a nightmarish reality for me almost every night," Beverly explained as he nodded to show that he understood. Doctor Spitzer had a perplexed look on his face as he tried to conceive a logical answer to what could possibly cause these new episodes.

She continued, "as you know, my life was not easy in the slightest. I had no other family to help me. My world was torn apart in an instant. Growing up in an all-girl orphanage, I never got the chance to live or experience the rest of my—" she turned away.

"Your childhood," he said, then handed her a tissue.

"It wasn't only that…, I can still remember the nights when I would be visited while the other girls slept," she said as Doctor Spitzer turned to her with a concerned look.

"I do remember you mentioning this. Who would visit you, Beverly?"

"I honestly don't know, Doc, and can vaguely remember all the details. During the middle of the night, I would see a shadowy figure standing in the corner of my room, staring back at me. It would just linger there in the darkness, motionless, then poof, vanish. But it was only during the last few months that I started to see these visions again," she said sobbing as the tissues fell from her hands onto her lap. Beverly turned her head and made direct eye contact with her psychiatrist. Tears glistened in her eyes with an eerie dissonance that revealed a pain locked deep within her otherwise emotionless face.

Doctor Spitzer stared down at his notepad for a moment, then back to her, "I do recall the past descriptions of this shadowy figure in your room. As you lie awake and paralyzed, correct?" She nodded as he continued, "Beverly, what you're describing to me is very similar to what you had experienced during your childhood," he said, pulling out a separate smaller notepad from his jacket pocket.

Doctor Spitzer leaned forward in his chair, "you've also told me before that you have never been physically harmed and usually would forget everything once you're fully awake." She didn't respond, only listened as he continued, "Beverly, all of these visions, are manifested in your mind while half-asleep. I'll prescribe you some medications that will help you," he said, then scribbled something down in his other notepad.

"Doctor, but—" she said, turning to him.

He interrupted her, "Beverly, everything that you have told me thus far is a chronic case of sleep paralysis, where you're partially awake while still in a dream-state. I've seen cases like these before, and it's all related to your post-traumatic stress. With my assistance, we can resolve this together," he explained as she stared back down at her lap.

Spitzer glanced down at his gold Rolex watch, then hastily continued, "unfortunately, we've run out of time, and I'm booked solid for the rest of the day. We'll have to reschedule in a few weeks, but take these for now," he said, leaning over to hand her several small pieces of paper.

She didn't extend her hand, so he laid them across her lap. "One is a benzodiazepine, for when you feel anxious, the other is Trazodone to help you sleep and improve your mood. We'll discuss anti-depressants when we meet again." Beverly looked over to him with a blank stare, then back down at the papers he had given to her.

A phone intercom beeped on a small table next to his armchair. He simultaneously rushed his hand over to press the button. His secretary responded, "Doctor, your new consultation appointment is here."

"Thanks, Autumn. Give me a few minutes I'm about to wrap things up here." He replied with relief, then released his finger off the intercom button. Beverly collected the tissues and prescriptions on her lap, then raised herself off the couch.

"I'm sorry I can't describe more to you, but it feels so real sometimes. Part of me knows it's just my mind playing tricks on me…but the other part of me doesn't. I hope you'll understand what I can't describe to you," she said with her head lowered. Doctor Spitzer nodded, then placed his hand over her shoulder as he escorted her to the door.

"I understand, and it's okay to feel this way, Beverly. Rest assured that none of this is real, and it's only your imagination while half-awake. Like I mentioned earlier, this is triggered by chronic stress and lack of sleep. With these medications and regular sessions with me, I'll help you overcome this. I'll see you in a few weeks, okay?" He reassured her as they walked toward the door. Beverly made eye contact with him and forced a closed smile of relief that contrasted her distraught face.

"Thank you again for everything, Doctor. I know I sounded a little bit crazy telling you all of this. But, I always trusted you and hope that these medications could make me feel whole again," she said, then shook his hand before exiting. Doctor Spitzer closed the door behind her, then looked down at his notepad with guilt if he had failed her. He knew deep down Beverly's traumatized past still haunted her to this very day. He had to now struggle in his own mind, on how to comprehend these new visions.

He sighed, then waited for a moment before opening the door again to the office lobby. "I'm ready for Mr. Jones's appointment. Please send him in." Doctor Spitzer walked over to his office window and looked out toward Central Park. He watched the withered leaves slowly fall from the trees below, then somberly proceeded back to his leather armchair. Another new customer for his mundane practice entered the room, closing the door behind him.

CHAPTER TWO

Beverly Hollinger pulled into the driveway of her two-story condominium, located in the quiet upstate New York town of Silver Lakes. She placed her car in park, then leaned over to grab the prescription bottles from the glove compartment. With hazy recollection, she recalled the faded memories of her childhood as she stared down at the medications. The unexplainable nightly visitations she had encountered in the city orphanage, along with experiences from recent. *Is it all just in my head? How could it be anything else? Doctor Spitzer sees it, so should I.*

Beverly placed the bottles back into the glove box, then exited her all-wheel-drive, dark-green Subaru sedan. From across the street, her neighbor glanced over his shoulder to examine his recently moved-in neighbor as he tended to his flowers. Beverly gave a quick wave without receiving the same gesture in return as he turned his attention back to his tulip bed. Beverly had seen him outside doing yard work over the last several days but had never bothered to introduce himself or extend a welcoming invitation. The only thing she knew about him was his surname, Mr. Kelly, which was hand-painted in white across his bright red mailbox.

Beverly disregarded his unfriendliness and walked over to her front door. The key slid into the lock, as she stared down the street for a moment to watch the leaves hypnotically dance in the breeze, before settling on the deserted streets. The sudden ring of her cell phone made her jump as it echoed in the silence of the small cul-de-sac. Her neighbor paid no attention, as his focus was caring for his flowers, now withered and decimated from last week's unexpected early frost.

"Adam, you scared the shit out me! I literally just got back from the city. I'm sorry I didn't let you know what time I was coming home," she said as she walked into the house. Before closing the door, she caught her neighbor staring over before turning away. She pushed the door shut, locking it with chain and deadbolt.

"It's okay. I know how shitty the service can be on the interstate. I'm glad you made it home safe and hope you had a great time with your friends," Adam said as she paused for a moment to collect her thoughts.

Beverly leaned over to pet her German Shepherd, then went into her innocent alibi, "It was fun for sure and we went downtown to see a play. It was decent, nothing to write home about," she said with a quick laugh. "I'm pretty tired, though, and will probably get ready for bed soon," as she walked to the kitchen to pour kibble into Tiny's bowl. She went upstairs listening to Adam talk about his day, then turned on the faucet to prepare a hot bath.

"Glad everything went well, hon. Hopefully, I can get some time off in the next few days to come over and see ya. So you know, I did come by earlier to walk Tiny for you. Also, remember that our camp trip is next weekend," Adam told her as she walked into her bedroom,

She pulled down the bedsheets, then grabbed her bathrobe from the closet. "Thank you, and of course, honey! I can't wait for our trip too and will see you soon. Sorry, I'm just exhausted from this weekend and will talk to you tomorrow, okay? She wished him a good night, then laid her phone on the nightstand. Not accustomed to the silence of living alone in the suburbs, she turned on the radio to accompany her for the night.

The evening sun sat above the horizon, illuminating a golden aura across her bedroom wall. Beverly walked toward her window as the street lights flickered on, and noticed her neighbor had retreated into his home for the night. His once-thriving garden was now slowly dying and left unattended until sunrise. She took in the panoramic view of the pine, maple, and oak trees off in the distance before drawing the curtain shades closed. Beverly slowly took off her blouse as she stood in front of the mirror, which hung on the closet door.

In the reflection, she examined the small multi-colored bruise on her upper right arm by her shoulder. She disregarded it, then unclothed herself. The radio and nightstand lamp were left on as a beacon of solitude throughout the rest of the evening. She had recently moved into her new home last week and still hadn't gotten used to not having any roommates. Every passing day she continued to reflect on her past and remained grateful for all of the success she had earned through hard work and perseverance. However, there were other memories she wished to forget.

Beverly was ten-years-old when she witnessed the breaking news event, which led to the brutal slaying of her parents, along with forty-seven other innocent lives. That night, her parents were attending their favorite downtown Brooklyn theater, "The Night Owl," before the unthinkable had occurred. Moments before the event, she had given her babysitter Denise, a hard time about going to bed. Unaware of what would tragically unfold across town, young Beverly demanded to stay up past her bedtime to finish watching her favorite cartoon. Denise finally caved into her simple demands, after receiving the innocent guilt treatment from Beverly's gentle blue eyes and smile.

Beverly was an only child, used to getting her way, and knew exactly how to do it. She lived a happy childhood, tucked away in a quiet neighborhood in Brooklyn, New York with her family. Her mother, Judith, worked as a part-time hairdresser and stayed at home the majority of the time to attend to her daughter's needs. Her father, Johnathan, a New York native, was a white-collar life insurance broker in Manhattan, who provided a comfortable lifestyle for his family.

Her father was always adamant for families to have the best life insurance policies in case of the most unpredictable events. He always put his family first and urged his clients to do the same. *Leave them something behind. A rainy day fund*, he would always tell them. In reality, though, no one could ever accurately predict when that big storm would hit, only to plan for the worst and hope for the best. He still continued to advocate and heed his own advice, unaware of his own family's unforeseeable bleak forecast.

On most weekends, her parents would routinely bring her along to see the theatrical shows and plays. Beverly loved to watch the magic come alive on stage. The actors, costumes, and props that were used created a fantastical reality for her. She loved the comedy and drama alike. It formed a perfect circle in her imagination, which opened new doors to her own creativity and motivated her to pursue acting in middle school. Tonight, Denise would be the only audience for many of Beverly's original plays, and recited lines from her favorite classics.

Even though Beverly begged to go with them, she understood that her parents needed a night to themselves. Disappointed at first, she was still ecstatic to know that her favorite babysitter was coming over for the evening. Denise Bedford was twenty-two, and had known the Hollingers for the past several years and considered part of their family. She was Judith's favorite client and had been initially offered to babysit in exchange for a free haircut every month. Denise was their reliable go to on last-minute bases, even though Beverly was nearing an age where she could be left home alone.

Beverly didn't defend this fact to her parents since she loved it when her babysitter would come over. Beverly adored her like an older sister that she never had. Denise also enjoyed their time together and never too eager to send her off to bed early. Judith would sometimes joke to Johnathan in her Bostonian accent, *they ah like sistas from another mothah*. He agreed, but didn't want any pressure to have another child; one was enough for him.

Quarter to ten in the evening, Beverly laid heavy-eyed on the couch next to Denise as they watched her favorite cartoon until, within a split second, Beverly's childhood and innocence were shattered. A breaking news broadcast interrupted their program as the camera focused on the outside of a worn-down brick building. They both sat in silence as the news reported the aftermath of a crazed gunman who carried out his heinous and cowardly act. The field reporter gave vague details of a mass shooting that took place at the local downtown theater, where they both knew her parents were attending that evening. Denise held her tight that night as they cried in each other's arms.

They witnessed the chaotic events unfold in front of their eyes as if in slow motion—a grueling slow-motion, where time briefly came to a standstill, like a photograph imprinted in her mind. Knowing the outcome was grim, they decided to keep the TV off and lie next to each other in Beverly's bed for the rest of the evening. She prayed that her parents, at the last minute, decided not to attend the show. Instead, they would walk through the front door any moment, oblivious to what had just occurred. She desperately awaited their laughter downstairs after enjoying a night out together. Unaware that they had only escaped their deaths by mere happenstance.

Reality finally set in, as the house remained silent throughout the night, washing away any hope she might have had left as tears ran down her face. Denial and fear eventually led to sorrow and anger. Swirling and thrashing, wave upon crashing wave, against the innocent pristine shores of her consciousness. The chaos from the broadcast wasn't a new thing for her as she was born in a post 9/11 world of domestic and foreign terrorist attacks. However, she never believed the evil of this world would take the lives of her parents. Watching her life and whom she loved, washed out to the mortal sea, taking them away from her, forever. Not knowing what else to do, Denise called the police and held Beverly close, trying to console her the best she could through the endless night.

Then came the knock at the front door. During the early morning before sunrise. A knock that would radiate throughout her mind for an eternity. Denise stayed with her until officers arrived to notify them of what they already knew deep down inside. The pain and sadness radiated to her core—as if she had swallowed boiling liquid metal—and felt it run through her veins before dissolving into her heart, mind, body, and soul.

Beverly, now emotionally numb, remained quiet as the police made their way inside after her babysitter invited them in. Denise looked back over her shoulder toward Beverly, who watched them through the railing at the top of the staircase. Through watery eyes, Beverly stared back at Denise for some sense of security and comfort, as the officers explained the situation from the other end of the room.

The officers made their way over to Beverly to try and comfort her, explaining that she would have to go with them to the station. One officer went to pick her up, which caused a hailstorm of fury as she ferociously fought back with fear and defiant anger. Beverly let out a blood-curdling scream, which could be heard throughout the quiet neighborhood, as they forced her from her home, and sequentially her childhood.

Two officers stayed behind to talk to Denise while the Sergeant placed Beverly in the cruiser, as she continued to kick and scream for help. Denise watched helplessly from the porch, like a parent witnessing their child being swallowed up by the riptide, as the Sergeant closed the back door to the police car. The emergency flashers turned off as they made their way down the street that early misty spring morning. Denise lost sight of the tail lights in the fog, as neighbors gathered outside to witness all the commotion. That was the last time Beverly would ever see her home and parents again.

Tonight, Beverly tried to repress those memories, as she made her way to the bathroom. She left the door, half-opened across from her dimly-lit room as the rest of the house resided in complete darkness. She hung her yellow smiley-face towel over the rack, then placed her bathrobe on the sink. She looked through the half-opened doorway into the narrow hallway illuminated by her bedroom lamp.

Where is Tiny? She wondered, knowing he was probably still downstairs, finished with his late dinner and resting on the couch after a hard day. She chuckled at the thought as she slipped into the warm bath. She grabbed a small bottle of body lotion and slathered it in one hand, applying it against her skin.

Reclined with her eyes closed, she tried to forget about today's meeting with her doctor and focused only on the good that had came into her life. She thought of

Adam, her new condo, and promising career. She had some remorse for making up a story of why she had to go down to the city with short notice. However, she didn't want to appear crazy to him. He is her first love, as this house is her first real home.

I'm no longer afraid. Never again. I will not let this fear overpower me. She sighed a breath of relief as she laid back in the tub. Beverly rested her eyes and remembered her accomplishments despite all the hardships. Clinging only on to the good memories, and not the evil ones that had once encapsulated her entire life. While laying in the comforting water, she reflected on these conflicted memories before falling asleep.

No matter how hard she tried, Beverly would never forget the long six-year struggle of bouncing between multiple orphanage shelters throughout the inner city. She never made what-you-would-call genuine friends during her involuntary orphanage residency and had no other extended family to adopt her. Her mother had no other siblings, and both her grandparents had passed away when Beverly was too young to had known them personally.

Her father's father had also been long deceased, while his widowed spouse lived out her remaining days in a Connecticut nursing home with dementia. Her father's only older brother Charlie, lived precariously on the streets of southern New Jersey battling opiate addiction, which he never won. He always adored the shore is the only thing she could remember him saying when she once met him a long time ago. In the sense of the long-term solutions, every foster family would never show any interest in adopting her due to her cold demeanor and post-traumatic stress disorder diagnosis in her file.

The staff observed how distant she was from the rest of the other children. Beverly usually would be seen playing by herself or drawing obscure pictures somewhere off in the corner. Despite this, they were never concerned, since reports rarely showed any outlandish behavior or emotional outbursts. She never had any verbal or physical altercations with any of the other girls, but it's been documented that she was picked on from time to time. Beverly remained introverted and reserved during her early-teen years, and had little interest in socializing or discussing her feelings, eventually burying them deep inside.

Denise would attempt to visit her during the first two years but had no luck connecting with her the way she had before. Beverly lost her sense of self and was no longer happy or thrilled to see Denise as if her memories were long forgotten and erased. Beverly had been mentally detached from all her surroundings and to anyone who attempted to pry in. Eventually, Denise would stop visiting knowing full well she wasn't the same little girl she had once known, and no longer knew how else to help her through this. The on-staff physician would order sedatives and anti-depressants for her, which seemed to help, but knew that time was the most beneficial medicine for her. *She needs to forget. She needs to move on*, he would say to the other staff members.

Hope was not all lost in her later years at the facility. Beverly obtained her GED at the age of seventeen through the orphanage's internal school system. Shortly after, she received a court order for emancipation, which granted her adult status. Beverly spent every opportunity to read any book that the orphanage library had to offer her. She loved reading fiction but also had an interest in history and math, and focused on numbers because it always connected with her, and on paper, it was universal. She continued to study history even though some darker topics regarding—tyranny, famine, slavery, and war—would upset her.

There was no sugar coating it for her, as it kept Beverly up late at night with insatiable curiosity. Questioning to herself with such things as; *Where did the idea of evil originate from? Why are humans so innately angry and violent?* She never wanted to go down that same path of no return and began opening herself up to the world again.

Deep down, Beverly wanted to be like everyone else. First and foremost, she had to tear down the walls of isolation and bitterness. After deciding to secretly heed the advice of her staff, who talked amongst themselves, she did want to move on. She wanted to forget. She needed her walls of internal conflict to come crashing down, to one day pave a new path toward peace and understanding.

Venturing out of the safety of her mind, she took the small but necessary steps to socialize with the other girls in her ward. From there, it all begun to blossom as she made a few good friends toward the end of her stay. Susan, her city social worker, pleased with Beverly's progress, wanted to see how well she could adapt back into society. Susan used her personal connections to get her a job at the local cafe, then helped her move into a state-operated all-girls rooming house. This small yet significant achievement allowed her to leave the orphanage and live on her own with several other roommates in the same situation.

Beverly had her doubts and concerns about adjusting to the real world, but still grateful she was finally free, independent, and happy. After a few years, she saved up enough money to rent an apartment with two young women, whom she had met from work. With her inheritance money, Beverly went to school at a local community college to study accounting, then found an entry-level job in her early twenties at a large downtown firm. Later, she met Adam and transferred to a division in upstate New York for a new beginning and to escape her past.

Beverly woke to water trickling from the bathtub spout onto her toes. A disorienting haze lingered in her mind as she laid motionless in the bathtub. She slowly regained consciousness from the slight sensation of water, but her reflexes did not react or pull away from the stimulus. Without motor or sensory afferent nerves acting the way they biologically should, she no longer could feel the wetness around her body, only the subtle sensation of droplets. Numbness and mild allodynia surrounded her from head to toe in this all-to-familiar paralyzed state she recalled from her childhood. Her face grimaced as she struggled to break free from this modern-day sorcery.

From downstairs, she heard a faint muffled barking that gradually intensified as she sat alone with her thoughts in overdrive. Beverly's heart raced as her palms grew clammy, hoping to escape this watery white acrylic sarcophagus. Tiny, her fearless German Shepherd, barked like a ravenous wild animal fending off a recent kill from another predator. She focused on his barks and growls for a sense of security and morbid curiosity. Louder and louder it became, followed by snarls and soft whimpering. Then came a sudden yelp, a short cry for help, which echoed throughout the entire house.

Everything went silent except for her bedroom radio, which only emanated a barely audible muffled static. Out of the corner of her eye, the hallway ceiling lights flickered behind the half-opened door. Beverly's heart pounded inside her chest, as beads of sweat formed across her forehead. Blood pulsed through her limbs like ants crawling up and down her body in single-file lines. Her eyes were heavy from exhaustion as she fought to keep them open since it was the only sense she could rely on for survival.

Beverly's labored breathing contrasted with the subtle sound of an opposing respiratory pattern to hers. A surge of fear and helplessness flowed through her body like streaming bolts of electricity. She had to react fast because the ability to move a single muscle fiber was no longer an option for her. *This is not real. This can't be real. It has to be all in my head.* She couldn't yell for help, nor had anyone to help her. Every vocalization settled deep within her throat. Screams slipped out as moans as she laid there paralyzed and vulnerable. Helpless and afraid, she prayed if this was just another awful dream, as her mind remained fully aware of her surroundings.

The intruder's breathing grew heavier, making her certain of whomever it was, had made it upstairs to accompany her for the evening. She listened intently to the person's expirations, which had no associated footsteps to follow. The lights flickered, as its breathing ceased to apnea, with the house falling under complete silence. The radio in the other room went dead. Tiny, her one and only protector, was silenced and defeated. Now, the only thing she could hear was her own heartbeat thudding rapidly in her chest. She tried to get up to shut and lock the bathroom door but still had no control over her body despite the exhausting desperation for survival.

As Beverly struggled to move, she noticed something out of the corner of her eye. A dark figure slowly emerged in her periphery, facing away from her in the hallway. Not the same shadowy figure from her childhood and recent encounters, but something more demonic and surreal. She never saw its true-form nor experienced these visions in her new home. It had only been during the last few months she had experienced them again back home in Brooklyn. When Beverly decided to move out of the city to rural New York, she thought she would have left the nightmares behind. She hoped that the doctor was right, and this was all just a manifestation in her mind. *That's right, Beverly. This is all caused by your post-traumatic stress. It's all just in your fucking stupid imagination.*

From her obscured bathroom view, she couldn't distinguish what the person looked like, or it is was even a person at all, but she was dead sure that it was the latter. The dark figure guided itself along the hallway with an almost animalistic apex predator demeanor. It slowly crept near the doorway, then stood hunched over in a desperate search for its next meal. The entity's body was pitch black with a texture of static electricity, fading in and out like an old transistor radio, as it struggled to conjure itself between our universe's spatial dimensions.

This had been the first time she could ever recall having a full close-up glimpse of it. It had a slender frame with no visible muscle tone, along with slow, calculated movements that made her skin crawl. The entity's long dangling limbs were disproportionate with its overall lanky non-humanoid body. The eerie encounter reminded her of an old traditional grey-alien movie abduction scene, but more menacing and demonic. It was truly from another world, she thought while trying to break free from the paralysis.

Beverly laid catatonic and helpless awaiting her grim outcome as she scanned her memories. Every other encounter she had had from before was brief as it always appeared to her as a tall shadowy man standing from across the room. It would just linger there quietly and stare from the same corner of the room, then vanish as quickly as it manifested itself. In most instances, she would forget the vision entirely as if it was only a bad dream. *This time it wasn't just a dream. It had to be real, right?*

Consciously aware of its surroundings, this supernatural intruder appeared hesitant as it advanced to the entrance of her bedroom. It stopped short, then peeked in with its long fingers wrapped around the door frame. Beverly held her breath and shifted her eyes as far as she could toward it, which was the only control she had over her body. Her heart pounded as if it was about to burst out of her chest at any moment. Despite its unknown intentions, the entity turned away from the bedroom and made its way down the hallway, disappearing from her limited view. The lights stopped flickering and returned to the on-position.

Beverly looked down at her feet after a small droplet fell from the faucet. She gasped out the breath she desperately held, as several droplets of blood fell onto her toes. The viscous fluid slowly trickled out, drop by drop. She panicked as the blood ran down her feet and into the water. Before she could wrap her mind around what was happening—the spout gave way like a geyser spewing copious amounts of blood, changing the water to a crimson red.

The water overflowed the rim like a fountain, spilling onto the tile floor. Immediate and impending doom overcame her as the lights began to flicker quickly with a disorienting trance-like strobe effect. The rapid-fire of light to her retinas forced her eyes shut, as a low foreign vibration penetrated her mind. She was lost and afraid, like a small child alone in a large open field, running for shelter during a tornado warning. This unpredictable and unimaginable storm had finally touched down tonight.

The dark figure crept in through the doorway as she reopened her eyes. The entity's movements were disorienting, as if in slow motion from the flickering strobe-light effect. It peered in through the half-opened door, hunched over, stealthily making its way into the bathroom. The door slammed open on its own as the entity entered and slid across the blood-covered tile floor. The clawed feet screeched across the tile as it inched its way closer to her. Beverly could only scream on the inside with complete terror, knowing this was how her life would end.

"Beverrrrlllly," it muttered with a horrific low, drawn-out hiss. "Beverlllly," the entity straightened to an erect posture as it towered over her and stared into her eyes.

"It's not fucking human!" Beverly whimpered to herself as she desperately tried to move her body, without any success. Its head was in a downward position, and face protruding outward like a snout. The entity's eyes glowed with magnificent green balls of energy, which weren't fixed in an exact location, as they shivered back and forth with intensity. The awful shade of green was otherworldly and hauntingly hypnotizing to her.

The entity produced a slow and steady grin that streamed across its demonic face. Its mouth wrapped around its entire head and began to open wider. The grisly smile exposed a desperate look as if it had been waiting a long time for this moment. Saliva dripped from its mouth and glistened off the various rows of non-uniformed, jagged teeth.

"Soooon Beverlllly, very soooon," the voice penetrated into her mind as its maniacal grin changed to disappointment and frustration. It slowly walked backward toward the door, hunched over as the lights went out, leaving her alone in formidable darkness. The door slammed shut as she cried hysterically until drifting in-and-out of consciousness.

Beverly woke in a haze with the lights back on as Tiny licked her petrified face. She jumped in a panic, splashing the frigid water onto the floor, while her favorite radio station played alternative rock B-sides from her bedroom. There were no signs of blood anywhere as she climbed out of the tub, trying to reorient herself to her surroundings. She patted her dog on his head with a shriveled wet hand, then grabbed for her towel.

"Tiny, I must've fallen asleep. It felt as if I was in the tub for days." Beverly said as she dried herself off and threw the bathrobe around her, tying the back strap in front of her. "You wouldn't believe the nightmare I just had," she said, then gave her dog a hug, relieved that they were both safe. Tiny looked up to her, then back over to the wide-open door. "Tiny, did you barge in here to rescue me?" Beverly laughed, feeling it was all just a bad dream. *Or was it?*

To rule on the side of caution, she grabbed a pair of scissors from her cosmetic drawer. With Tiny by her side, she stuck her head out of the bathroom—to inspect up and down the hallway, which had no signs of an intruder—followed by her body. Beverly stepped softly into her bedroom, again to only find nothing. She sighed, then quickly spun around and froze as she faced her closet door.

"Okay, you can do this. There's nothing in there, but your cheap shitty wardrobe." Beverly said, gripping the pair of scissors tighter to counterbalance the sweat on her palm. The makeshift dagger in hand—prepared to stab anything that would pop out at her—was brought up over her right shoulder. With her free hand, she opened the closet door, only to find her clothes hanging neatly and undisturbed. She relaxed her grip, then rested her arm back down by her side.

Beverly grabbed her phone and turned on the living-room lights at the end of the hallway, then proceeded downstairs with utmost vigilance. The top of the staircase had an open view of her living room and kitchen, except for two blind spots. One was the far left of the living room, near the couch and patio sliding glass door. The other was her laundry nook past the kitchen island table. As Beverly reached the bottom step, she peered around the corner toward the blind spots and found nothing out of place. The burden had finally lifted from her thoughts.

For the first time, she pieced together the shattered details, as if it wasn't all a dream. The experience still infested her mind, like a horrible bedbug outbreak that you couldn't seem to get rid of. *It had to be real. All of this had to be real.* Frightened and paranoid, she checked to see if all the windows were closed, and found the front door deadbolt still locked. "No, this all has to be in my head," she said out loud as she looked to Tiny, who panted with content as he followed her around the house.

She calmed herself, relieved that no one or nothing else was in her home. Placing the scissors on the kitchen counter was her acceptance of the situation. *Should I tell Adam? He may think I'm absolutely bat-crazy. An effin loony bird that flew over the cuckoo's nest, who would be locked up once word got out to anyone. He would leave me! Beverly, calm yourself down, listen to your damn psychiatrist and take those fucking medications!*

Beverly stumbled over to the living room, nauseous, stressed, and tired, then dropped herself onto the couch with her palms against her face. She turned over on her side and cried, as Tiny leaped onto the sofa next to her. Beverly pulled a fleece blanket over her and cuddled against his warm fur. Terrified to fall back asleep, she grabbed for the remote and turned on the TV to watch the late-night infomercials.

With one eye half-opened, she thought she had noticed a shadowy figure on the infomercial call out her name. She opened her eyes to find nothing unusual—only some over-weight man in his late forties, ironically trying to sell butter dispensers—then ignored it due to exhaustion before slowly falling back asleep. Tiny rested by her side, as night turned to day, without any further bad dreams.

CHAPTER THREE

Beverly woke to a phone ring, as the morning sun anxiously peeked in through her patio sliding glass door. She lifted her fatigued head off the couch as her cell phone vibrated and raced across the table. Her blue fleece blanket was sprawled over the floor, as the television cycled through repeats of the morning news and weather-traffic reports. Tiny was nowhere to be found, as her restless haze lingered over her.

Beverly grabbed for her phone off the table and raised it to eye level. Half-asleep, with blurred vision, she noticed it was a quarter past 10 am, and there had been several missed calls from Adam and an unknown number. She got up and stumbled toward the kitchen to religiously turn on her coffee maker, before checking her voice-mail.

"One missed message...Beverly, this is Doctor Spitzer, sorry to keep calling you. But I need to get a hold of you to clarify a few things. I know I may have rushed you out of my office yesterday. But I've had a lot of new clients claiming similar experiences you've been having recently, and can't figure out why. I couldn't go into more detail at the time, but I know of someone who specializes in this sort of thing and could possibly help you. I feel there's some truth to it all, but I couldn't express my own opinions at the office. I hope you understand. I'm calling you from my personal number, so give me a call back when you get this message. Thanks, take care and talk to you soon."

The disorienting mental fog lingered as she replayed his message. She placed the phone tightly against her ear, uncertain of what he meant by others having the same experiences and that there's more truth to this. Standing in the kitchen with a splitting headache, she poured coffee into her mug and took a sip with trembling hands. She saved the message, then placed the phone down, staring toward her living room with an empty and restless gaze.

The doorbell rang, which drove another blow to her headache. Startled, she dropped her mug and watched it fall as it shattered against the kitchen floor. "Shit!" Tiny came bolting out of nowhere, barking with his teeth exposed. "Calm down there, Tiger," she said, walking toward the door, then patted him to reassure and quiet him. She opened the front door to find Adam standing there.

She tried to recollect her thoughts before speaking, "Adam? Sorry I didn't pick up your phone calls. I must've overslept a bit. I haven't been getting good rest lately."

Adam walked inside and kissed her, "it's okay, babe. I just wanted to see how you were doing? Sorry I haven't been able to see you since you moved in." Adam said as he gave Tiny a pat on the head before walking into her living room. Tiny backed away from the door, then walked over to his empty dog bowl.

"I know, honey. I've also been busy getting things situated, and had to prepare for my trip down in the city," she said, then smiled. "I'm glad you stopped by, though, and still looking forward to our getaway next weekend." Beverly said, giving him a hug and passionate kiss as she ran her hand through his short stylish black hair. Adam was twenty-eight years old, two years older than Beverly, and stood six feet tall, three inches above her. He embraced her as they held each other in the living room.

Adam Grove was born and raised in Silver Lakes, and similar to most people from this town had a stable family upbringing. Like Beverly, he was an only child and had a close-knit relationship with both of his parents. His entire world was enclosed within this small town but would never consider it as living in a bubble. Every road and every hangout spot had been explored and re-explored. The same faces and shared memories are where he, and many here would agree, drew their comfort. A simple picturesque of an all-American midnight summer dream-town, suspended in time of a self-absorbent golden era.

He kissed her soft lips, then said, "I'm looking forward to it as well. I think we both need to get away for a bit. I've noticed you have been stressed lately. I can't deny the fact you have really worked your ass off to be here and closer to me. I just want you to know that I'm proud of you, sweetheart." Adam said, looking over her shoulder toward the shattered mug and coffee spilled on the kitchen floor. "Did I startle you or something?" Gesturing with his head toward the mess with a stupid boyish smirk across his face, that she always found obnoxious, but utterly adorable.

"Of course not. I just accidentally knocked it off the counter as I tried to grab for my phone to call you back," she said, then innocently smiled. Beverly playfully strutted over to the kitchen, looking back over at him. She grabbed a paper towel, then leaned over to pick up the ceramic glass chards. Adam followed her and placed his hand on her shoulder. Then it hit her all at once. Today's forecast neglected to mention the ever-looming storm clouds inside her head.

"Let me help you," he said as he bent over to pick up the small pieces she had missed. There was an awkward silence as he noticed a tear running down her cheek. "What's wrong, honey? No need to cry over spilled milk, right?" Adam joked and noticed her lack of coordination as she fumbled with the roll of paper towels in her hands. He grew concerned, knowing she didn't quite look right to him and hesitated to ask again, "Is everything okay, Bev?"

Beverly stopped in her tracks, like a deer caught in the headlights, and looked toward him with tearful eyes and trembling hands. "Can I tell you something, Adam?"

"Always, honey. What's up?" He said as he continued to focus on cleaning the mess, prepared for what would come next.

"I've meant to tell you this for a long time," she said, before another awkward pause.

"Oh, boy," he said, trying to control his natural instinct to overthink things.

Beverly noticed his uneasiness and brushed her hand against his to reassure him. She cleared her throat, paused, then spoke with clarity. "I think someone is stalking me," she said, mustering up all her strength and courage to tell him.

Not knowing what to say next, they stared at each other while kneeling on the floor. "Can you hand me some more paper towels?" Adam asked as he stared down at the mess on the floor.

"You don't believe me?" Beverly responded, disappointed, with an embarrassed tremble in her voice as she stood back up.

"Bev, I'm not saying that I don't believe you. I just don't how to respond to that. Did you see someone? How long has this been going on for? Is it an ex-boyfriend I need to straighten out for you?" Adam said, followed by an obnoxious laugh, another quirk that he had, in which she didn't find cute. Beverly stood in the kitchen, carefully choosing her words before continuing.

"No babe, you don't have to beat anyone up for me," she said, going along with his nonchalant sarcasm. "Honestly, I don't know who it might be, but I've experienced this before. I never told you any of this because I was scared to tell you." She said, turning her head toward the floor. He finished cleaning the mess, then stood to face her.

Beverly mustered up all her strength, then looked

him in his eyes, "The reason I was in the city yesterday, was so I could see my psychiatrist. The one I used to see when I was a child. I didn't want to lie to you, but I felt ashamed of the fact that I needed help. I didn't tell you because I thought you would think I was crazy, and leave me." She explained as another tear traced down along her cheek.

Adam brushed her tear away with his hand, "Beverly, you don't have to ever hide anything from me. I know what you've had to go through and also know that I'll always be here for you. I'm not sure what you are going through right now, but I would never think you were ever crazy. If anything, I'm the one who is crazy...crazy for you," he said with a smile, then embraced her in his arms.

She kissed him and smiled, "Thank you, I appreciate that. These visions began after my parents died as if someone was watching over me, but not in a good way. These nightmares feel so real at times and don't know what to think anymore. I know it doesn't make any sense trying to explain it to you. But several months ago, before relocating up here, to be closer to you. I began having these visions all over again. I thought they would go away if I left the city behind. I really thought that it would solve all of this," she said, pausing for a moment. "But they haven't stopped...

they're only just getting worse," she said with her head against Adam's shoulder.

"I know your past still haunts you, but you're safe now. You're with me, away from the city and your past. We have our whole future to look forward too. I also would never think you were crazy. I can promise you that." Adam said to her as she looked up at him. He dried her tears with the clean paper towel, then smiled with that same stupid grin he always had. The cute quirk she always will love.

"I appreciate you understanding this. I know I'm unloading a lot on you right now. I feel this is all just caused by stress and lack of sleep. That's what the doctor thinks anyway. But these nightmares are getting worse and much more vivid. I honestly feel as if somebody was watching me," Beverly said as she grabbed her phone off the counter and shook it in front of him. "My psychiatrist tried calling me this morning and left a voice-mail, saying he may know of someone who's experienced in treating this sort of thing." Beverly looked desperate for a sympathetic response from Adam.

"Yeah, if that is what you think you need, you should consider it, then give it a try. I just want you to be happy and feel safe. I think that our camp trip next weekend would clear both of our heads," he said, then kissed her before stepping back out of the kitchen. Adam made his way toward the front door. "Honey, I'm glad you feel comfortable opening up to me and all, but I really should be getting back to work now. I just wanted to check in on you."

"Thanks, I know, and I'm sorry to unload this on you all at once. But I can't keep hiding this from you. Beverly walked Adam to the door and kissed him goodbye.

"No need to be sorry, I completely understand. On that note, I would be paranoid too living next to that guy. He is one strange dude," Adam said loud enough that Mr. Kelly looked over and grunted to himself, before going back to his yard work. They both laughed as he gave her another kiss goodbye. "Don't worry about anything, babe," Adam said as he opened the door to his jeep, started the engine, then smiled back at her.

Beverly watched him pull out of the driveway as he waved back to her. She looked across the street as her neighbor turned his head away again. She uncomfortably stood outside in her bathrobe, as he kept glancing back over at her. Beverly shivered as a brisk autumn breeze caressed her exposed skin, then went back inside, locking the door behind her for the evening.

CHAPTER FOUR

Beverly tried to forget last night's events, which seemed like a fruitless endeavor that yielded an endless void in her mind. She paced her living room while staring down at her phone, deciding to call Doctor Spitzer tomorrow—when she had mentally regrouped. She staggered to the kitchen and prepared a small pasta dinner for herself, then poured a tall glass of red wine to unwind for the evening.

After her meal for one, Beverly cuddled up on the couch with her Tiny fur ball. She turned on the TV to watch her favorite crime-drama show before getting distracted by Adam's text messages. Tiny jumped to the floor and fell asleep alongside her. Wishing for more pleasant thoughts, she closed her eyes and focused on Adam and their camp trip together in the Adirondacks next weekend.

The evening twilight quickly faded to nightfall as she fell asleep on the couch with her blanket covering mostly Tiny on the floor. A buzzing sound stirred her awake along with static white-noise emanating from across the room. With her eyes now wide-open, she laid on the couch as her fear and anxiety boiled over the metaphorical pot. Her body movements and sensory became dull to respond on command. Every experience had always felt new to her as if it was the first occurrence. In her peripheral vision, she could see the static lines emanating from her television screen.

Half-asleep, Beverly's eyes traced the room, noticing Tiny was nowhere to be found. *Some guard dog you are.* The silence of the night was interrupted by a shrill piercing static that penetrated her mind. Beverly panicked, realizing she could no longer move her body as the screen faded to blackness and silence. She laid on the couch, knowing last night wasn't a dream. The mental bridge of connecting the dots had finally made the mental synapse, and that this was truly happening—a reoccurring nightmare manifesting into existence.

The couch laterally faced the television, and her feet pointed toward the front door. With nowhere else to turn to, she stared at the brass door handles, which she unmistakably saw move ever so slightly. *This can't be my imagination.* The handle rattled violently, followed by a loud rap against the door. A knock that propelled her mind back into her childhood, fading into her subconscious. The banging continued, endless and relentless. *Go away!* The pounding intensified as she helplessly watched the door handle swing back and forth.

It's not real. This isn't happening to me! She repeated over and over in her head, trying to make sense of everything logically. If one can't explain things rationally, that is when our good-old friend, amygdala, comes out to play. Fight or flight can be a very useful and effective response for a person—who could, of course, move their body. The knocking finally ceased as the door handle returned to its neutral position. The relief was brief yet rewarding, as her logic finally kicked in, *It must have only been my imagination*, she thought before drifting back to sleep.

Playful laughter from a small child cackled next to her, then faded to the far corner of the room. Beverly slowly woke to soft giggles from a little girl on the other side of her kitchen. She heard the gentle voice but couldn't make out her exact location or what she was saying. The conversation was not directed toward her, but to someone else in the room whom she also could not see nor hear.

The giggling stopped, followed by distress in the child's voice. "I don't want you to go," the girl said in a somber tone, but loud enough for Beverly to hear.

There was a period of silence, then sobbing and then again followed by silence. Soft footsteps pattered against the hardwood floor as a little girl ran passed the kitchen and through the living room toward the staircase. She quickly ascended the stairs, then thudded across the hallway above Beverly's head.

Paralyzed on the couch, Beverly caught a quick glimpse of the small child with her long wavy brown hair flowing behind her. The face was hidden from view but looked somehow familiar to her. *How did she get in my home?* An overwhelming subconscious maternal instinct told her that the child needed her help. She struggled to move but couldn't find the strength to do so. She looked down at her feet, then focused on moving her toes, thinking it was a good place to start. Staring down at her feet took all her concentration and effort to move one toe. *Damn it, move!* Exhausted and frustrated, she felt if she was performing a rare hidden talent of telekinesis.

As if some miracle or cheap parlor magic trick, she began to gain control. First, by wiggling her toes, feet, then legs, followed by regaining complete consciousness and mobility of her body again. Beverly hopped off the couch, trying to catch her breath, feeling if she had just ran a marathon through the Sahara. Rain pattered against the patio glass door next to her couch, intensifying her thirst. She turned toward her television as credits from her favorite show scrolled up the screen.

Tiny hadn't moved from where he slept on the floor, as she barely missed stepping on top of him. Beverly rubbed her eyes and collected her thoughts, then calmed her breathing as she tried to rationalize this new vision. *It's all a dream. It has to be. At least it wasn't as bad as last night*, she thought as she shook her head in confusion. She went to the kitchen to get a glass of water for her parched throat. The initial sip was sore to swallow.

Beverly looked over to Tiny sleeping and smiled, then turned off the kitchen lights as flashes of lightning illuminated her living room. She cautiously walked upstairs and felt absurd to be paranoid in her own home. She checked her bedroom and bathroom regardless, only to find nothing out of the ordinary. "Is my house haunted?" She said, shrugging it off as nonsense. She didn't believe in the supernatural but did believe something else was going on inside her head.

I need to call Spitzer tomorrow. He'll know how to make this all go away. Beverly desperately hoped as she brushed her teeth, glancing periodically over in the hallway. She slammed the toothbrush down in the sink, "I can't fucking live like this anymore!" Beverly went to her bedroom, locked her door, and turned on the small lamp on the nightstand. She quickly crawled into bed, pulling the blankets over her head.

Beverly dreamt of the time when she was brought inside the 32nd police department precinct by two officers. She was held in the arms of Sergeant John Potowski, who was a seasoned veteran of NYPD. He had also been one of the officers who delivered the news of her parents that dreadful morning. Beverly no longer cried, while temporarily comforted in the arms of the sergeant. Beverly held onto him with one arm and the other on a teddy bear he had given to her. She glanced around the front lobby with puffy blue eyes as several people waited in chairs against the wall.

Suspects, secured in handcuffs, sat in the processing section as an officer searched through their belongings. A second officer behind a tall desk recorded their demographics and took their photographs. A warden, escorted them one by one down a separate hallway, through a thick metal door like an assembly line. Beverly squeezed her teddy tighter, then leaned over Potowski's shoulder for a better view. She sniffled her runny nose and watched one person in particular with inquisitive child-like curiosity.

An intimidating bald and heavy-set man in his late thirty's stood in shackles as a younger officer patted him down. Beverly thought the man was much bigger than her father and startled by all his frightening snake and goat-head markings across his skin. The man's numerous tattoos covered him from head to toe, along his neck, arms, and legs, which were, in a way, hypnotizing to her. She noticed an outline of two black teardrops underneath his right eye. *Why was he sad? Did he also lose his parents?* Young Beverly innocently wondered.

Additional officers gathered around the prisoner and turned him around, which brought him in direct eye contact with her. Beverly was startled and thrown off by his sudden awareness he had of her in the room. He smiled, which was far from comforting, making her turn away. She clutched harder onto Sergeant Potowski, digging her nails into his back. The Sergeant and other officers noticed this and shoved the man in the other direction to get his attention. One officer grabbed him aggressively and escorted him out of the room. They vanished behind the metal door at the end of the corridor, never to be seen again.

Beverly was carried off in the other direction toward the right side of the lobby. The long stretch of hallway led to a room on the far right filled with several chairs, toys, a couch, and a desk that were surrounded by cartoonish wallpaper. Not from her favorite cartoons—but of generic giraffe and elephant characters, which appeared more frightening than friendly to her. The escorting officers left the room, as Sergeant Potowski brought her inside and sat her down on the couch near an overfilled toy bin.

Potowski placed his hand on the top of her head, "Beverly, you are in the safest place in all the city right now. We just have to talk to this nice lady for a bit." Beverly looked up to the sergeant as she rubbed the tears from her eyes.

"Hi, what's your name?" The city social worker, said in a comforting soft voice. Beverly turned her head as she held onto her teddy, not wishing to respond.

"I'll let you gals be to get better acquainted with each other." Sergeant Potowski said, then leaned over to Beverly. "Goodbye, sweetheart. I wish you the very best," as he brushed his hand over the top of her head and the teddy bear, then stood up to leave the room.

"No! Don't leave me!" Beverly cried out, locking eyes with his.

"It'll be okay, sweetheart. You're a strong little girl, Beverly. I have to go now and help other people who also need my help. Susan is really nice and will be there for you. You're going to have to trust me, okay? Your teddy bear will be there to protect you. He hugged her, then walked toward the door. "I'll see you again, Beverly. But for now, goodbye." He nodded to Susan, then exited the room.

"How is she?" A man said as he walked past him in the hallway.

"She's definitely distraught but is one tough cookie. Tougher than these other scum bags we bring in here, day after frickin day," Potowski said.

"We live in a world of chaos, Sergeant. And it's this very chaos, that upsets me. Especially when it involves a child, the true victims in all of this," he said as they walked down the hallway.

"This is very true, Doctor Spitzer. We live in a sick world," Potowski said as they parted ways in the lobby.

"Beverly, what is the name of your new little friend there?" Susan said, trying to break the silence. Beverly didn't respond as she stared down at her teddy bear, wiping away her tears.

"I know you are scared, honey. I'd be too. I couldn't even imagine what you might be going through right now," as she handed her a tissue. "But I need you to know that I'm here to help you. We all are." Beverly reached her hands out to accept the tissues, then wiped away her tears and runny nose.

"I miss my Mommy and Daddy," she whimpered, dropping the tissues on the couch.

"I know, sweetie. Trust me, I know." Susan leaned over and embraced her with a hug, forcing back tears herself. Susan squeezed Beverly tighter as if she was cradling her own daughter tonight.

Beverly slept, as Tiny remained downstairs undisturbed in his own blissful slumber. Silence encapsulated the mid-October night in her cozy rural New York neighborhood. No familiar sounds of sirens, cars, or late-night party-goers wandering the streets below, which she grew accustomed to back home. Only a gentle rain tapped against her window and rooftop as distant rumbles of thunder ruled over the night sky.

Beverly had recently moved into her new house a week ago with high expectations. She had been promoted with her voluntary transfer to an office farther north of the city. There had been nothing but joy during this transition, as she wanted to be closer to Adam and get away from the world she had despised. However, tonight, the dread of isolation was plentiful and tormented her thoughts from the past. Sometimes, our minds can be a dangerous place to tread alone at night.

Beverly first met Adam at a Brooklyn pub less than a year ago. He visited the city with his friends that weekend, which wasn't all by near happenstance—secretly coordinated by her mutual best friend, Kristen Citdel, who arranged the place to meet. She had gone to middle school with the popular athletic Adam Grove in Silver Lakes and were friends to this day.

Kristen knew how great of a guy Adam was and how lonely Beverly could feel at times. She wanted to play matchmaker for her best friend and knew they would hit it off great together. She had told Adam about Beverly in advance, wanting him nonchalantly to meet her in Brooklyn. Kristen wanted nothing but success and happiness for her best friend and to have her one-day experience a simple life outside the confines of the city.

Beverly tossed and turned in her sleep before settling onto her right side. She fell back asleep, facing away from the street light coming through her window. A sudden, body-sized pressure sat near her legs, which stirred her awake. She looked toward the foot of her bed without seeing anything unusual. She glanced back toward the wall at the cast of shadows from the street lamps. Beverly turned onto her back and quickly nodded off again. Then within moments, another strong force flopped on top of her bed. *Tiny?*

She became fully alert with eyes wide-opened in a paralyzed state. The little girl sat at the foot of her bed with her knees tucked toward her chest. Her hands covered her face as her silhouette hid her features in the darkened room. Beverly held her breath as she watched the small child sway back and forth, sobbing to herself.

Beverly stirred with fear and confusion, along with sympathy, wanting to console the scared child. Beverly laid there paralyzed and quietly observed the same loneliness, similar to when she was a child. In the corner of the room, she saw another figure standing off in the darkness. The shadow began moving forward and walked toward her bedside as its features became more evident.

Beverly gasped for air, letting out a slight moan, realizing her nightly hallucination were that of her mother and younger self. "Mommy don't go, don't go," the young girl muttered as she continued to sway with her hands still buried in her face. The child sobbed to herself as a third dark figure emerged into view near Beverly's head, staring down at her. Her deceased mother called out to comfort the young girl sitting at the foot of the bed.

"I'm sorry, Beverly. Your father and I are both really sorry. We couldn't stop it. We just couldn't stop it," her mother said as Beverly noticed the dark figure at the top of the bed reach his hand around to gently brush it against her face. The sensation sent wave upon wave of chilling electricity throughout her body.

"There, there now, Beverly. It'll be okay. Your time will come, just not yet. You're not ready yet." The incorporeal being said with a low intimidating voice, then disappeared behind her peripheral vision. Beverly drew her attention back to her mother with desperation.

"I just couldn't stop it, Beverly. I'm sorry." Her mother repeated before walking backward, then disappearing into the darkness as quickly as she first appeared. The warmth of her mother's presence was extinguished as a fleeting memory trapped in her mind, tucked away like a personal scrapbook. Alone again, without the safety of her mother, a sense of impending doom returned as darkness swallowed the room. The small girl kept sobbing while swaying faster and faster at the foot of her bed.

"Stop what? Mom, don't go!" Sadness and grief flooded her mind, as the small child's crying ceased, then turned to her with a blank stare. Beverly's fear ensnared her, as the small child crawled on all fours like an animal on top of her. It climbed over Beverly's chest, knocking the breath out of her lungs as the demon girl lowered its head over her face. Beverly wanted to scream as the child came only a few inches away and whispered into her ear.

"You couldn't save them. You can't even save yourself!" The small child hissed in a low otherworldly tone. The child's face was no longer of her younger self, but now of a decayed rotting corpse. The room temperature dropped below freezing as the demonic young doppelganger straddled over Beverly's chest. She could smell the wretched stench of rotting flesh from its breath as it formed condensation in the cold ambient air.

The entity's eyes were pitch black with no reflection of any light or soul inside. Frost and ice formed along the windowpane as the shadows from the street lamp posts moved away from the wall toward the bed like black boa constrictors. They wrapped around Beverly's entire body, snaring her in a vice as she struggled to breathe, suffocating her slowly. She tried to force out a scream, which was nothing more than the last bit of air squeezed out of her lungs. The fire in her chest intensified with the desire to take in a breath but painfully denied by the weight of the small child and shadows tighter grip.

"You caused them to die! You let them die because you are weak, Beverly." The demonic girl said as she leaned in closer, drooling over Beverly's face as it readjusted its grip over her. The shadows and child sunk more painfully into her. Beverly closed her eyes, accepting her fate. In a state of profound hypoxia, she took a moment to think of her mother, then mustered all the strength she needed to fight back before it was too late.

This isn't real, none of this is real! She opened her eyes, directly staring back at the child sitting on her chest. She glared deep into its eyes as they shifted from pitch black to shivering green balls of energy. She glanced past the child, allowing herself a view of her lifeless feet. She took her eyes off the girl and began to focus on her toes. Beverly concentrated on moving her feet while slowly being suffocated under the child's weight. The shadows clutched her tight as the dark entity emerged from behind her bed.

"You are weak and pathetic, Beverly. Your time will soon come." It said to her as she started to move her feet. The small girl's eyes changed from green to a bloodthirsty red.

"No, I'm fucking not!" Beverly screamed, jumping up from her bed, gasping for air. She flailed her arms hysterically in front of her, reaching for the demon child. Beverly looked around the empty room as daylight began to break. She raised herself out of bed, drenched in sweat with trembling hands from fear and anger. Frustrated only to find nothing to take it out on nor of any explanation on what had just occurred. Tiny continued to bark outside of her room as she stared toward the foot of the bed with complete exhaustion and relief it was over. The morning light slowly peered in through her window like a long-awaited friend.

Beverly got out of bed and opened the door to let Tiny in, "I'm sorry if I scared you, buddy. You probably think Momma is crazy. Hell, I'm talking to you right now and hallucinating visions of my mother and demons. I really need to call Doctor Spitzer tomorrow," she said, then noticed the time, and rushed to get ready for work. She dragged herself to the bathroom, sleep-deprived, and not looking forward to starting the first day at her new job.

She hurried downstairs and realized there wouldn't be enough time for breakfast. Instead, she poured dry kibble into Tiny's bowl, grabbed her keys, then rushed toward the front door. She casually waved to her neighbor as he was taking out the trash. He watched Beverly reverse out of the driveway and speed down the road, as the autumn leaves floated back down toward the street behind her.

CHAPTER FIVE

Beverly accelerated into the parking lot of her new job with a few minutes to spare. She pulled into a parking stall not far from the building with plenty of spaces to choose from. Two dozen cars were parked spaciously throughout the lot, which was adjacent to the red brick building. Her anxiety subsided, as she was already accustomed to heavy traffic at her old downtown firm, where it was near-impossible to find anything last minute.

Her reflection in the visor mirror showed dark circles underneath her eyes and a pale, drained complexion. Beverly was a woman of natural beauty, who had never been too fascinated with spending a lot of time on her appearance. However, today, she felt hopeless and regretful not to had the time to at least apply some effort. It was her first day and wanted to be somewhat presentable. She knew she had woken up on the wrong side of the bed this morning—and recalled the competition she had to deal with during the time spent working at their headquarters.

She reached into her handbag for a hairbrush, found it, and ran it through her messy hair. She applied concealer to cover the dark circles under her eyes. She stumbled out of the car, dropping her brush, then leaned over to pick it back up, "Get a grip girl. You got this." She said to herself, trying to refocus, then straightened her posture and proceeded to the front doors of the small single-story building.

She walked confidently through the office lobby toward the front desk. "Hello, my name is Beverly Hollinger. I'm the new senior accountant transfer from Brooklyn. Sorry for running a little late today," she said to the young secretary who looked up from her cell phone.

"Nice to meet you, Beverly. I'm Junie. And don't worry, you're on time for our standards. People seem to show up when they please," she said, then laughed. "We're pretty relaxed around here. I couldn't imagine the hustle and bustle of working down in New York City," Junie said with a smile from behind her desk. "You can wait over there for the time being," as she pointed to the pair of red chairs in the lobby. "I'll contact Mr. Schwartz, to show you to your new office," she said in an upbeat yet annoying bubbly voice before staring back down at her phone.

Beverly walked toward the waiting area feeling dead on the inside with each step, yearning for a large cup of coffee. It felt as if an hour had already passed, as she continued to wait while half-asleep. Beverly looked at her watch, which showed a quarter past eight. She forced herself to stay awake, thinking about the phone call she would have to make with her psychiatrist later today. Beverly dozed off, while listening to her surroundings, and imagined her name being called out from a distance. She replayed the visions of the last two nights in her mind. Her thoughts were sloshing around like an overloaded washing machine, rocking violently back and forth.

Her name was called out to her with the same slow demonic hiss from the night before, then took on a more human quality, as she stirred to wakefulness. "Beverly?" She heard as if whispered in her ear. "How are you doing, Beverly?" She opened her eyes, startled to see her new boss standing there, then jumped out of her chair, almost elbowing him in the face.

"I'm doing fantastic. How are you?" Beverly responded in one breath as she eagerly shook her boss's hand.

"I can tell you're a little bit of out of it today," Paul Schwartz said with a smile, then chuckled. "I bet you're exhausted with the transition from moving up here. I understand entirely, and I planned for it to be a laid back orientation day. I'm thrilled to have you on board with our team," he said, gesturing for her to follow him as he escorted her down the hallway. "I've heard a lot of good things about you and saw you've done some extraordinary work for our main Brooklyn office. I know you'll fit in perfectly here. We may be a slower pace then what you're used too. So, I'm sure you can handle your new lead accounting role with ease."

She opened the door and overwhelmed to see her spacious new office with an actual window to the outside. "This is wonderful, thank you! Much better than the small cramped cubicles I'm used too." She responded with a smile from ear to ear.

"I'm glad to hear it, Beverly. We are a close-knit family, and you'll have no problem fitting in here." He said, then handed her the branch's orientation paperwork for her new job duties. "Review these packets and become familiar with some of our procedures and protocols. Nothing too much different than corporate, all the changes are highlighted in the packet. Our IT support will be over in a few hours to get your computer in sync with the one you had in Brooklyn, and then we shall take it from there. Glad to have you on board with us, Beverly. I'll check back in with you later this afternoon. Let me know if you have any questions," he said, then smiled before walking out of the room.

Beverly sat down in her office chair as he closed the door behind him. "This is absolutely amazing!" She said out loud as she swung around several times in her chair, then examined the numerous drawers in her desk. She got up and walked over to the large window overlooking the small pond outside. An old oak tree stood majestically as it leaves laid scattered across the ground. Several ducks floated over the water, while the others basked in the morning sunlight. Beverly smiled, then returned to her desk to start her day.

After an hour of reviewing the orientation paperwork, she began to drift off to sleep, recalling last night's events. She forced herself awake and placed the papers back on her desk as she reflected on her life. She felt that her vision of her mother was, in some way, a sign of communicating with her. As if to tell her that everything will be okay. She disregarded all the negative thoughts she had experienced before, focusing only on her mother. Even though she wasn't religious, Beverly searched deep down within her self-doubts to realize that this was, in fact, truly a sign.

Acknowledging this career opportunity as a blessing, she didn't want to take it for granted or screw it up. She remembered all the hard times and thankful for all her recent success. She leaned back in her chair to rejoice in the progress she had accomplished. Beverly reflected on her entire life from losing her parents at a young age, the orphanage, her friends, the internship to becoming certified, her new home, and Adam. *And Adam... None of these new possibilities would have been possible if I hadn't met him.* Beverly closed her eyes as she reclined back in her chair. She began to envision her mother again, then fell back asleep.

A muffled voice circled inside her mind as she swam deep within her dreams. "Beverly...Beverly?... Are you okay?... Can you hear me?" The voice said louder, followed by a sudden jerk of her chair. She leaped out of the chair and fell to the floor, frantically picking herself back up again, drenched in sweat with trembling knees.

"Sorry to startle you like that, Miss Hollinger. My name is Kevin Berkley from the IT department. I'm here to get your computer connected to your previous account server," he said as she got back into her chair without any finesse.

"Oh, I'm sorry, Kevin. I had a long day yesterday, trying to get everything moved in," she said with an embarrassed smile and laugh. "I wasn't expecting you this soon," as she looked down at her watch, noticing that several hours had already passed.

"It's okay, I should have knocked first, but it's nice to meet you, Beverly. I just have to access your old IP address with a remote server, then link your account so it can connect with our system and…" Kevin continued to explain the process further, which droned on in Beverly's head. He awkwardly made his way toward her desk as she offered him the chair. He took a seat, then went to town on her desktop, lost in his own world of software codes and algorithms.

"I'll let you have at it then. I'm going to grab a coffee," Beverly said with a smile, turning to him as he barely noticed her still standing there.

"No problem, this shouldn't take too long." He responded with full concentration on the computer screen.

"Okay, I will be back in a few, you want anything?" He gave no response. She left him to his duties with embarrassment on her face, which went unnoticed. She poured herself a cup of coffee, then proceeded out the back door, double-checking that it wouldn't lock behind her. She ventured outside, still in a daze, toward the pond below her office window, then sat on a wooden bench next to the old oak tree.

She blew on her coffee to let it cool in the crisp autumn air. The small sip scalded her tongue as she spat it out on the ground. The pain lingered for a moment as she swished her tongue back and forth. The sensation, unpleasant as it was, gave her reassurance that she wasn't lost within another dream. The aroma of cheap watered-down caffeine reached her senses and rejected it, as she tossed its contents out onto the patch of dying grass below her.

Beverly looked around the courtyard, then back toward the tree as a few more of its leaves floated free from their branches onto the grass. The ducks, who were once sunbathing, were now gone. They left on their own free will, or perhaps, of an atavistic genetic instinct passed down from every generation, to fly south for the winter. What was left, was herself, the stagnant pond water, and her overwhelming thoughts, as the vibrant colored leaves laid lifeless on the earth beneath her.

All her built-up emotions stirred, then boiled over as a sudden burst of pent-up energy. She leaned over on the bench, crying and weeping to herself. She had never experienced this raw outburst of every emotion in her life since her parents died. For the first time, she had been alone with herself and nature. To finally be able to let go of all her surroundings and memories for a brief passing moment—all the city-goers, roommates, past life, everything, gone.

Beverly wept until she could no longer shed another tear, then lifted her tired head toward the balding oak tree. She picked up one of the brightly colored leaves off the ground and twirled it between her fingers. She wiped her eyes with her other hand, then released the leaf, watching it gently float back toward her feet. "I can't live like this anymore," she said, reaching for her phone to call Doctor Spitzer. It rang to voice-mail and she quickly hung up.

Beverly regained her emotions, wiped away her tears, and cleared her throat before calling him back. It rang through again to voice-mail, but this time left a message to meet with him urgently. She hung up and dialed his office number, saved on her phone contacts. His secretary answered and scheduled her for an appointment for next Monday. Beverly confirmed, then hung up her phone, staring somberly off into the distance toward the rolling hills. With bloodshot eyes from the tears and exhaustion, she stood with a new sense of empowerment, then made her way back inside to finish out her first day.

CHAPTER SIX

Beverly pulled into her driveway and parked, then leaned over, fumbling for her prescriptions out of the glove box. The sedative effects of Xanax had already set in during her ride home from work. The calming euphoria, or placebo effect, had taken the edge off for the moment. Beverly waved to her neighbor, who had just finished raking up the fallen leaves into several smaller piles. The various mounds were scattered throughout his yard, resembling a bizarre indistinguishable pattern from afar. Perhaps from space, it could have resembled a galactic message or possibly a runway, she chuckled at the thought.

"Shouldn't your grandkids be helping you with your landscaping?" She shouted over to him in a friendly manner, hoping he would lighten up. Mr. Kelly, a disheveled elderly man in dirty torn overalls, looked over to her as he tied a bag with leaves spilling out from the top. He turned away with no expression or response as he dropped the last bag off by the curb, then returned to his garage. "Well, okay then. They probably fucking hate you too," Beverly muttered as she grabbed the house key from her handbag.

The evening had already set over Silver Lakes, as a cold breeze brushed against her back. The street lights flickered on behind her as she fumbled with her key into the lock. She looked over her shoulder, noticing that her neighbor had already closed his garage door and slithered back inside for the evening. She took a second to glance around the neighborhood, observing that everyone else was as equally reclusive. She received the same cold welcome from the neighbors a few houses down, along with the older couple at the end of her cozy little cul-de-sac.

To think of it, Beverly recalled no real interaction with anyone here and still hadn't seen or heard from the neighbors who lived directly next to her. They had never come over to introduce themselves or answer their door on multiple occasions. She knew somebody was home since their lights were always left on at night. It was also two weeks until Halloween, and there were no decorations, no jack o' lanterns, no children. *Where was the holiday spirit?*

Beverly began to think that her quiet neighborhood was a place where nobody had the will to live anymore. As if she had taken up residence in a cemetery, waiting to collect its new souls. She enjoyed the peace here but compared to the city, it lacked all the interaction and liveliness she had been used too. Beverly wasn't thrilled to be in the middle of everything on God's green Earth, but there was no compromise here. She had an overwhelming sense of loneliness in this town, feeling cut off from the rest of civilization.

Beverly walked through the front door as Tiny frantically begged for her attention. He jumped on her and nuzzled his snout against her side as she knelt over to greet him. "Hey there, buddy! How was your day? I'm so happy to see you, too," she hugged him, then patted the top of his head. Beverly stood over him, noticing that his dog dish and kibble were scattered across the kitchen floor.

"Did you do this, poopy?" She said in a childish voice, looking down at him as he wagged his tail, happy to see her. He barked several times at her, then walked around in a few circles before going back to the living room. She grabbed the broom from the closet to clean up the mess. Tiny ran back over, wagging his tail after she revealed his favorite savory can of dog food.

Tiny inhaled every single bite as if he hadn't eaten all day. "You're one silly pup. You know that?" She said and laughed, which was cut short as she looked past him toward the staircase, "I'm exhausted, Tiny. You may be having dinner alone tonight." She said, bringing him outside to use the bathroom, then went to the kitchen to pour herself a glass of water. She took the prescription bottle out of her purse—took half of the sleeping pill that her Doctor prescribed for her—then sent upstairs for the evening.

Beverly got ready for bed, closed her bedroom door, locked it behind her, then turned the handle to confirm. She checked her phone, only to find no new missed calls or texts, then set the ringer to silent. She set the alarm for six, anticipating an earlier start tomorrow. Looking forward to a good night's rest after all the horrible previous nights she had dealt with before. Beverly crawled into bed as the drowsy effects from the pill slowly began to take hold, forcing her eyes closed.

During the middle of the night, she woke to her phone ring, as it vibrated across the nightstand. The room was dark except for the light emanating from her phone as the ringing continued. "I thought I put the damn thing on silent," Beverly said as she raised her head up out of bed to see who was calling her this late. She picked up the phone but didn't recognize the number or why it hadn't gone to voice-mail yet.

"Hello…?" Beverly answered in a soft and hesitant voice as she waited for a response. "Hello?" She repeated more irritated, staring back down at her phone as it was still connected to the caller. Loud static emanated from the speaker, forcing her to pull away. The shrill subsided as she placed it back to her ear. "Hello!"

A low background static with an audible garbled voice came through in choppy fragments. Beverly got out of bed and walked around the room, trying to get better reception as the voice continued to fade in and out. She went to her bedroom window and found a better signal, "Whoever this is, it's not funny," growing more impatient and agitated. In response to her anger, the static became more intense and shrill, forcing her to pull the phone away again.

The voice had a hostile tone to it as she tried to make out what they were saying. She listened to the muffled chatter, as a distant sound of a dog barked through the static. Beverly panicked, as Tiny barks echoed in unison with the ones through her phone receiver. She ended the call, grabbed a baseball bat from her closet, turned on all the lights, and carefully made her way downstairs. Tiny snarled and growled at the front door, then jumped onto the window seal to investigate outside.

Beverly positioned herself several feet behind the front door with a Louisville Slugger gripped tightly in her hands. "Who is it, Tiny? I hope it's just Adam calling me drunk from a friend's phone or something else stupid." She walked toward her German Shepherd, who continued to growl at the window, before letting out a yelp. Tiny jumped back and ran behind her, whimpering as she stared over at the window. Beverly jumped as the phone rang again in her hand from the same unknown number.

She answered, trying not to panic, "Go away! What do you want from us?" Beverly said with her ear still against the phone, the static intensified, sending low vibrations throughout her body. Then a deep, otherworldly voice penetrated into her mind with full clarity. LET ME IN!

She yelled back into the phone, "go the fuck away!" Not thinking straight, she threw the phone at the door, watching it shatter to pieces from the impact. *Shit, that was stupid.* She thought, looking toward the door, hopeless and scared. Her mind, now numb from all the accumulated fear and anger, sent a cold fire coursing through her veins.

Tiny stood like a statue, not knowing what to do or how to protect them from the intruder. With a sudden crash, a rake slammed against the glass window breaking Beverly out of her trance. Tiny rushed the window, barking and baring all his teeth. The rake slowly slid down the glass, which sent a blood-curdling shrill throughout her body. Then a pair of green eyes appeared, shimmering like emeralds outside the window before vanishing again.

A loud thud slammed against the front door, sending Tiny into a frenzy. The pounding continued as the handle swung violently back and forth, desperate to get in. "Get back, Tiny!" Beverly pushed Tiny aside, then stood defiantly with the baseball gripped tight in hand, prepared for her one and only last stand.

"Come and get it, bitch!" She yelled as the door slammed wide-open, revealing the shadowy humanoid figure standing in front of her as its eyes shifted to bright red. Beverly involuntarily lost grip over the bat as it fell to the floor. Paralyzed in place, she stared directly into its hypnotizing eyes. No longer able to think straight, the world around her became distorted and ceased to make sense.

The entity stood seven-feet tall, hovering outside the doorway, not advancing any further. It stared into Beverly's eyes, then spoke into her mind. "I have always been here, Beverly. I will soon come for you. Remember. I am always watching, " she heard its thoughts penetrate straight through her as a horrific low-pitched vibration—radiating throughout her entire mind, body, and soul. The entity moved backward as it floated several inches above the ground.

The front door slammed shut, while at the same time Beverly woke in her bed with the thud of her own bedroom door slamming shut. She jumped out of bed, screaming as she fumbled her fingers in the dark to turn on her lamp. Beverly fell to the floor in hysteria, then crawled toward the bedroom door. She reached for the knob, relieved to find it still locked. Turning with her back against the door, she cried herself back to sleep from exhaustion.

CHAPTER SEVEN

Beverly woke on the floor, leaned against the door as her morning alarm chimed. The sun came through the window, as the rays flooded across the floor, accompanied by its warmth over her. She forced herself up to turn off the alarm, then checked to see if anyone had tried calling her last night. No missed calls, and the phone was still intact. *"Well, I'm not taking those pills anymore."* Beverly said as she hesitantly opened her bedroom door, checking up and down the hallway before sneaking over to the bathroom.

"Beverly, what the hell are you doing? There's nothing out there," she said out loud, still in a morning haze. She took a shower, changed into her dark blue business attire, then went downstairs to have breakfast as Tiny patiently waited for her. "Good doggy, today will be a better day," she said, patting him on his head. Tiny looked up at her panting, which resembled a smile to her. "You probably think I'm slowly losing it, huh?" She chuckled to herself, shaking her head as she poured kibble into his empty bowl.

Beverly sat down at the kitchen counter and ate her breakfast next to Tiny, who effortlessly devoured the contents of his bowl. "Easy there, Tiger. Remember to chew your food; it isn't going anywhere," she said, standing up to get prepared for work. Before leaving for the day, she took a quick look around the house to err on the side of caution. She examined the front window, not noticing scratch marks or any other signs of entry near the front door.

Beverly exited, then walked toward her car as Mr. Kelly raked up the same leaf piles from yesterday. She grabbed her keys from her purse, trying not to stare, but noticed he had stopped what he is doing to look over at her. Caught off by surprise by his unexpected deranged smile, she dropped her keys to the ground.

"Have a good day at work," he said with an eerie grin across his face, which soon faded as he went back to raking the leaves.

"Thank you...good day to...you too, Mr. Kelly," she responded with a hesitant stutter. Beverly picked up her keys, then got into her car, locking the doors behind her. She turned the ignition and reversed out before quickly slamming on the brakes to avoid hitting a passing vehicle. Mr. Kelly walked over and gestured to roll down her window. Beverly pulled out into the road and complied with his request to hear what he had to say.

He leaned his elbow over her opened window, "That was a close one, you got to be more careful. They almost gotcha," he said with a grin on his face, which morphed into a discolored, crooked smile.

"Yeah, I know...," she responded short, then quickly rolled up her window on him and continued down the road. In her rear-view reflection, Mr. Kelly stood halfway out in the street, watching her go down the road. He held his rake with a smile from ear to ear before losing sight of her around the bend.

Beverly received a call from Adam as she pulled into work. "Hope you have a fantastic first day at work," he said through her speaker-phone.

"Adam, today is my second day, but thank you for the reassurance," she said, parking her car.

"Sorry, I thought you had Columbus Day off."

"That was last week. Regardless, I'm glad you called anyway. I would've tried to call you last night but fell asleep early. Would you like to come over tonight, if you can?" She said more as a statement with desperation in her voice.

"Sure, babe. I have a few clients in the afternoon, but I'll stop by. Is everything okay? You sound a little flustered."

"Yeah, I'm good. I just want to see you, that's all," Beverly said, walking toward the office building.

"Okay, sounds good, I'll let you know if I'm running a little late."

"Awesome, thanks, hon. Talk to you soon, gotta go now buh-bye," Beverly rushed him off the phone as she went inside.

Beverly passed the secretary's desk saying good morning to Junie, as she made her way to her office. She turned on the computer, prepared to work on the first project assigned from yesterday. Beverly summoned up all her strength to keep everything locked deep inside and remain focused.

She imagined a world where everything was normal, a world where she was in charge and without any problems. After the first hour of getting back into her groove, Beverly finished her new assignments before lunch. Mr. Schwartz gave a small knock on her door before coming in as she was tackling a few outstanding account receivables and invoices.

"I have to say, Beverly. You're everything I was hoping for and more."

"Thank you, sir!" She said with a prideful smile.

"Please, call me Paul. Also, we're having a small welcoming party slash company meeting at noon to welcome you to our branch. We are providing lunch, and shall see you there," he said, then smiled before walking out. Leaning back in her chair, Beverly felt she had made the right decision to relocate here. Finally, recognized for her hard work, instead of being a nameless face out of a sea of many.

After finishing her last assignment by noon, she made her way toward the conference room to meet some of the other co-workers. With complete surprise, she walked into the room and greeted by a dozen blue and white balloons, along with a crowd of co-workers sitting around a table.

A catered lunch scattered the table with cold-cut sandwiches, snacks, and a blue frosted cake with "Congrats Beverly," written with white icing. In weird unison, they turned and gave a round of applause as a few rose from their seats to introduce themselves.

"We're all glad to have you here, Beverly," One co-worker she hadn't met yet, said with a smile. Beverly took a step back, claustrophobic and overwhelmed by it all.

"Why, thank you, guys. You didn't need to go all out for me but I appreciate the kind gesture. I'm not used to this sort of thing," she said, forcing a nervous smile.

"We know. You're probably used to the hustle and bustle of the busy city life, but we're all like one big happy family here. Everyone wanted to welcome you to our branch appropriately. Now come over here and have some cake," Paul said with a hand gesture and smile. Junie took Beverly's hand and walked her over to the table.

"I would just like to say thank you for all your hospitality. Again, I'm not used to this sort of thing. I can't even remember...," Beverly stopped and chuckled. "The last time I was the center of this much attention," as she tried not to get choked up from their generosity and kindness.

"It's okay, Beverly. We like to make all of our new employees feel welcomed into our family and—" Paul said, interrupted by Beverly's cell phone ring. She took it out of her pocket, trying to hide her embarrassment, which quickly changed to excitement as Doctor Spitzer's number appeared on her screen.

"I'm so sorry, guys. But I really need to take this call," she said in a desperate voice as she rushed out of the room.

"No worries, Beverly. You know where to find us. Alright, everybody, let's dig in!" He gestured to his staff as Beverly made her way toward the door in haste.

"Hello, Doctor Spitzer?" She answered with both hands over her phone.

"Beverly, I've been eager to speak with you. I have some urgent information that may help you. Listen to me carefully. What you've been experiencing is far more of an importance than what I previously conveyed from our last meeting. I have a few things to tell you in person and have a dear friend and colleague of mine who will explain more soon. He will be back in town this Sunday. I need you to make sure you can meet me at my office next Monday?" Beverly paused for a moment and leaned against the wall with her hand over her mouth in disbelief. "Beverly? Are you still there?"

She gathered up her courage and cleared her throat, "yes, of course, Doctor. I'll be there. I just... need to know what is real anymore. It feels as if I'm living two separate lives. Can this all be real?" She asked with hesitation.

"I don't want to give you any wrong information, so my colleague will go over everything during your next appointment."

"Okay, Doctor. I'll definitely be there. I just need answers. Please help me," she said in a somber tone.

"We'll do our best. Just hang in there until then."

"Thank you, Doctor. I'll try too, but it's getting worse," she said before being interrupted by her boss.

"Is everything okay?" Paul said as she jumped, almost dropping her phone.

"Yes, sorry about that, I'm okay, really. I just had a family member call me about something." She looked down at her phone and saw Doctor Spitzer had already hung up.

"Hopefully it's nothing serious. But, please come back in so everyone can introduce themselves and allow us an opportunity to hear more about yourself." Beverly agreed with a half-smile of dread.

"I just don't have much to say, Paul. I'm just your ordinary city girl," she said, which only went on deaf ears as they made their way back into the conference room. Beverly decided to play the part as her boss closed the double doors behind them.

CHAPTER EIGHT

Late in the afternoon, Beverly pulled into her driveway. She dialed Adam's cell phone on her way home, which went directly to voice-mail again but found him waiting patiently by the front door. Beverly hurried to get out of her car to greet him with a long-awaited hug. "I'm glad you were able to meet me," she said, holding him tighter.

"I'm sorry I didn't get back to you when you called on your lunch break. I've been buried with clients during the last several days. How do you like your new job?" He asked as they made their way toward the house. Before entering, they noticed Mr. Kelly across the street raking leaves, which appeared if he had just spread the previous piles from earlier.

"That guy gives me the total creeps," she said as they ignored it and walked into the house. She recollected her thoughts, "I enjoy my new job, everyone there seems really friendly and laid back." Beverly said, placing her handbag on the kitchen counter.

"Yeah, I can believe it. It's a different atmosphere up here. Probably no comparison to your life back in the city. We're just a small community of simple folk." Adam said, with a laugh, as he patted Tiny, who kept sniffing at his hand.

"I can see it. It'll take some time to get used to it, though. I would go through an entire day without anyone noticing me or asking me how I was doing, or for my life story as they did at the office today. I just made up some ordinary things so they wouldn't ask me any more questions," she said sighing.

"There's nothing to be ashamed of Beverly," Adam said as he took her hand.

"I know. I just don't want to share that part of my past with everyone. I only tell people whom I can trust. She said and kissed him. "That's why I had to tell you everything that has been going on with me recently." Beverly paused for a moment, "I needed to tell you the truth."

Adam rubbed her hand as she continued, "these visions are more frequent, intense, and terrifying the last several days. I'm meeting with my psychiatrist next Monday so he can treat this properly. I hope you understand what I'm going through. I'm not crazy. I just need a little help."

Adam held her as he continued to stare into her eyes. "I don't think you are crazy, I'm just trying to piece this altogether too, so I can understand what you are experiencing. What do you see, hon?...in these visions?"

Beverly went into detail about last night and explained how she was in bed, then received a phone call in the middle of the night from an unknown number. Then went on to tell him how she had investigated downstairs after hearing someone trying to break into her house. "Half of it seems real, but half of it feels like it's all a dream. I remember going downstairs last night, then suddenly, a rake slammed against my window and then—"

Adam took a step back, "wait, what? Where did you see this?"

Beverly pointed next to the front door, "I saw it strike against the window over there, then slowly scrape down the glass. Sorry, it's all just coming back to me now. I heard this loud bang against the front door, then the handle shook as if someone tried to get inside. It was all hazy after that. I just remember waking up in bed, but I'm certain it wasn't a dream." Beverly said, lowering her head, ashamed for not remembering all the details, like a young child trying to interpret the real world to a grown-up.

"Over here?" Adam said as he walked toward the window, to investigate for any signs of an intruder. He scanned the double-paned tempered glass window, knowing it wouldn't leave a trace. Adam glanced across the street as Mr. Kelly grinned back over to him with his rake in hand.

"That mother fucker!" Adam rushed over to the front door, slamming it open.

"Wait! Where are you going?" Beverly followed outside after him, recalling his slight temper at times, but never to this severity. Adam pulled up his sleeves as he walked across her front yard and street.

"Hey, you! Yeah, I'm talking to you. You fucking son of a bitch! Why are you always looking over at my girlfriend's house?" Adam crossed into Mr. Kelly's yard, coming only inches from his face, then knocked the rake out of his hands. Mr. Kelly turned his head slightly to where it had fallen, then back over to face Adam.

"Boy, I don't know what your problem is? But I suggest you get on out of here before there's a real issue," he said, appearing not one bit surprised by Adam's erratic behavior.

"I better not see you look in her general direction ever again! If I so much as hear a single word of it, I'll be over here so fast to shove that rake so far up your ass; you'll be doing handstands to rake up your fucking leaves! You got that?" Adam said, grabbing him by his overalls, clenching them in his fists as he pulled him closer.

"Adam, wait! Stop!" Beverly screamed from across the street as Mr. Kelly used the distraction to knock Adam's hand away, then shoved him back.

"Boy, if you touch me again, there will be serious consequences. I don't know what your deal is. But if I see you near, or on my property again, I'll beat your ass, then call the cops and press charges, saying it was all in self-defense." Mr. Kelly said, looking him dead in the eyes as he readjusted his overalls.

Enraged, Adam continued to question him, "someone has been stalking my girlfriend and tried to break into her home last night. Coincidently, she saw a rake hit her window before they attempted to come inside." Adam stepped back as Mr. Kelly reached down for his rake on the ground.

"I don't know what to tell you, kid. Weird things happen around here at night. You'll one day find that there is more to fear than me," he said with a smirk across his face.

"What did you just say, old man?" Adam said as he clenched his hand into a fist by his side.

"You heard me, boy. I suggest you get out of here if you know what's good for ya," he said as Adam swung back his arm about to throw a punch. Beverly ran up from behind to intercept it by grabbing his upper arm.

"We need to go now!" Beverly said as she tried to pull Adam away with all her strength.

"You best listen to your lady before you soon regret it," Mr. Kelly said, belting out a hearty laugh. Beverly walked Adam across the street as he continued to look over his shoulder to face him.

"You son of a bitch, this isn't over!" Adam yelled back as she forced him around toward the front door as hysterical laughter echoed from across the street. She pushed Adam inside, then slammed the door shut.

Beverly glared at Adam, "what the fuck was that all about?" Scolding him as Tiny circled them, not knowing why she was upset.

"I know it was him! I am trying to protect you, Beverly," he said, trying to calm her and himself down.

"I don't want you to make matters worse. I'll have to take it day by day. He creeps me out for sure, but I don't even know if it was him. If I have proof, I will get the police involved." Beverly said, grabbing his arm as Adam's fists finally unclenched and relaxed.

"He mentioned something about weird things happening here at night. He has to be up to something," Adam said, catching his breath.

"I don't know what he meant by that either. All I know is that he's an odd retired senior from across the street. He's probably senile and has a couple few loose screws, so I don't want you starting some sort of feud to make things worse, okay? Is that crystal clear?" She said, waiting for a response, then continued to explain, "I appreciate you trying to be my hero and all. But I'll find a way to figure this all out. I just need to speak to my psychiatrist, who knows somebody that specializes in this sort of thing."

Adam interjected, "I'm sorry, sweetheart. But your psychiatrist can't help you if your neighbor is the one causing all this. I'll try to restrain myself, but if he ever comes over here again or tries to confront you. I want you to tell me. I would be over in a heartbeat to take care of it." Adam said, taking her hand as she looked in his eyes with nothing else to say. "Let's just forget about it, okay?" he said as she nodded her head, trusting his judgment.

As the evening progressed, they sat down for a quiet dinner and discussed their camping plans together. "The weather might be a little chilly this weekend, but I'll, of course, build a fire to keep us warm at night." He said with a smile, then pulled out a map from his backpack. "I know of the perfect place in the Adirondacks that's two and a half hours north of us," Adam said, pointing to a spot on the map. "The campground is located in Twin Peaks, which is near a small town tucked away in the mountains several miles from route 30 off of Interstate 87."

"Isn't everything closed this time of year? I thought Columbus Day was the last weekend to camp," she said, glancing down at the map.

"Yes, they are, after Labor Day to be exact. But I know someone who manages the property up there. He's an old friend of mine that'll unlock the gates to the entire campgrounds for us. I used to go there every year during the off-season with my friends. It will be amazing, just you, me, and nature. We'll finally be able to get away from it all," Adam explained as he finished his dinner.

Beverly continued to look at the map, then back up to him, "it sounds wonderful, sweetie. I have never been camping before. This town is the closest thing I've ever been to nature unless you consider Central Park," Beverly said and laughed as she drank her wine.

"I'm really looking forward to sharing this experience with you and hopefully many more years to come," Adam said as he rinsed his plate off in the sink. Beverly blushed, then placed her empty wine glass back down on the counter.

"Oh, is that so?" Beverly said as she slowly got up and walked toward him. Adam dried his hands and embraced her in his arms. She took his hand, then passionately kissed him. "Let's go make some more great memories," she whispered into his ear. Beverly led him upstairs to her bedroom as Tiny watched from the living room.

In the heat of passion, Beverly threw Adam onto the bed and positioned herself over his lap. She straddled him and kissed him, then turned her head as her flowing brown hair flew over her shoulder. Beverly looked deep into his eyes as she held his head and kissed him feverishly, biting his lower lip. She arched her back, then slowly unbuttoned her top as he reached behind to unhinged her bra. Adam aggressively yanked the sides of her blouse, sending several buttons flying across the room. She smiled and tilted her head back, guiding his hands over her exposed breasts.

He noticed a bruise on her upper arm but ignored it as he shifted his body to lay atop of hers. Adam slowly kissed down her neck toward her stomach. Beverly placed her hands on the back of his head, "I want you inside me," she moaned as he unbuttoned her pants and went down on her. She grabbed his hair as he continued to pleasure her, "I want you so fucking bad, Adam." Beverly said with a tremble in her voice, as he continued to make love to her for the rest of the evening.

Several hours later, in the middle of the night, she slowly woke as Adam slept with his arm over the sheet across her chest. She laid motionless on her back, fully paralyzed, focusing on her breathing. Beverly watched his arm slowly rise and fall with each breath, hoping the paralysis would subside. She felt a low rumbling vibration throughout her body, drawing her attention in front of her.

A dark humanoid figure stood from across the room, staring back at her. It had no physical features that she could relate too. Similar to the entity from last night, but now veiled in complete darkness without any distinguishable characteristics. It stood motionless, like a three-dimensional shadow contrasted against the darkness. The entity stepped closer and observed them laying next to each other. Beverly's breathing became labored as her eyes traced its movements from the foot of the bed. Every attempt to move her body was in vain. She called out for Adam, which only verbalized as a faint moan, barely escaping her lips.

Beverly watched as the dark figure climbed onto the foot of her bed, then sat quietly to study her for several more minutes. The dark, faceless entity tilted its head toward its shoulder with curiosity like a cat playing with its prey, ready to pounce. It slowly brought its long slender fingers toward its non-distinguishable face. This particular entity didn't have the same glowing eyes from before, only a bottomless pit of darkness. She laid there, not knowing what else to do or how to wake Adam. Beverly wished he would sense this otherworldly presence and spring awake to fight it off. For him to finally know once and for all this wasn't solely a manifestation in her imagination.

The entity tucked in its arms and legs inward, as to curl into a ball, then slowly unfurled itself in a diving motion toward the sheets. With one slow uniformed sliding movement, the being submerged its head underneath the blankets. A painful shock of electricity ran across her legs as it made its way upward toward her chest. It slithered further until it laid directly on top of her.

The sheets rose above her as its knees pressed against her body. The entity, now hidden underneath the blankets, raised itself in front of her. Adam removed his arm, then rolled over onto his back, unaware of her and his own danger. She turned her eyes forward again as the dark figure's head emerged out from under the sheets. His darken void of a featureless face was now only inches away from hers.

The entity stared into Beverly's eyes then turned its attention toward Adam, then again back to her. It leaned over and whispered its thoughts into her mind. "Can I come inside too?"

Beverly screams escaped as soft whimpered moans as she tried to break free from her paralysis. Tears ran down her cheeks as Adam laid silent, asleep, and unaware of its presence. The entity concealed its head back underneath the sheets, then raised itself above her. Shocks of electricity radiated throughout her helpless body. An intense pressure pressed against her pelvis, followed by something unpleasant penetrating inside her.

The terrifying sensation lasted a few seconds, then stopped as the electrical sensation dissipated. The comforter fell back toward Beverly's body as if nothing had occurred, just a hallucination in her half-asleep dream state. Beverly's paralysis wore off as she jumped up in bed, screaming at the top of her lungs. Her skin was moist from hot sweat, with a tingling sensation that continued to linger.

Adam woke from her frantic cries, and out of instinct, grabbed Beverly to console her. She flung her arms outward, trying to fight him off during the hysteria. He quickly scanned the room to find nothing out of the ordinary. In the moonlight, he saw Beverly's panicked face. "Honey, it's me. Is everything okay? It was only a bad dream," he said as he tried to put his arm around her.

"No, it couldn't have been a dream! I can't fucking live like this anymore!" She yelled as tears streamed down her face.

"What happened?"

"I don't want to talk about right now. These fucking nightmares have to stop!"

Adam turned toward Beverly and kissed her on the cheek, "I'm here for you, Beverly. We'll find a way to fix this together, okay?" He said as he rubbed his hand across her back to comfort her.

"I know you want to try and help me. But in all honesty, I feel there's no hope left. I'll completely understand if you want to leave me," she said as he wiped away her tears with his hand.

Adam grabbed her by the chin, turning her head to make eye contact with him, "I swear to God or to fuck whomever. I will never leave you, Beverly. There's always hope left in the world, it may not be easy to find, but together we'll keep searching for it," he said, getting her to smile.

Beverly kissed him, then lowered herself back into bed and cradled herself in his arms. "Let's try to get some sleep, honey. I'll never let go of you tonight or ever. You're safe now," Adam said as they laid next to each other in the dark, not knowing the following steps to take, as he held her during the rest of the night.

CHAPTER NINE

Quarter past seven in the morning, they sat at the kitchen table, eating their scrambled eggs in silence. Neither wanted to bring up last night's events, to avoid any unnecessary awkwardness. Beverly lacked the desire to explain every detail of what she could barely remember in the first place. Instead, they sat mutually quiet at the table, sharing the same feeling that it was a new day, and knew as long as they were together they could resolve this. Adam reached over and held Beverly's hand as she finished her coffee.

"Hang in there, honey. Two days from now, we'll be off on our camp trip together. Afterward, you'll be refreshed, clear-minded, and able to sort this all out during your next appointment," Adam said, kissing her hand before standing from his chair.

"Thank you, Adam. I appreciate you wanting to help me. I'm feeling much better today," Beverly said as Adam ran his hand along her shoulders while walking toward the kitchen.

"You better get going, or you'll be late," he said, placing his plate into the sink. "I'll feed Tiny and clean up for you," he said as Tiny stared down at his empty bowl.

"Thanks, hon. I'm looking forward to seeing you this Friday," she said, grabbing for her purse, then kissed him goodbye.

"I am too. Trust me, you're going to love it up there," Adam said as she made her way to the front door.

"I can't wait! Have a good day. Love ya!" Beverly said, blowing him a kiss before closing the door behind her.

Adam finished washing the dishes, then decided to spoil Tiny with a half-can of wet dog food and some leftover bacon. He went to gather his things, then remembered he had left his phone in her bedroom. He stood at the bottom of the staircase, glancing toward the top as a shiver ran through his body.

"Why am I getting creeped out by this? This is all just in her head," he said, before walking upstairs. He entered her bedroom, scanning from corner to corner, only to see sheets spread across her bed. He grabbed his phone, placed it in his pocket, then made his way toward the hallway. He stopped in the doorway for a second, then turned, deciding to make her bed before he left.

Adam pulled the sheets off her side of the bed and noticed something peculiar. A series of burn markings were underneath the top comforter. He lifted the sheets, only to find none of them had burned through. He didn't see any particular pattern to it, except that they were only isolated to her side of the bed. He tossed the sheet into the air, watching it fall and reposition over the bed. After a second glance, they were gone and thought it was only his imagination. He tucked the sides under the mattress while an uncomfortable intuition stirred in his subconscious.

Adam rushed back downstairs, "alright, Tiny. I'm outta here, see ya later, buddy." Adam locked the door behind him and got into his car as he collected his thoughts. He noticed Mr. Kelly in his mirror, trimming several overhung branches in his front yard. Adam decided to heed Beverly's advice and ignore him to avoid any unnecessary problems. As Adam reversed out of the driveway, he caught a glimpse of him smirking off in the distance. Adam raised his middle finger out the window as he drove down the road.

Beverly pulled into the parking lot of her office. She said good morning to Junie, who sat behind her desk, playing on her phone and taking pictures of herself in ridiculous poses. Junie Smith had just recently graduated from Silver Lakes high school. She had worked part-time during her senior year, which eventually led to a full-time position. Junie, like the majority of her other high school graduates, lacked any ambitions to one day leave their small community behind.

From time to time, they would make small talk amongst each other in passing. Beverly soon realized her passions were for simpler things, like what was new on social media, reality TV shows, and People's magazine. The only topics she would go into depth with were centered around bleak discussions about the latest celebrity's public outbursts, fashion trends, or relationship infidelities. Beverly didn't consider her unintelligent or incapable of achieving more, but maybe lacked the motivation and drive to do so.

Beverly spent most of her childhood trapped within the confines of the orphanage. She felt fortunate that her social worker pushed her to evolve into the woman she had become today. Eventually, Beverly molded her own identity, independence, and destiny. Beverly may have easily turned out like Junie if she hadn't expanded her own horizons, or had lived out a private, comfortable childhood lifestyle with her parents. Happy and content, without the flames of hardships to sharpen the steel that resides inside all of us.

Growing up in a large city, Beverly felt small and alone, yearning to escape and move on to something different. Beverly knew they had that commonality with each other despite their opposing upbringings. Coming to a conclusion about her own life, it's either a deep-seated fear or a lack of drive that holds someone stationary within their bubbles of comfort. Junie's personality and friendliness reminded Beverly of her best friend, Kristen. Not only were they both from Silver Lakes, but also shared similar down-to-earth traits inherited through their small-town upbringing. However, Kristen always wanted out of this town and did everything possible to make that happen.

Beverly knew Kristen would never return to Silver Lakes since she's a self-proclaimed city girl now. But that big city lifestyle was everything Beverly wanted to escape from, which had been loneliness, isolation, and despair. She desperately hoped that this rural town would one day fill that void. The idea of where the grass was always greener on the other side persuaded her actions.

This concept appealed to her; the pleasant thoughts of having a fresh new start with Adam, job-position, and a new home that would help her grow as a person with a new identity. Beverly felt everyone was friendlier here, but she was still hesitant to shed her mask of comfort and allow for her true individuality to shine. In a way, she still struggled with the same fear of change, like a prisoner locked within her own mind. Beverly made her way to her office, feeling motivated after reflecting on her own weaknesses, hoping it would one day be her strengths. She sat in her chair, ready to tackle the balance sheets and prepare the company's monthly profit and loss statement.

Beverly had worked for NY Skylines, Inc, a large electrical parts distributor, for five years and managed the accounting books for large sums of money, inventory, expenses, and sales at her last position. Corporate had noticed their sister branch contingents were not as profitable as their city counterparts, so she had been promoted to relocate up north. Hoping to straighten out the discrepancies within their profit and expense margins and to fix these issues before corporate finally decided to close down their long-time coming, non-profitable branch, indefinitely.

Beverly continued to work on account payables through her lunch break to catch up and keep her mind occupied. A sudden lower abdominal pain gnawed at her as she remembered her experience from last night, the good and the bad. She sat silently, rubbing her stomach and recalled the realness of the nightmare and how despicably physical it felt. While shedding a tear, she knew how vulnerable and helpless she had been with these new visions, which continued to haunt her night after night.

The pain subsided as she packed up her things for the afternoon. She closed her window blinds overlooking the stagnant pond below. Outside, the leaves had all fallen off the bare tree and laid scattered across the landscape, slowly decomposing into cellulose skeletons. She turned off the light and went down the hall toward her boss's office. Her mind raced as she quickly conceived a new alibi to avoid mentioning her psychiatric past.

"Paul, are you busy?" Beverly said, with a gentle rap against his half-opened door.

"Not at all, come on in," Paul said as she pushed the door open as he worked on revising a client-vendor spreadsheet. "Can you believe it, Beverly? Our clients are leaving town left and right! Account receivables have been dragging for the last few months. We had a slight increase in sales during the early summer with solar parts and installations, but not by a whole lot. Maybe due to the fact that we live in a densely wooded area. We just aren't hitting the mark, " he said as he turned to her.

"I noticed that too. I'm working on the profit and loss statements to see where we can cut back and how much we currently owe to our vendors," Beverly said from the doorway.

"Good work, Beverly. We'll need all the expertise we can get. I swear the last person we had could've been outworked by a chimpanzee."

"Well, I hope I don't drive you bananas in the process," she said with a smile, knowing how corny her joke sounded.

"Ha, I like you, Beverly. What can I do for you too help with your transition here?" Paul said with his contagious laughter.

"You guys have been great so far! I just have one favor to ask you," she said, then continued. "I know it's my first week and all, and this is very short notice…" Beverly said as he smiled, waving his hand for her to continue. "Well, the phone call I received yesterday during our luncheon was from a family member back home. And…it's sort of an emergency that I need to attend to over the weekend and most likely on Monday as well," she said, somberly.

"Beverly, I'm so sorry to hear this. Take care of your family first, and don't worry about coming in on Monday. Hell, take tomorrow off if you need too. I know you're working very hard on these financial statements, but they can wait until you get back. If you were in sales, it would be a different story," he said, chuckling to himself.

"Thank you, Mr. Schwartz, I appreciate that very much so."

"You're very welcome, Beverly. Take care of yourself. I hope you have a good weekend. I'll see you when you return," he said to her.

"Thanks again. I'll see you next week." Beverly closed his door, then walked passed the front desk, noticing Junie had already left for the evening. She exited the building, then got into her car, relieved, knowing she had the camp trip to unwind from everything and prepare for Monday's appointment. On her way home, Beverly called Adam to tell him that she could leave anytime tomorrow.

"That's great news, honey. I should be over around noon. I'll also call my friend and let him know we'll be arriving earlier." Adam said as he recalled in the back of his mind of what he thought he saw this morning. "I cleaned up a bit and fed Tiny before I left," he said, neglecting the anecdote that could ruin the mood. He didn't know what he saw or if it was even real or just his imagination.

"Thanks, honey, I appreciate everything you do for me. I shall see you tomorrow!" Beverly said, before saying goodnight as she pulled into her driveway. She got out of her car and noticed a package left on her front doorstep. Beverly cautiously walked toward her porch to retrieve the box, labeled from an unknown sender. Out of paranoia, she looked around her quiet neighborhood, then across the street. There was no one in sight, including Mr. Kelly, who was religiously outside, tending to his dying garden or an endless pile of leaves.

She picked up the box and brought it inside with her. "Hello there, buddy!" Beverly said to Tiny as she went to the kitchen and placed the package on the counter. "How was your day?" She said, patting his head, then led him out back to relieve himself.

She turned on the TV as the news broadcast discussed the latest crime shootings that occurred last night in the city. One from an incident of domestic violence, which quickly turned tragic, leaving four displaced children in the aftermath. The other was an armed robbery at a bodega near Queens, where an elderly woman was hospitalized with minor injuries. There's been ongoing breaking news of an active hostage situation at the Harlem flats where civilians taunted the police, on the very streets, they were trying to protect.

Beverly shook her head in disgust as she made her way to the kitchen to prepare Tiny's dinner from a can. "Only if we can be like you, Tiny. Grateful and appreciative of just being alive," Beverly said as she turned her attention back toward the mysterious package.

"Who could this be from? Adam? Mr. Kelly? Perhaps, it's a bomb." She said, laughing out loud while opening the box, then pulled out a gift, wrapped in brown kraft paper. She grabbed a pair of scissors to cut the string, which held it together. She tore through the wrapper, like a small child on a Christmas morning, to reveal two books inside, along with a note: "*Hope this helps! Review some of it over the weekend before we meet on Monday. Take care.*" Beverly examined the two books, one titled, "Sleep Paralysis: Myth and Science" and the slightly smaller book, "Lucid Dreaming: The True Awakening."

After realizing it was from her psychiatrist, she felt grateful for all the effort he had put forth to try and help her. She looked down at the books feeling overwhelmed with the amount of information on the subject. Beverly had never heard of any of this before, only the term sleep paralysis, which he had diagnosed her with before prescribing those useless medications. It finally dawned on her that there's more to all of this than just merely taking another pill. She picked up the thicker book on sleep paralysis, along with a glass of wine, before heading toward the couch. She sat down as Tiny munched on his dinner in the kitchen.

Beverly reclined on the couch with the encyclopedia-sized book over her lap and a wine glass in her hand. "I usually prefer to read Bachman before bed, but I guess this will have to do for tonight." She said as she fingered through the index and titles for each chapter, with topics ranging from biblical to modern times. One section caught Beverly's eye as she read every word with insatiable curiosity.

The chapter discussed the non-canonical passages from the book of Enoch regarding the Bible's Genesis epoch, which referenced Lilith as the first woman before Eve. The description explained that Lilith had been made from the same very clay as Adam and considered herself an equal, refusing to be subservient to him. The chapter went into more detail, describing Lilith as a rebellious soul who questioned God, which led to her banishment from the Garden of Eden.

Old Hebrew legends from the lost dead scrolls explained that the archangel Samael—considered both good and evil while condoning the sinful acts of man—seduced Lilith to be his bride. Samael was the grim reaper, angel of death, and still argued by some if he was more destructive and sinister than the most powerful fallen angel, Lucifer—battling over the title of Satan. In both Hebrew and Arabic, Lilith translated to Night or Night Hag and had been feared for stealing babies while they slept. The book also stated she was well known as a demonic succubus, which targeted men with her nightly sexual encounters as an act of revenge toward Eve and mankind.

Beverly saw similar connections with several other stories that were mentioned in the text, along with photos of Roman-era paintings. Other pictures were of statues that depicted a succubus with her male counterpart described as an Incubus. "Thanks, Doc! I'm sure this won't give me any nightmares tonight," she said out loud, recalling last night's vision. She continued to read further as she took another gulp from her wine glass.

She grabbed for her side after a sudden deep sharp pain dug into her lower abdomen, slowly subsiding as before. She read through the chapter's introductions of each demonic entity. She came across many names she had never heard of before; Batibat, of the Philippines, Pesanta of Catalonia, Pandafeche of Italy, Popobawa of Africa, and Domovoi, which caused bruises at night. There were also numerous stories passed down to generations regarding the chest crushing old hag visitations from Newfoundland and the British Isles. She read brief articles in early American history from the Salem witch trials, where the corpses of the accused would be unearthed by colonists—only for the sole purpose to have their hearts removed from their chests, then burned for confirmation.

Beverly took a deep breath as the list continued on with Liderc, a shape-shifter from Hungarian lore, along with more similar entities. One chapter referenced the D'Jinn from ancient Egyptian times, which caused horrible dreams they called Karabasan, which is the term now used for the nightmarish creature from Turkey. Arabian lore simply referred to them as Jinn, describing them as a supernatural species who lived amongst us, which coined the modern-day term, Genie. She sipped her wine and scanned down the list of contemporary folklore where Vietnamese refugees in America had unexplainable deaths at night, which their culture thought to be caused by a creature called the Dab Tsog.

Beverly continued to read about other eastern folklore from Japan, which had stories about the Kanashibari, described as spirits who took on the form of their deceased loved ones. Then on the other page, an entity called the Baku, which had been described as a dark, hideous beast who "ate hope, motivation, and the inspiring dreams from its sleeping victims," Beverly read out loud while turning to the next page. She came across the more well known Anglo-Saxon and old Nordic folklore that referenced all these same entities, simply as the Mara or Mare. This was the origin of the contemporary name for nightmare. *The Night Mara.*

"Holy shit! I never knew that!" Beverly said out loud, then closed the book, realizing every culture all had the same similarities she had been experiencing. There were slight variations in their stories, and every creature went by different names, but never-the-less they were all one and the same. Despite how disturbing these stories were, she found refuge in the idea that she was no longer alone. Coming to turns that everyone around the world, and throughout different eras, had shared the same underlying symptoms in one way or another.

She placed the book onto the table in front of her, then reclined back to finish her wine. She quietly thought to herself, how mankind, from every corner of the globe, are somehow united with all the same fears and experiences from eons ago. *Why is that? Why are we then still so divided and violent toward one another?* With all our minuscule differences, we continue to have territorial disputes and conflicts over resources and religion. *Why does humanity still embrace war, when, in fact, everything we all have in common, are the same fears?* She shrugged it off as random thoughts from having a few glasses of wine and exhaustion. Tiny jumped onto the couch and cuddled next to her. Beverly pulled the blanket over her, turned off the TV, and fell asleep.

During the middle of the night, Beverly sprung awake after the TV newscast began talking about a mass shooting. Beverly laid there in a haze with her head slightly raised near the armrest of the couch. She listened to the newscaster talk about a mass shooting at a downtown Brooklyn theater. She sat up with the blanket still around her as Tiny slept by her feet. The volume blared as she recalled herself, turning it off before falling asleep. She looked around for the remote without any luck, then was interrupted during her search when the newscaster called out her name.

"Beverly, we're so sorry to inform you that...we just couldn't find him," the newscaster said as she stared at the TV in complete confusion. The broadcast showed breaking news but displayed the date of October 20, 2014, at the bottom of the screen, marking the sixteenth anniversary of the event, which she buried deep inside. "Yes, Beverly. I'm speaking to you. We know that you're all alone tonight. And it appears that we couldn't find the other person responsible for killing your parents. Oh, wait, this just in, as we speak... breaking news," he said with a grin, "we have stopped the investigation indefinitely. Sleep well tonight, poor sweet little, Beverly."

The TV screen went to whitish-grey as static blared throughout the house. Beverly covered her ears and sobbed as anger swelled inside. Her posture became rigid, her jugular engorged as she clenched her hands into a fist. Beverly threw herself off the couch, then leaped toward the television. She grunted, lifting it from its stand and threw it onto the hardwood floor. Shards of plastic, metal, and glass shrapnel flew across her living room, ricocheting into the kitchen.

Tiny opened his eyes and barked hysterically, which snapped Beverly out of her dream-like state. She turned to him, confused about why she was standing in the living room, trembling with uncontrollable rage.

Beverly looked down at the remnants of her television sprawled along the hardwood floor. She consoled Tiny, then stumbled her way off to bed. Halfway up the staircase, she glanced over her shoulder at the demolished television, then over to the book laying open on her table. *This can't be real. I must have been sleepwalking or something.* Beverly made it to the top of the staircase and thought. *The Night Mara?*

CHAPTER TEN

Beverly woke with Tiny sound asleep against her pillow and snoring in her face. She rubbed her eyes, then swung her legs off the bed without disturbing him. While sitting at the edge of the bed, she noticed the sunlight penetrating vibrantly through her window. She checked her phone and found she had overslept well past noon with several missed calls and texts from Adam, "Shit!"

Knowing he was on his way, she returned his call as it only rang through to voice-mail. She stumbled to the bathroom to get ready for the trip as Adam sent her a text message, "20 out." Tiny looked up with exhaustion from the bed after hearing all the commotion, then jumped to the floor. He followed her to the bathroom and positioned himself directly underneath her feet.

"Come on, Tiny. I have to get ready," she said with a sigh, then chuckled as Tiny fell back asleep underneath her as she brushed her teeth. Even though she had nothing packed from the night before, she knew

Adam would be well prepared for this trip and that she could travel light. *It would only take ten minutes max to get ready*, she thought as she got out of the shower and grabbed for her towel.

She went to the closet to retrieve her backpack, which was shoved toward the back underneath piles of clean clothes she hadn't put away yet after moving in. She fumbled with her bag, which had been filled with things from her commuting days in the city. She pulled out a small can of pepper spray, makeup, and some crunched up magazines, then tossed them to the floor. She collected a change of clothes, toiletries, and a few other essentials, cramming them all in. Beverly noticed an old teddy bear tucked away in the far corner of her closet. She stared at it for a moment, then shut the door, throwing the backpack across her shoulders before going downstairs.

Adam stood in the living room, waiting for her as he examined the shattered TV across the floor. "Earthquake?" Adam asked, sarcastically, and puzzled. "You alright? You left your door unlocked last night," he said with a concerned expression as he tried to move the broken television.

"Don't worry about it. I was messing with the wires in the back, then poof it landed on the floor," she said, grabbing her book off the table and placed it into her backpack. "You know us women and lifting things," she fired back, wanting to change the subject.

"You should have waited for me, babe. I could've helped you when I came over today," he said, stepping over the pieces.

"It's okay, I'm independent and don't always need help with everything. I was just a little careless, that's all. It's called an accident, Adam, sheesh. I can freakin' replace it with my next paycheck." Beverly said as she walked toward the kitchen counter, shoving the other book into her bag.

"Okay. I was only offering to help you," Adam said as Tiny made his way downstairs to the kitchen.

Beverly zipped her bag, then turned to him, "I know that Adam, and I appreciate all that you to do to help me. But, I'm okay. Sometimes, it's like you don't think I can handle anything on my own," she said, lowering her voice, not wanting to be confrontational.

"I know you're a tough city girl." Adam joked as Beverly knelled to feed Tiny, then hugged him goodbye. "Who will watch him for you while we're away?"

"Junie, the secretary from work, offered to check in on him. I didn't have the chance to make a spare key yet, so I'll have to leave mine under the mat."

"What, really? Aren't you worried about that lunatic from across the street?" Adam said with a concerned look on his face as they prepared to leave.

"It's fine, Adam. He's probably crazy, but I don't think he's that crazy. Besides, I forgot to lock the door last night anyway." Beverly said while pretending to hold an imaginary rake, shaking it in front of him, as he didn't find the humor in the joke.

"Come on! Let's get out of here! Let us be free!" Beverly said, joyfully skipping toward the door to patronize him some more.

"Alright, but use my spare key instead," Adam offered, with it in his hand before exiting the house. She took it and locked the door behind them, then placed it under the welcome mat.

"This is a quiet little town on a small dead-end street. It'll be fine, Adam. Stop worrying so much," Beverly said as she turned to him with a smile. Across the street, Mr. Kelly was on the top rung of his ladder, clearing the roof gutters from the last batch of leaves. Beverly got his attention by yelling over to him as she waved her hands over her head with a smile. "Have a great weekend, Mr. Kelly! Adam and I are off on an adventure together. See you later, alligator," she said, waving enthusiastically. Mr. Kelly looked over and shook his head before turning away to attend to his autumn chores.

"Can we go now? What has gotten into you today? Is this how you are when you get to sleep in?" Adam said rhetorically, as she playfully ignored him with a smile, throwing her backpack into the back seat of his Jeep.

"What's the hold up then? Let's do this!" Beverly said as she kissed him, then ran over toward the passenger side.

"Was that wise to tell him you were leaving town, after placing your key under the—" he trailed off, noticing Beverly had already gotten into his car. Adam glanced across the street at Mr. Kelly, who paid no attention to him, as he continued with his weekend home projects. Adam shook his head to all of the nonsense and got into his car. He pulled out of her driveway in a hurry and drove down the road, vacation-bound.

A quarter past three in the afternoon, they continued north on Interstate 87 with no traffic ahead for miles. The clouds were sparse; the sun was bright; the weather was mild. Adam leaned over to kiss Beverly, then smiled. "We're making good time and should be at our exit within an hour," Adam said as he turned the radio station to 102.7 EQX.

"No rush, I'm enjoying this. Wait! I love this song!" Beverly yelled out enthusiastically, swiping his hand away from the radio as she rocked out to the intro for Alice In Chain's "I Stay Away." Adam smiled as she grabbed his hand and hung her other out the window, watching it go up and down with the wind. "We definitely lucked out with the weather this weekend. It's perfect for a road trip," she said, squeezing his hand.

"I know, right. It's an amazing October weekend. Perfect for your first great outdoors camping experience." Adam passed a flatbed truck in front of him and pointed to the sign that they were now entering the Adirondack's national park reserve. "We have about 30 miles before we need to turn off the highway. I'm going to stop for gas and let my friend know we're getting close." They continued up the steep incline as the open landscape gradually narrowed into an enclosed roadway, surrounded by steep rocky cliffs with lush, colorful mountains off in the distance.

"It smells wonderful up here! And so many trees," she said with a smile as she leaned her head out the window.

"Those are all the evergreen trees. I bet you're not used to seeing those back in the city," Adam turned to her, enjoying the excitement on her face. "I find it funny how I've gotten to know this area so well over the years. Believe it or not, I've been here more often than in the city. Heck, I can't even tell someone how to get to Central Park from Times Square. However, I could name every mountain peak within the state park. I guess I'm more of an outdoorsman's type." Adam explained as he passed over a suspension bridge as several people were in the water below with their canoes and fishing boats.

"I do have to say, with all certainty, I'll always love this place more than anywhere else. It's a tradition that I can never get tired of," Adam said, turning to her.

"I can see why. It's so beautiful here. Thank you again for bringing me along for this adventure." Beverly said, looking out her window toward the small cape-style beach homes scattered along the lakeside. The late afternoon sun reflected ribbons of gold, which glistened across the water as boaters anchored and cast out their fishing rods. Several small children swam and waded by the shore as their family prepared a barbecue picnic for a birthday party celebration, with several silver balloons tied to the dock.

"I'm happy to have you a part of this whole experience with me. And hopefully, with some luck," then turned to her and smiled, "we could continue this tradition for many years to come." Adam said, squeezing her hand before quickly letting go to grab the steering wheel on both sides. He changed lanes abruptly as a large, lifted pickup truck with over-sized tires accelerated toward them. The truck tailgated inches behind his rear bumper. To try to avoid them, Adam jerked his car into the middle lane before regaining control again.

"Assholes!" Adam yelled out the window, flipping them the middle finger as they sped by with diesel fumes billowing out of the vertical aftermarket exhaust pipes behind their cab. The occupants were four college-aged men oblivious to anyone on the road. The carefree passengers stuck their heads out the window with beer cans in hand, screaming along to heavy metal music. They continued to accelerate, passing them, as a noxious plume of exhaust smoke momentarily obscured their view. Two large flags flew opposite of each other on the rear corners of the pickup truck; one was the Confederate "Bars and Stripes," the other, a "Don't Tread On Me" flag. Adam put the gas pedal to the floor to catch up but was left far behind as they went over the hillside.

"Douche bags," Adam yelled out, laying on his horn as he corrected his car in the center lane. He turned to see if Beverly was okay as she was tossed back and forth in her seat. She raised her hands in front of her to brace the dash for impact but regained her composure and unexpectedly smiled back at him.

"Is that what you and your friends were like back in high school?" She let out a laugh, looking over to him as he shook his head, not wishing to answer.

"Yeah...we liked to party from time to time, but these types are unfortunately common up here. Bunch of frat boys who have an excuse to leave the establishment and feel they can do anything they want too. My friends and I had a few run-ins with douche bags like these before. Usually, while we were camping, or at some dive bar in the middle of nowhere, that didn't care to serve the underage." He explained as they approach the gas station off-ramp.

"Will they be there too?" She said as he turned off the exit with a sign reading, "Twin Peak- 40 miles west."

Adam looked over to her, "No, hon. We're going to a closed campground that my friend oversees and will let us in for the weekend. Besides, there are so many places up here where people go and do whatever..."

Adam rubbed his hand against her shoulder as he pulled into the small gas station.

There was a small convenience store, which had four gas pumps, and one diesel off to the other side of the parking lot. Adam noticed the large pickup truck with its flags dangling off the back as he pulled into the station. His anger crept back to existence like reuniting with a long-awaited friend, as one passenger stood several feet from the pump. The man smoked a cigarette toward the side grass area, as the driver pumped the fuel. They talked amongst each other, not noticing Adam had pulled up next to them.

"Don't do anything stupid," she said with a stare, that Adam even knew not to question.

"I would never," he said, making eye contact with her before they got out of the car. As they walked to the store, he looked over his shoulder toward the truck to see if they had recognized him from the highway but found them caught up in discussion. When he turned around, the store's double doors slammed open, barely missing Beverly's face. Two guys walked out, laughing amongst each other, with 18-pack beer cases in each hand.

"Hey! Watch it, you fucking pricks!" Adam said without hesitation as they both continued toward the pickup truck, not paying any attention to him. Beverly looked over to Adam. "Okay, I'll drop it," he said, grinding his teeth, as they both went inside. He grabbed a few snacks, then paid for his gas as Beverly went to use the restroom. Adam left the store on a mission, thinking this was his perfect opportunity, only to find that the truck had already left.

Beverly got back in the car, as Adam pumped the gas and called his friend to let him know they were on their way. He put his phone back in his pocket, then placed the pump on the handle before getting back in his Jeep. "You ready?" Adam said, resting his hand over her leg as she smiled, nodding in excitement. They went back down the local side road with a wooden sign reading, "Welcome to the Adirondacks, Where Magic Meets Nature."

CHAPTER ELEVEN

Adam drove another twenty miles uphill, through winding roads, before returning back to a long flat stretch of highway surrounded by dense evergreen forest. They passed over a covered wooden bridge, then through several small towns separated miles of each other. A vast and seemingly endless river ran parallel along the road, weaving in and out, before breaking into a large lake toward the southwest. Beverly watched from the window as a flock of Canadian geese flew in formation over the trees, heading south for the winter.

"This must be a frickin' nightmare during a snowstorm," she said as they drove up another steep incline.

"I honestly have never been up here during the winter, but could only imagine. Everyone must be well prepared before a big storm. I'm sure anyone who lives here owns an all-wheel-drive vehicle," Adam said as she looked out the window. There were no familiar cityscapes, skyscrapers, billboards, or large corporations she had been accustomed too—only the occasional local mom-and-pop stores and homes surrounded by miles of forest and farmlands in-between.

Nothing here compared to any other memories or experiences she had seen before, leaving a profound imprint on her mind. Even towns like Silver Lakes, rural as it seemed, came across more urban than this new environment to her. Despite these differences, she instantly fell in love with the majestic serenity and isolation of being swept away from it all—no materialism or bombardment of advertisements, displaying how their corporations could enhance one's life.

The people out here must know what real living must truly feel like. Not some collective vision of how life should be, provided by the media, authorities, and consumerism. She rejoiced with every small town they traveled through, how quaint and uniquely self-sufficient they appeared from her window. They're not deprived of anything in the slightest. Yet, some biased outsider's perspective could possibly consider them backwoods, or perhaps even third-world. Despite all these misconceptions, everyone still had the same basic necessities and resources available to them, providing an unembellished lifestyle they sought fit. This way of life had always been what Beverly dreamed and wished for.

They passed by a sign welcoming them to Twin
Peaks as Beverly's heart filled with excitement and
happiness. A single-story red brick schoolhouse stood
across the street from an old early eighteenth-century
Protestant church, which towered over the town. Local
farmer markets on the town green sold fresh apple pies
and jams, along with vegetables harvested from their
crop orchards. As if plummeting headfirst back into
colonial-America, Beverly momentarily disregarded
her troubling nightmares and worries. Subconsciously
leaving them all behind on the open highway. Hoping
to never come across them ever again.

Blanketed with a soothing calmness and a sense of
wonder, Beverly daydreamed about her own future as
she stared out the window, falling under its spell. Adam
pointed out the historic sites, shops, and an organic ice
cream stand, now closed for the season. They pulled off
of Main street onto a narrow road heading north for
several more miles. Beverly remained in a comforting
state of bliss as she reclined in her seat, embracing the
essence of all her surroundings.

"We're here!" Adam said, driving down a tertiary
road that led to a dirt parking lot. They drove past a
small rustic building that had "Adirondack's National
Park Ranger" written in white across the front.

Clouds of dirt shot up from behind his tires as he pulled his jeep toward a green park ranger truck parked near the entrance of the woods. A large metal square bar barricaded the road, which led to the vast wilderness beyond. The campgrounds weren't visible from the entrance, masked by the dense forest canopy of evergreens and thick oak tree branches. Vibrant golden leaves glistened in the sun as it set over the treetops.

A tall, rugged, bearded man with a dark green uniform emerged from his truck, then gestured with a quick wave toward them with a stern militant expression across his face. Adam turned toward Beverly, who appeared apprehensive, with a smile before they both stepped out of his jeep. "Kyle, mountain man, Johnson, how the hell are ya, brotha?' Adam said enthusiastically as he gave him a handshake while throwing his left arm around his shoulder, pulling him closer.

"I've been good, brotha! Great to see you again and glad you could come up this year." Kyle said as he patted Adam on the back, then turned to Beverly as she walked over. "You must be the woman, Adam keeps talking about, probably during his sleep, too," he said with a quick laugh. "I believe we've met briefly before, but I can't remember when or where, though,"

Kyle said with a smile, then shook her hand as they exchanged reintroductions.

"Yes, we did. Glad to meet you again. Adam mentioned the tradition of you guys coming here during your high school years. After hearing how great it was, I had to accept his offer to experience it for myself," she said, smiling over at them.

"We definitely had some amazing experiences here. Unfortunately, it seems we'll never find the opportunity for everyone to get back together again. I know it's a long trip coming up here, but I'm glad you both were able to finally make it," Kyle said to Adam.

"It's a long drive, but a beautiful one," Beverly added. Kyle nodded in agreement, then brought up the whereabouts of his other friends, who he hadn't heard from in some time.

"Yeah, I rarely hear from any of them either. John has a family life now, and I only speak to him on rare occasions, even though he lives just a few towns over. I'll periodically see Eric when I come down to visit him in the city since he never comes up to Silver Lakes anymore. I also haven't spoken to Rich in over a year after he moved to Texas for a prestigious IT position." Adam explained to him, then reminded Kyle how he had met Beverly through Kristen.

"That's where I remember you from! The weekend when we went down to Brooklyn to meet Eric and Kristen. That was definitely an awesome night. You're like part of our crazy family now!" Kyle said, then smiled at Beverly.

"It was amazing! I would have never met Adam if it wasn't for Kristen trying to pressure me to go out that night," Beverly said, looking back over to Adam. Kyle mentioned how he used to have a crush on Kristen throughout high school but explained how it would have never worked out.

"She is definitely a stubborn one-minded woman, that's for sure. Hope you didn't take it personally," she said as he shrugged it off.

"Don't tell her I said that though, it was just a stupid high school thing. Besides, I have a great lady waiting back at home for me now, so I best get going soon. Hit that old dusty trail." Kyle joked as he walked back toward his truck to grab the keys for the gate.

"I'm happy for you, bro, and also congrats on being a father soon too," Adam said to him, as Kyle poked his head up from the door.

"Thanks, Adam, but I still have some time until

fatherhood. She's only in her first trimester," Kyle said non-enthusiastically.

"Congrats to you both!" Beverly said to Kyle as he walked over to unlock the singled barred gate.

"Thank you, it's something I am still trying to wrap my head around, but I'm slowly getting used to the idea of the family-life every day. But, I truly miss the good old days, though." Kyle said as he pushed the gate open, then walked back over to hand the key to Adam.

"I hear ya, brother, but you'll totally make a great Dad. I can see how responsible you have become. Hell, you're park ranger management now, so hopefully, that supports you guys." Adam said as he shook Kyle's hand, taking the key from him.

"It's okay, not spectacular money, but in exchange, I do receive some great New York state benefits. I still have to work a part-time job at the local auto shop and do some odd jobs around town to make ends meet." Kyle explained with tiredness in his voice. Beverly listened to them talk as she questioned her previous thoughts of envisioning a perfect little town where no one had to struggle to live. She soon realized there wasn't such a thing of a simple life where the grass was always greener on the other side.

"Sorry to hear that, Kyle. You're a good person and hope things work out for you soon…Hey, maybe we can meet up for lunch before we head out of town," Adam said before they parted ways.

"I can't guarantee anything, but I'll try my best. Just remember to lock the gate before and after your stay. Also, leave the key in my office mailbox before you leave. It was great seeing you, Adam," He said, placing his hand on his shoulder. "Hopefully, we can get together again soon and catch up. Enjoy yourselves this weekend, and take care of your girl, Adam." Kyle said goodbye as he gave Adam a hug, then shook Beverly's hand again.

"Thank you," they both said to him. Kyle nodded before getting into his truck then drove out of the parking lot, picking up a small cloud of dust behind him. He disappeared around the bend, as Beverly and Adam were left standing alone with the vast wilderness behind them.

"Okay, let's get this weekend started!" Adam said, turning toward Beverly as she smiled, then walked back to the car. Adam drove several feet past the gate and got out to close it behind him. He took a moment to look around and recall the memories he had had with his friends over the years, momentarily regretting not being close to them anymore. This was one tradition he held on too and had been eager to finally share the experience with Beverly, who waited patiently in his front seat.

"She's perfect," Adam said to himself as he shrugged off his worries regarding his old friendships and memories. He knew life continued to move forward and now had to search inside to accept this fact. He couldn't allow himself to be afraid any longer of adulthood and being responsible for his actions. Adam locked the gate chain with the padlock, then walked back toward the car, feeling this might be the last time he would ever see this place again until he started his own family. He cleared his mind, then got back into his jeep, ready to enjoy the start of his new life with the woman he loves.

The sun had already set over the tree line, barely shimmering through the dense forest canopy, which towered over the small desolate road. Fractionated beams of sunlight streamed through every twist and turn as they made their way through the campground. They passed through the section with private rental cottages and RV hookups near the recreational area designed for families who still needed to cling onto their modern-day conveniences. They continued down the road on a gradual decline, penetrating deeper into the wilderness, as the sunlight was slowly consumed by the darkness of the forest.

"This is spooky. I kinda like it." Beverly said as she was tossed around by the bumpy roads, staring out at the various trails and vacant camping lots.

She envisioned what it would look like during the regular season, and pictured families creating cherished moments over the summer. Now everything laid dormant with lingering energy, full of ghostly laughter and memories from the not too distant past. They crossed over a small one-way bridge separating them from the main section and continued the rest of the way off-road. The family campgrounds were no longer visible, as she caught her first real glimpse into the world of the great outdoors.

The vibrations from the trails tested his jeep's suspension, as it rattled the interior cab. "Just a little further," Adam said as he squinted, then turned on his high beams to navigate the tight and narrow path that led them to a stream several feet ahead.

"I was happy with everything we passed so far," Beverly said with a hesitant laugh.

"I wanted to give you the real deal, just a little further. Hold on," Adam said as he approached the edge of the stream. He came to an abrupt stop that looked like a dead-end, as his headlights illuminated the landscape ahead. The water ran low and steady over the flat rocks, which lay scattered across the creek, as a hilltop rose into the late-evening sky.

"It's very peaceful here," Beverly said before being jolted back into her seat as he drove forward into the stream. He passed over the rocky terrain as his jeep jerked violently back and forth, until reaching the solid ground on the other side. "Is this part of the campgrounds?" Beverly said, concerned as she grasped the sides of her door and armrest to stabilize herself back into the seat.

"Well, not exactly, but this is where we would go camping just beyond the campgrounds to be closer to nature. "Trust me, this isn't my first rodeo," Adam said as he navigated off the trail, searching for landmarks he remembered like second nature from years ago. "See that huge rock over there?" He said, pointing off in the distance.

"No, but I guess I just have to trust you," Beverly said as they continued up the hillside, dodging several large trees as branches scraped across the roof and sides of his jeep.

"Yup, just what I thought. There it is. See it over there?" Adam pointed, with a smirk across his face.

"No, not really, hon. Is this the spot?" She said as he passed by a large boulder, which flanked the small clearing in between the trees and flat ground. Illuminated in the jeep's headlights was a small hand-made stone fire pit and a view of the river below, dividing the hillside from the cliff embankment on the other side. The forest stretched on for miles into the velvet horizon as two silhouetted peaks stood like giants off in the distance.

"Here we are," Adam announced, parking his car near the stone pit, then turned to kiss Beverly. "Let's get to it, shall we?" He said with excitement radiating from him like a small child stepping through the entrance of Disney World. They got out of the Jeep as Adam left it running to use the headlights to unpack their supplies.

"This is wild. I can't wait to see everything during the day," she said, looking around in wonder.

"I told you, hon! I knew this would be mind-blowing for you. And here you thought, our little town was quiet," he laughed as he grabbed a bag from his backseat.

"You weren't frickin' kidding. This is amazing,

Adam." Beverly smiled and walked over to help him. They unloaded most of the supplies, placing them on the ground into organized piles in front of the jeep's headlights.

"Let's first set up the tent, then we can get the bonfire going," Adam said as he pulled out his trusty old patched-up tent from its sleeve cover. "I've done this so many times I could literally set this thing up with my eyes closed. But I wouldn't mind the extra hand and to show you how to set up your first tent," he said, holding the rods and canvas. Adam explained to her how the rods inserted through the loops, which supported the frame. He had a smirk on his face as he slowly guided the pole between her fingers. Beverly innocently giggled, helping him slip it through the final loop, before securing it into the ground with stakes.

"See, that wasn't too difficult," he said as she smiled, tossing the sleeping bags, pillows, and their backpacks into the tent. Beverly peeked inside for the first time with hesitation and curiosity.

"That's because you have me around," Adam said as he dragged the ice cooler toward the other side of the tent.

She climbed back out with a grin across her face, then went over and passionately kissed him, "I know! I do have you in my life. And for that, I'm very fortunate. Thank you for everything, babe. For being there for me. For all of this," she said, looking him in the eyes.

"I'm fortunate to have you, too," Adam said, staring back at her. The headlights illuminated Beverly's face, which was flushed with a warm, vibrant tone, similar to the day he had first met her. He kissed her with one hand behind her head and the other across her lower back. "Come now. We have a lot of work left to do, honey. Then we'll have plenty of time to enjoy a bonfire amongst the stars."

"I can't wait! Let me know what you want me to do?" She said as Adam grabbed a few grocery bags off the ground.

"Oh...you know what I want...," Adam said as Beverly grinned from ear to ear. They gathered the rest of the supplies and laid them next to the tent. Beverly moved two folding chairs and the cooler near the makeshift stone fire pit. Adam crumpled up several pieces of newspaper, then tossed them into the center. He carefully placed a few logs he had picked up before their trip and stacked them in a vertical triangular formation.

"Wow, honey! Look up! Isn't that the most beautiful thing you have ever seen?" Adam walked behind Beverly as he placed his arms around her and kissed her cheek. "The stars are absolutely amazing here," she said as he embraced her from behind. Far from any large city, the stars were unbounded without any light pollution to obscure the night sky.

Tonight, the entire observable galaxy looked back down on them on Terra Firma. Lustrous strands of the Milky Way galactic outer rim stretched through the heavens with a brilliant display of the eloquent cosmos. Celestial bodies followed their orbits with calculated precision as they continued their free-fall toward the fiery center of our self-contained system. A force that is unseen by the visible naked eye, with their strings of attachment eternally present, as they ride the gravitational waves of space and time.

"I've never seen anything like this before in my entire life. It makes me feel so small, knowing how vast our universe really is. Imagine, there might be a faraway civilization somewhere out there looking back toward us, feeling the same way." Beverly said as they continued to stare out into the night sky.

"I'm sure there is life out there…somewhere. But I don't believe in all those crazy conspiracy stories, though. Like all these wackadoos who think they have visited us here on Earth," he said as he continued to hold her. "If a species could travel light years to a planet with sentient life on it, I think they would have better things to do then mutilate cattle and probe farmers. I've read some interesting articles though, where—"

Beverly suddenly jumped as a beam of light streaked across the night sky. "Well, what the hell was that then?" She said as Adam began to laugh to tears. "What's so funny, Adam?" She said with a serious tone, playfully pushing him off of her.

"Relax, babe, it's just a shooting star," he said, trying not to ridicule her.

"What's a shooting star?" Beverly naively inquired with all honesty. She had never been outside of the confines of the city nor ever heard of the term before. Even modern astrophysicists, who had been raised under the incandescent lights, wouldn't realize their own passion until they ventured far away from home. All that was needed is that single humbling moment of looking up into the night sky above a rural landscape for the first time. Sometimes, escaping from the presence of light and to embrace the dark, is where we truly find ourselves.

"It's a small meteorite or debris passing through the Earth's atmosphere. It's completely harmless, and we'll see them all night long. Some folklore describes it as heaven's announcement of a baby's birth or even someone's death. There's also an old English nursery rhyme, starlight, star bright, first star I see tonight, I wish I may, I wish I might have the wish, I wish tonight. Then you make your wish, and with some luck, it will come true," Adam explained to her.

"Well…," she turned to him with a smile. "I wish that this night will never end."

"You're also not supposed to say your wish out loud, like when you blow out your birthday candles," Adam said with a laugh as she scrunched her face, pretending to pout. He continued, "well, having said that. I'll try my hardest to make sure that this night will never end. And to lessen your worries. I'll also make sure to give you more nights like these," he said, embracing her in his arms as they kissed beneath the stars.

Later in the evening, as Adam prepared dinner, he explained to her that they would need to collect more kindling to start the fire. He went to his jeep, and started up the engine, then turned on the headlights. "I need you to collect all the small branches you can find," he said, pointing toward the woods. "Everything is wet out here in the open, and we'll need drier ones to keep the fire going. I'll go over there, and you can look over on the other side of the tent. Just grab whatever you can find," he said, noticing her face scrunch in slight protest.

"I'm scared, though," Beverly said while walking in the other direction, trying to not make a big deal out of it.

"Don't be silly, there's nobody else out here. I'll just be right over there," Adam said, parting ways in the opposite direction.

"That's what I'm afraid of," Beverly muttered, then sighed as she walked to the other side of the jeep, where they previously drove up the embankment. She turned to find Adam already on the other side of the tent, away from the headlights, leaning over to pick up branches along the ground. It was a cloudless night with the moon providing additional light, but not enough to penetrate through the tree canopies. Beverly went back to the tent to grab a flashlight, then noticed Adam was no longer in sight.

Beverly hesitated to go out alone but summoned up all her courage to venture back out into the woods. She wandered from the camp, trying to suppress her fears of getting lost in the dark. She held the flashlight in her hand, slowly scanning the light in front of her. Beverly carefully balanced the flashlight in her underarm to free both hands. She leaned over to collect the fallen twigs and small branches, then brought a pile over to the fire pit. "Is this enough?" She called out to Adam, without receiving a response.

Beverly shined the flashlight over to where Adam had been several minutes ago. She passed the beam of light from one end to the other, only to find nothing but silhouetted trees against the moonscape. A dense fog layer lingered along the ground and reflected back the light, obscuring her view. A sudden chill rushed through her body as branches cracked in the woods behind her. She turned while shining the flashlight back and forth feverishly, trying to locate the source of the noise. "Adam…you better not be playing a prank on me," she yelled on deaf ears, as the branches snapped closer to where she stood.

Beverly, armed only with her flashlight, tiptoed across uneven ground to investigate. She lost track of the jeep as she made her way forward into the shrubbery. The rustling continued fifteen meters in front of her as she directed her flashlight toward that direction. She jumped and accidentally dropped her flashlight after a swift movement rustled off in the distance. The light flickered off-and-on several times before returning back to normal. She squatted and picked it back up with trembling hands as her heart thudded faster inside her chest.

Beverly traced the light back and forth as the rustling ceased, followed by an unsettling silence. With unsteady hands, Beverly trained the flashlight toward the direction from where the movement originated. Focused in the light and off to the distance were a pair of fixed eyes intensely locked onto hers. The glowing eyes sent a harsh shiver down her spine as beads of cold sweat formed on her forehead and the back of her neck.

With a quick blur, the figure dashed out from the bushes at a sharp angle away from where she stood. Beverly followed along with her flashlight, trying to reveal its identity but lost sight of it. The quadruped creature finally stopped dead in its tracks, then faced her. Her flashlight caught up to make contact with the beast. Its eyes glared back, revealing a small doe that was more startled than she was. Beverly sighed a long breath of relief, then laughed uncontrollably. "Beverly, get a fucking hold of yourself," she said out loud, shaking her head toward the ground.

As she collected her emotions, a hand swiftly came down over her shoulder. She leaped forward with a shrill scream escaping from her lungs. Adam stood there, laughing hysterically as the deer galloped back into the woods. "I see you got acquainted with the local wildlife," he said, hollering with laughter. She sighed loud enough for him to hear, then slapped him against his chest.

"It's not funny, Adam. I didn't know what it was, and you went off gallivanting, nowhere to be found," she said, turning her head away, embarrassed.

"I'm sorry, hon. I went deeper into the woods to get some better kindling. I see you gathered a good-sized pile, so we should be all set for the night. I'm sorry for scaring you like that, babe." Adam said, giving her a comforting hug, then kissed her. They made their way back over to the fire pit, holding hands as he suppressed his laughter with a smirk still across his face.

He turned off his headlights and engine, then placed two lanterns, one on the hood of his jeep, the other near the fire pit. Adam grabbed a bottle of lighter fluid and sprayed it evenly over the logs and kindling, saturating the newspapers. He took a torch lighter out from his backpack to light the bottom of the pile. The flames shot wildly into the air, illuminating their remote backwoods campsite.

Beverly turned to him with a smile as she watched Adam go back and forth, blowing on the fire before it finally caught evenly across the logs. "Could you grab me the food and skillet? They're in the backseat," he said as he attended to the fire. She climbed in the car, then came out with a cast-iron skillet, along with a small bag of chopped onions and peppers. She placed them on the two TV stands, then opened their cooler, pulling out a container of diced chicken breasts already prepped for dinner. "Wait until you have my world famous chicken fajitas over the campfire," Adam said as he got up from the fire pit. The flames burned with intensity, illuminating the surrounding woods with a comforting glow.

"That sounds wonderful. I'm starving!" She said, accepting Adam's kiss first before going back to prepare the food. Adam placed a metal holding rack over the fire pit, "Aren't you impressed that I'm so well prepared?" He looked over to her, then back to the pit with his hands stretched out above his head toward the fire, as to showcase his skills. The flames eventually calmed down to a slow, steady burn.

Beverly laughed and playfully shoved the skillet to his chest. "I won't admit it until I experience your culinary skills first hand, mountain man," she said as he laughed. They both sat in folding chairs and poured wine into their plastic cups, watching the cast iron simmer on the metal rack above the settling fire. Beverly talked about her new job and Monday's appointment.

"Doctor Spitzer gave me two books to review," Beverly said, pulling them out of her bag and described in detail what she had been experiencing. "It's actually pretty fascinating. I never knew there were so many cultures that had so many similar experiences like mine", she said, refilling her cup.

"I hope they can help you with this, Bev. I could see how it has stressed you and put you on edge at times." Adam said as he glanced over the books in the flickering light of the fire and lantern. "This is very fascinating, but I don't think it's supernatural at all. Hopefully, they have medications or something to fix this sleep paralysis thing. I don't know too much about the topic, but I definitely could see the fear in your eyes the other night."

She nodded her head and placed the books back into her bag. "I don't believe it's supernatural either and I apologize putting you through all of this, it just feels so real sometimes. I'm hoping with both of the doctors' help, they could figure out how to make this all just go away."

Adam gently took her hand as she looked down at the ground, feeling ashamed. "I'm sure they can help you, hon. Let's not worry about it this weekend. Come on, let's eat!" he said as she looked up toward his warming smile.

After dinner, Beverly and Adam rejoiced by the fire while holding each other's hands without the need for conversation. She took a sip of her wine while being serenaded by the peaceful tranquility of the dancing flames and floating embers. The fiery glow illuminated the surrounding woods as crackling pops from the burning logs disrupted their silence. Thoughts from her past crept through the darkness as if it was calling out to her. She stared back down at the fire, warming her other hand for a moment, hoping that it will all just fade away. By then, it was too late.

Beverly stood from her chair to grab a blanket and a drink of water. When she returned, she found Adam asleep with his drink still in his hand. She smiled as she took the cup away from him and placed it on the ground. She pulled the blanket to his shoulders and kissed him gently on the cheek. Beverly sat back in her chair and stared into the flames as the shadows hypnotically danced amongst the trees. She sighed a breath of relief, then reflected on her life, while periodically gazing up toward the star encompassing night sky.

Beverly slowly nodded off in her chair, opening her eyes from the occasional pops of the crackling fire. She finally fell back to sleep and dreamt of her younger self wandering the wilderness alone during the late-summer afternoon. She felt at peace, gliding effortlessly above the ground in the tranquility of her own dream-scape. She passed through the forest as the sunlight penetrated through the trees, emanating a warm and comforting embrace across her skin. Small animals grazed across the ground as she explored the landscape with innocent wonder. She continued on this automatic trajectory toward an open field of ragweed and flowers as they dispersed their seeds in the late afternoon summer breeze.

Beverly drifted through the fields with her hand outward, passing through the tall grass. The sensation ran across her fingertips like soft paintbrushes against her skin. Off in the distance, she noticed the sun setting over the horizon. Her peace and comfort were disrupted by uneasiness as she continued to float toward the woods. Blue skies shifted to a blend of orange, purple, and red. Approaching the woods ahead, Beverly's involuntarily flight slowed as darkness lingered in the far horizon. The mountain peaks off in the distance resembled two black pyramids, penetrating into the heavens.

The entity from her dreams manifested in the periphery of the weed fields off to the left. The same otherworldly creature from earlier visions had slowly crept its way toward her from the tall grass. The entity advanced further as the weed fields parted around it, breaking the stocks into well-defined crop circles. Glowing green eyes traced her flight across the landscape as her peripheral vision lost sight of the beast at the edge of the forest. Then without warning, she lost the ability to fly and came crashing to the ground. She landed on her chest, knocking the breath out of her as she slowly lifted her head to orient herself to her foreign surroundings.

Beverly's legs trembled and buckled underneath her as if she was learning to walk for the first time. With all her strength, she pulled herself up off from the ground. Her blissful dream slowly became her worst nightmare as she ran deeper into the woods, lost, alone, and afraid. She tripped over logs and branches that scattered along the foggy forest bed. The sun had vanished past the tree line, taking the light along with it. Beverly slowly regained her balance and sprinted down the trail until she came across a fire off in the distance. She frantically tore away at the tree branches blocking her path, then came to a sudden stop near a clearing.

Beverly looked onward toward a raging fire near a stone altar, "Dad, Mom!" She called out as her parents stood in the forest clearing ahead of her. Several dozen people in black cloaks gathered next to them, forming a semicircle with their backs turned to her.

"Beverly, you're just in time. I'm glad you could come and join us," her father said as he turned to her with a wide smile. In synchrony, everybody gathered around the altar turned toward her. She stood trembling as the occult cleared a path down the middle. Her stomach swam to her throat, as the dark entity stood in the center, over the altar. The demonic beast was sacrificing a deer atop the stone slab as it dug its long slender hands into the deer's belly, pulling out its entrails. The dark entity looked over at Beverly, raising the bloody innards toward its face, then tossed them to the ground.

The supernatural entity looked deep into her eyes, then spoke directly into her mind. "Makes for good practice, before it's your turn," it said, as everyone had fixed smiles on their faces. The entity reached back into the chest cavity and removed the heart. It dangled the pulsating organ above its mouth, squeezing the blood from the chambers over its rows of jagged teeth. The beast made an unearthly growl, then tossed it into the fire. The flames shot up violently, illuminating the forest around her, before quickly fading back to darkness.

Beverly sprinted to her left, pushing her parents aside as she ran off into the wilderness toward the east. Her breathing, now labored as her heart pounded inside her chest as she continued to run without looking back. The darkness closed in on her, distorting her vision as branches brushed against her like dead bony hands springing back to life. She stopped at the edge of a cliff, almost losing her footing as rocks tumbled thirty feet below toward a raging river. From across the ravine, she noticed a familiar light glowing like a beacon of hope from the other side.

She turned around with her heels against the edge, only to find nothing chasing after her. Without wasting the opportunity, Beverly regained her breath and strength, then began to descend the cliff in the dark. She scraped her knees against the jagged rocks, almost losing her footing as she made her way toward the bottom. Once Beverly felt the solid ground beneath her feet, she quickly turned to the other side of the stream. "It can't be!"

Beverly saw a bonfire illuminating a silhouette of a woman sleeping in her chair. There was a thin dark wire suspended in the air floating across the water. It began to vibrate and glow, revealing a long silver cord that linked them together.

She walked over to the riverbed and knelt to see a moonlit reflection of her childhood face in a small puddle of water. She looked at her hands and feet, realizing she was trapped in her child-aged body that was tethered to the same silver cord. Beverly quickly looked up as branches snapped along the top of the cliff. *This all has to be just a dream.*

The drone of low vibrations radiated throughout her body as the dark figure emerged out from the forest. Voices of children began to fill her head, "Beverly, Beverly, stupid and sweaty. Always sitting in the corner with nothing to say, only to one day grow old, hefty and smelly." The cackle of childish voices and laughter from the orphanage echoed throughout the forest and within her mind.

"Get the fuck out of my head!" Beverly screamed, staring back up toward the cliff.

"Ah Beverly, so young, naïve and vulnerable," the dark entity said in a menacing tone, now standing before her. The being suddenly directed its attention across the river at her adult-form sleeping in the chair.

Beverly knew now she had to protect her physical body and fight back at all costs. She regained her focus and remembered that this was simply another bad dream. The entities green eyes changed to a bloodthirsty red, locking onto her unprotected physical form. Beverly concentrated on returning back to her body, then slowly floated off the ground and hovered backward across the river toward her adult-self resting in the chair. With one swift tug of the silver cord, she was pulled back with intensity, slamming backward into the chair.

Beverly leaped out of her chair, trying to scream, but out of breath to do so. Adam continued to sleep undisturbed next to her. The unbearable impact into her chest lingered as she struggled to catch her breath. Desperate to remember what had just happened, she looked around the empty campsite. The memories were only on the tip of her subconscious and no longer within reach.

The bonfire had exhausted except for a few smoldering logs left behind in the pit. The forest was in complete silence and darkness as the cloud layer covered the night sky and obscured the moon and stars. She couldn't stop shivering as each breath escaped her mouth in the form of condensation.

"Adam! Wake up!" Beverly yelled, shaking him awake.

"What is it?" He muttered as he looked over with eyes half-closed in a daze.

"We need to get inside the tent now," she said, taking his hand, then led him into the tent, zipping it closed behind her. Beverly grabbed every blanket she could find to throw over them. She pulled herself closer to Adam, holding him tight for warmth and security. Beverly pressed her body against his, trying to remember her dream. In the silence of the night and within the comfort of his arms, she fell back asleep.

CHAPTER TWELVE

Beverly tossed and turned between the blankets, then reached over to discover Adam was no longer inside with her. The front entrance was zipped halfway with the sun shining in. She crawled out into the daylight, shielding her eyes with the back of her hand, and found Adam preparing sandwiches for lunch. Beverly welcomed the warmth against her skin as she stumbled for a moment before regaining her senses.

"Good morning, darling," Adam said, placing half of the turkey and cheese sandwiches into individual baggies. He put them in his backpack, then tossed two apples along with them.

"Yeah…good morning. What time is it?" Beverly said groggily as she walked over to grab some water.

"I don't usually like to keep track of the time when I camp. But judging by the sun, I would have to say it's probably around ten. I wanted you to sleep in," he said, handing her half of a sandwich on a paper plate. "I packed the rest for our hike. I thought it would be fun to head out into the woods and explore for a bit," Adam said as she took a bite of her turkey sandwich.

"Sounds good," Beverly mumbled, with her mouth full as she finished the last bite. Adam threw his backpack over his shoulder while she went to change into new clothes. "At least it is warm out during the day," she said, grabbing her camera and placed it into her bag.

"I didn't think it was that cold last night. But it's definitely a beautiful day to go hiking," he said, taking her hand. They walked passed the extinguished bonfire toward the woods that led down the embankment.

"Did you get a good night's rest?" Adam asked as he held a branch back for her.

"Yeah, sort of, I just had this bizarre dream where I was wandering through the woods as a child. Then I was suddenly awoken as if something slammed into my chest. I don't remember the rest of it, though. I guess we both fell asleep outside, and the cold air startled me awake." Beverly explained without a response as they descended down, holding on to the smaller trees to maintain their balance.

"The bonfire and wine really knocked me out last night. I was exhausted from the drive up and preparing for our trip," Adam said as he stopped at the bottom of the ravine to take a sip from his water bottle. He took a quick look around to remember where he used to cross the stream.

"I've hiked this area many times before, and know of a spot where we can cross over and get up the cliff easier. I didn't want to make this a strenuous hike for you." Adam explained as he went further downstream until coming across a natural dam, which divided the river from the more turbulent waters stretching further north toward the rapids of Raquette Falls.

"This may sound a little weird, but all this looks really familiar to me. I remember seeing this before." Beverly said, shaking her head while taking his hand to walk over the mossy rocks to cross over the stream.

"That does sound strange. Maybe you wandered over here last night to collect kindle," Adam said, helping her up the smaller incline, adjacent to the vertical cliff.

"Maybe, But, I don't recall going this far, though. Plus, it was night time and wouldn't be able to see anything," she said, breathing heavier as she climbed on all fours up the embankment. She followed Adam's lead, tracing his movements as he reached out ahead, holding onto a large rock and nearby roots to pull himself toward the top. He offered his hand to help her the rest of the way as she struggled with the last part of the climb.

"This is absolutely beautiful, Adam," Beverly said while taking several pictures of the river, which stretched out toward the horizon. Miles of trees full of colored foliage surrounded the mountains that stood off in the distance. "I take it that's where the Twin Peaks name came from," she said with a chuckle, then turned to Adam, who smirked back at her. She followed him over toward the other side that led into the woods.

An uneasiness brought her to a sudden stop as Adam continued to walk on without noticing. She looked over to her left at the embankment on the other side with their car, tent, and two empty chairs in full view. Beverly remembered this view perspective from last night's dream but couldn't recall any of the details. She made a short sprint to catch up with him as he had already made his way into the forest.

"Is everything okay?" Adam said after noticing she had run up behind him.

"Yeah, I was just taking a few more pictures," Beverly said as he looked down, no longer seeing the camera in her hands.

"Okay, just let me know if you need me to stop. I don't want to lose you while we're going through the woods," he said half-jokingly, half-serious.

"Maybe you should get a leash for me then," she said sarcastically, hoping he would lighten up. Adam continued through the woods, keeping an eye out for any landmarks that he and his friends made over the years. Up ahead were several faded red ribbons nailed to various tree trunks, which they continued to follow for another mile. They reached the other end of the forest and walked into the sunlight that shined through the other side.

"Can you hear that?" Adam asked as a steady drone of humming surrounded them.

"Yeah, are those crickets or something?"

"During the day? No hon, those are Cicadas."

"What are those?"

"It's an insect that spends the majority of their lives entirely underground only to surface every thirteen or seventeen years like clockwork. They're categorized by geographical regions and when they come above ground. The upstate New York group is referred to as brood two, and they surface every seventeen years. Ancients believed they were the sign of spiritual resurrection and immortality," he explained as Beverly looked over at him with a smirk.

"I know, I can be a nerd sometimes. But I find the rarity of these events fascinating, similar to the totality of a solar eclipse. It's nature working together in their unique, distinctive paths while still in sync and in perfect harmony. Like cogs turning in a well-designed machine," Adam said as she kept walking through the dense brush.

They crossed into the clearing, which opened up to a massive field, stretching on for another several miles before transitioning back to wilderness. They embraced the warmth of the late afternoon sun as they continued through the tall fields of withering ragweed and sporadic pockets of flowers. Beverly grabbed her camera to take several pictures of them.

"Those are called fire-weeds. They're not poisonous despite their name," he said as Beverly had already run her hand through them. "They're beautiful. I'm starting to remember the dream I had. You might think this is crazy, but I remember seeing these here in a field similar to this, but there were more of them though, purple ones too." Adam listened to her as he took a moment to rest.

"That's odd. You can only find these here, though.

Maybe you saw a similar field on the drive up to make you think of them." Adam said, scratching his head as he led her toward an open patch in the field. A warm autumn breeze caressed her skin as it blew the tops of the weeds back and forth in a synchronized dance.

"Maybe..." Beverly said under her breath as she followed several feet behind him. They reached a flat patch of grass adjacent to the woods and tall weed fields toward the north. Adam pulled out a blanket from his backpack and laid it over the grass, then took out the sandwiches and apples. They sat and talked for several hours, looking out toward the field as the sun descended over the woods and western skies. Adam leaned over to kiss her as he brushed his hand across her flowing hair. Beverly moaned as he slowly kissed down her neck while running his hand up her shirt. Adam helped remove her clothes as the warmth of the sun embraced her skin.

They both laid naked on top of the blanket, making love in the field during that late afternoon. The sunset passed over the tree line, stirring the evening winds with powerful gusts. She reached a blissful threshold, then rolled off of him after their shared climax together. She laid on her back as the slight chill from the wind rolled across the beads of sweat against her flushed skin. They gathered their clothes as she pulled a sweater over her head. Adam packed up the blanket and gathered the rest of their belongings scattered along the ground.

"What's this called?" Beverly said, pointing over to a small white flower on the ground next to her.

"That's what you'd call a devil's trumpet. They're pretty rare around here, along with the deadly nightshade flower. It must be a sign," he joked.

"A sign?" Beverly asked, looking curiously back at him.

"Well, there is an old Native American legend that if you ever come across one, it would bring you and your tribe years of bad luck," he explained.

"Really?"

"It's only a story, hon. I could imagine they told a lot of silly folktales by the campfire to scare the children. It was probably the only way to deter them from wandering around in the woods unsupervised."

Beverly ignored his interpretation of the tale and stared inquisitively at the twisting white petals. She stood quickly without saying anything, then looked over her shoulder in his direction of the ragweed fields off in the distance. Several patches ahead had been pushed over with the stems broken in the middle, forming a systematic pattern. The visions came flooding back into her mind as she stood there in silence.

"Let's get going. It'll be dark soon," Beverly said softly, picking up her backpack and throwing it over her shoulder. He agreed as they made their way toward the woods to be back at camp before nightfall.

"It should be just right over there," Adam said, searching for the markers on the trees.

"Are we lost?" She said no longer joking around with him.

"No, we are not lost, Bev. I just need to find one of the tree markers to get back on track," he said agitated as he continued to search for the faded red ribbons. "We're going to be fine as long as we keep heading east. We'll eventually run back into the ridge by the river." She didn't bring it up again and trusted his judgment to know where he was going. She followed close behind, as a sense of dread intensified inside her. The vision of floating as a child flashed in her mind.

He crossed back and forth, disoriented by the vast forest landscape. Darkness approached, as the sunlight dimmed through the canopies like a flickering candle. Even if a marker had been on a tree, it would be near impossible to spot it during this time of day. They continued to head east, stumbling over dilapidated logs and broken branches, slowing their progress. Eventually they came across a small clearing in the woods where the barrier of trees surrounding them and acted as an impenetrable wall, hiding the secrets within.

Several empty beer cans and garbage littered across the ground, assuring them they were not alone, but unsure for how long. On the other side of the clearing, near two oak trees isolated from the rest of the forest, was an old fire pit similar to the size of the one back at camp. It contained several logs recently burned as the ashes laid scattered near the charred wood. They both stopped at the same time after coming across a small stone altar next to the two oak trees.

"What the hell is that? We need to get out of here," Beverly said as Adam ignored her and continued to investigate.

"I don't know, Bev. It looks like some sort of devil-worshiping shit." Adam said as he carefully examined the stone while running his hand over the surface as his arm hair stood on end. The altar had perfectly smooth graphite that had to been brought explicitly to this location from the outside.

"Adam! We need to get the fuck out of here now!"

Beverly yelled, grabbing his arm to get his attention.

"Alright, relax, Bev. I was just curious. We can go now," he said, still intrigued by the altar. They turned without noticing the fresh blood dripping off the tree trunk and walked out of the clearing toward the other side of the woods heading east.

She took the lead and rushed through the forest as Adam tripped over tree roots trying to catch up with her. "Slow down, Beverly. You don't know where you're going!" She continued through the woods, not paying any attention to him as she kept a steady pace not to leave him behind. Beverly finally came to a dead stop after reaching the edge of the cliff, which overlooked the river below. He caught up to her out of breath. "How did you know...where...you were going?"

"You said to head east, right?" She said as he smiled as they walked along the cliff and found the embankment to descend down. They crossed over the river and made their way back up the hill to their campsite. She sighed in relief as the night encapsulated the entire landscape behind them. He started his car and turned on the headlights to illuminate the campsite as they prepared the fire for dinner.

"What do you think they were doing over there?" Adam said as he grabbed a beer from the cooler.

"I don't really want to talk about it right now," Beverly said in a flustered voice as she poured herself a cup of wine.

"Whatever it was, there were no obvious signs that they were around anymore. It was probably just a bunch of stupid high school kids imitating stuff they saw in a movie or something. Besides, we have only one night left here, and we should focus on the good memories and relax for the evening." Adam said, then began to prepare and cook dinner on the cast iron skillet over the campfire.

"I know. I just don't want to talk about it anymore. Like you said, we have one more night here, and I don't want to ruin the evening by talking about it," Beverly said, taking a seat and changing the subject. After dinner, they sat together relaxing underneath the stars as Adam explained the local wildlife and native American history of the Iroquois Confederacy. Later in the evening, he told her a few inaccurate ghost stories, one regarding the folklore from the Mohawk tribe. A tale of disembodied floating heads that still haunt the forest to this day, *within these very woods they set up camp in*, Beverly busted out with laughter.

"How do you know all of this weird stuff, bozo?" Beverly said as she playfully slapped his shoulder.

"I do know a lot of pretty useless information, huh? I just enjoy learning about the local history of where I grew up," Adam said as Beverly smiled to his honesty.

"I also find it very interesting, and as you know, I love learning about history too. We can't move forward unless we have a link to our past," Beverly said, slowly closing her eyes from exhaustion. Adam kissed her forehead and placed a blanket over them before falling asleep beside her.

The temperature plummeted to the low-forties as the fire continued to burn strong into the night. A flash of light passed overhead, slowly awaking her. Adam had still been asleep next to her as she got up to get a drink of water. Beverly tossed another log onto the fire, rubbed her hands near the flame, then stared up to the night sky.

Several more lights streamed across the ether. *Shooting stars?* She wondered, then noticed they appeared much slower, purposeful, and had multiple colors of red, green, and orange. *Airplanes?* She thought for a split moment as one abruptly changed direction, making its way across the stratosphere. Remembering what Adam had told her, she ignored it, then sat back down into her chair, throwing a blanket over herself and fell back asleep.

Later in the evening, a dog barked ferociously off in the woods toward the north. Beverly opened her eyes and raised herself from the chair as if hypnotized, heeding her subconscious to investigate. A haze lingered over her as she walked half-asleep passed Adam and the campfire. She stood at the edge of the woods, listening to the frantic dog barking off in the distance. "Tiny?" Beverly said half-asleep and delusional. "How did you get out here, buddy?" She said, catching a glimpse of him barking at a strange green light emanating from the woods.

"It's okay, Tiny baby. Mommy's here," she said in a trance, sprinting toward the forest. Beverly stopped short, as the dog stood facing forward, and away from her, with its muscles tensed and hair frayed. Barks transitioned to growls as saliva dripped from his jaws. She tried to console him from afar but was taken by surprise after he bolted into the woods.

"Tiny, wait! Momma's coming for you," she yelled, running after him. Green light slowly emanated through the darkness and reflected off the dense fog, obscuring her view. She stopped her pursuit after her vision of Tiny was no longer in sight. Beverly's haze subsided, followed by the sudden awareness of her foreign surroundings. The fear and a state of paralysis ensued as the green lights encapsulated her and the woods around her. An intense low vibration penetrated her body and gripped her like a vice.

Green fog gathered along the forest bed, reflecting the haunting aurora, which slowly snared her. Tears streamed down her cheek as she stood there alone, vulnerable, and helpless. Out of the forest, came several dark grey humanoid figures walking among the trees as the light illuminated their frail, slender bodies. The beings had large oval heads compared to their disproportionate bodies and long thin fingers which dangled by their sides. They stood five feet tall, with their silhouettes distorted over the ground from the light behind them. Their gait had a hostile otherworldly presence as they approached her from afar.

Beverly stood paralyzed as the beings circled around her with their elongated faces and large, pitch-black eyes staring back at her. She tried to scream, but nothing came out from her throat. The six beings walked around her as if to inspect and examine her from head to toe. She shivered as one of their long cold fingers ran across her shoulder toward her back. She tried to look away from them as they surrounded her. Off in the distance, she noticed the dark entity standing behind a large oak tree, glaring back at her.

Half of its body remained hidden behind a tree, as the other half was only a silhouette. It wrapped its long arms around the trunk with its fierce red eyes peering back at her. The emotionless humanoid beings continued to run their slender fingers across her body as she focused her attention on the dark entity staring back at her. A steady grin of sharp teeth stretched from end to end over the entity's mouth.

"Beverly, you can't escape me," its voice penetrated into her mind like a sledgehammer. The otherworldly creatures began to walk in different directions back into the woods, then disappeared into the fading green light. The demonic entity grinned back at her as its body slowly dissipated into the darkness. Beverly broke from her trance and found herself standing alone in the woods surrounded in the darkened silence. In a deep panic, she sprinted back toward the campsite leaping over fallen branches and rocks, disoriented on how she got there. The smoldering bonfire came into view as plumes of smoke billowed into the night sky. She screamed out for Adam before tripping face first over a log, hitting her head against a rock. Her consciousness slowly faded to darkness.

Beverly woke with her arms and legs snared in tight metal clamps, with her body spread across a cold, damp slab of granite raised off the ground. Muttered chants approached her from all sides as she desperately tried to break free. The figures emerged from the shadows and circled the altar with glowing red eyes veiled within their cloaked hoods. Emerald green light emanated from the surrounding woods accompanied by the shrill grind of machinery and trees cracking, splintering apart at their trunks.

The increasing tension tore away at her muscle fibers with every attempt to break free as she screamed out for Adam to save her. The occult encircled the altar and glared down at her with faceless orbs of red-light shimmering underneath their hoods. The cloaked acolytes forced her down and drew needle and thread to sow her mouth shut as she squirmed against their grasp. Her screams transitioned to moans, then to cries as they finished with their facial crochet.

The synchronized circle parted as a torchbearer walked beside the altar and set the wood piles ablaze. The heat from the flames singed her skin as the gathered followers watched her arms and legs blister, boil, and ooze. The agonizing pain slowly subsided to numbness as the thermal burns penetrated deeper into her tissue, destroying every nerve ending. Beverly fought to raise herself off the altar as her extremities and muscle tore apart from the bone.

Cackles echoed throughout the wilderness, followed by silence. The acolytes slowly backed away from the altar as she helplessly awaited her fate. Flames shot up sporadically, forcing her face away as the dark entity appeared before her. Tears ran from her eyes, then quickly evaporated off her scorched cheeks. Beverly laid there drifting in and out of consciousness as she stared up to the night sky, wishing to see one last shooting star.

The demonic beast towered over the altar as it swung its long slender fingertips across her neck, cutting into her flesh. The entity dragged its hand down her body then submerged them deep into her abdomen, pulling out her intestines and tossing them into the flames. Beverly jolted her body up off the slab in agony as she desperately fought against imminent death then fell back flaccid.

"I suppose, it is finally your time, Beverly," the being said as it fixated on her emotionless face, slipping out of consciousness. The beast lunged its hands deeper into the exposed abdominal cavity, snaking his arms toward her heart. Before Beverly closed her eyes and finally leaving this mortal plane, she turned her head toward the woods and saw a brilliant white light bouncing between the trees. The white light penetrated through the clearing, dissolving the occult acolytes and distinguishing the flames. The supernatural entity retracted his hands and backed away from the altar. "Until we meet again. My sweet little, Beverly," the being said as it vanished into the darkness. Beverly closed her eyes as the blinding white light consumed her.

Beverly? Beverly! Where the hell are you?" Adam yelled, jumping frantically from his chair and running toward her final scream. He wandered out into the woods with his flashlight and found her unconscious, limp body sprawled out on the ground. "Oh my fucking god, no!" He yelled as he lifted her bloodied head off the ground. She woke up in hysteria, kicking him in the chest while swinging her arms to fight him off.

Adam fell backward, then quickly sprung back to his feet, unfazed, "Beverly! It's me. I'm here now. Everything will be okay," he said as he grabbed both of her fists. Adam cradled Beverly in his arms, trying to console her as he rocked gently back and forth. She cried in his arms as he picked her up and carried her back to camp.

"Are you okay? What were you doing out there?"

He said as he helped her in the tent and treated her forehead laceration with his first aid kit.

Beverly laid on her back, trying to remain calm as he cleaned and disinfected her cut with hydrogen peroxide. "Fuck! That really stings!" Beverly yelled as he applied it to the wound.

"It will be over in a moment. But I think you suffered a concussion, babe," he said, patting forehead dry. Adam grabbed a washcloth to clean her bloodied face, then applied sterile bandages to stop the bleeding.

"I'll be okay," she said bluntly as he continued to treat her.

"You never answered my question. What were you doing out there in the woods by yourself?" Adam said as he finished wrapping the dressings, then kissed her on the forehead.

"I don't know, I must have been sleepwalking or something. I just remember having a nightmare, waking up, and seeing people out in the woods. I remember them coming after me, so I tried to run away to get back to you," she said with all sincerity. Beverly sobbed, ashamed that she can not remember any of the details. Adam got up from his knees, biting his lower lip with a scowled emotionless expression. He ran his hand through his hair, perplexed while trying to piece it all together.

"Well...You are safe now. I can promise you that," Adam said after a brief pause, before crawling out of the tent.

"Where are you going, Adam?" Beverly said as she wiped her tears away. She heard him rustle in his car for a moment. He slammed the door shut and came back into the tent with an ax in his hand. "What is that for?" Beverly said, frightened of the whole ordeal.

"You know, just in case if this wasn't all just a dream," he said, then zipped up the tent behind him and pulled the blankets around her. "You are safe now. Try and get some rest. We'll get your head checked out at the clinic tomorrow," Adam said as he brushed his hand across her blood-matted hair.

Beverly turned to him, "I'm sorry to have put you through all this. I honestly don't know what I saw out there," she said as he embraced her in his arms.

"Don't ever be sorry. Get some rest, honey. We'll leave tomorrow morning," he said, then kissed her.

"Thank you," she said as he turned off the flashlight and held her until they both fell asleep in each other's arms.

In the middle of the night, Beverly woke to a throbbing headache as she laid still, staring at the top of the tent, trying to make sense of it all. She felt a pang of guilt with always dragging Adam into all of her problems. Beverly knew deep down it was all in her imagination, and now had Adam thinking that people were out there harassing them. She tried to understand what was happening to her but could not come up with any real logical answers.

Beverly turned over and faced Adam, who slept with the ax laying on his opposite side. *How did it all come down to this? What is the fuck wrong with me?* She thought and ashamed of whom she had become. She cried to herself, wishing for it to all stop. Wishing for it all to end. She regained focus, then stared back at the tent ceiling with racing thoughts before eventually falling back to sleep.

A few hours later, a slow ripping sound ran along the side of the tent, jarring her awake. She laid on her back paralyzed as she stared up toward the ceiling. The fabric jostled back and forth from the outside as if trapped in a gale windstorm. Fear ran through her entire body, along with frustration and anger of being helpless yet again. A green light illuminated from outside of the tent as the scratching ceased, followed by a dreadful silence.

She tried to let out a scream but was unable to speak or move as she stared up toward the ceiling wishing for it all to just go away. The green light illuminated the night as silhouettes appeared on the outside of the tent with slender hands grasping along the sides, desperate to get in. Their fingers slid against the fabric producing an unpleasant sound as their large heads bobbed back in forth, trying to figure out a way in. She laid still, unable to turn and wake Adam up, no matter how hard she tried.

She laid there hopeless as a tear ran down her cheek. The green light dissipated, along with the shadows vanishing into the night as if they had given up. Then with a few seconds, there was rustling toward her feet, followed by a rush of cold air. She directed her eyes as far as she could toward the sound.

The entrance unzipped as long fingers grasped along the edges, trying to tear the rest open.

"Beverly…Its almost time," it said with a low pitched drawn-out hiss. Lingering fog and condensation from its breath obscured most of its head as its vibrant red eyes of piercing energy stared back at her. She tensed as the entity slowly withdrew its head from the entrance, disappearing into the darkness.

"Adam! Adam!" She regained her voice and mobility as she sat straight up hysterical.

"What is it?" He said, sitting up half-asleep.

"Something was out there trying to get in! Several people were trying to get into our tent! I saw them out there!" Beverly screamed as she slowly gained full consciousness. She tried to keep her composure while shaking with fear.

"You got to be fucking kidding me. Stay here!" Adam said as he crawled toward the entrance of the tent with his ax. He unzipped the canvas as the morning light trickled in. He looked back toward Beverly's pale, bloodied, and terrified face. Intense rage surged through him as he exited the tent, ax in hand, trying to find the intruders. "You mother fuckers! I know you're out there! If you fuck with us, you're going to regret it!"

He said while frantically searching their campsite like a madman.

Adam walked the perimeter checking near his car and pile of supplies. Everything was in their proper place and undisturbed with no signs of any intruders. Beverly peeked her head out of the tent as Adam paced back and forth with his ax in hand like a bloodthirsty barbarian. She saw the anger in his face as he tried to sort this all out in his head. "Whoever it was, they're gone now," he finally said as he looked back at Beverly as she crawled out of the tent.

"You believe me, right?" She said, starting to doubt herself as she looked around their deserted campsite.

"Of course, I believe you. I just don't know who it was or where they came from. These people could have followed us across the river after nightfall. We should have left, but instead, I put you in unnecessary danger," Adam said as he dropped the ax to the ground.

"It's not your fault. We both thought they had left a long time ago. There were no signs of anyone here," Beverly said, hugging him.

"Let's get packed up and get the hell out of here. Sound good to you?" Adam said, continuing to hold her in his arms.

She smiled, "Yeah, I think I have had enough camping for the weekend." They both started to gather the supplies, prepared to leave for back home.

"Sorry for such a shitty experience," Adam said as he started his Jeep. They both got in as he turned his car around to head back down the embankment.

"It's not your fault, hon. Sometimes, the things that we love from our past change over time. I enjoyed all the other experiences with you, though," Beverly said as she was tossed back and forth in her seat again. They made their way across the stream toward the main campsites. The early morning sun illuminated through the tree canopies as he continued toward the entrance.

"Can you grab me the gate key from the glove compartment?" Adam said, reaching his hand out for it. "What the hell!" He said as he pulled up to find the chain cut and padlock laying on the ground. The parking lot bar was swung wide open during his approach. Adam drove forward and found the same pickup truck from the highway parked in the lot. Four guys stood by the vehicle drinking beer with empty cans scattered underneath their feet.

Adam stomped the gas pedal to the floor and accelerated toward them. Out of brief rational thought, but without sympathy, he quickly swerved at the last

moment to avoid hitting them. Adam placed both feet
on the brakes as his Jeep came to an abrupt stop several
inches from where they stood. They both slammed back
into their seats as dust, dirt and small rocks erupted
into the air. The debris rained back down onto the four
guys who were ready to engage the maniac in the Jeep.

"Adam!" Beverly yelled out to him as he rushed
out of the car to confront them.

"I know it was you fuckers out there in the woods
messing with us!" Adam said, walking toward the driver
of the pickup truck.

"What the fuck are you talking about, you crazy
asshole?" He said dropping his beer can as his friends
took defensive stances around Adam.

"I saw your trash around the altar. And I also know
it was you and your shit hole friends who tried getting
into our tent last night. My girlfriend saw you guys in
the woods, and she busted up her forehead, trying to
run away," Adam said as he stepped closer to him.

"Altar? What the fuck are you talking about,
whack job? We just got here prick, so I don't know
what the fuck you and your psychopathic girlfriend
thought you saw last night." He said, facing Adam as
his friends followed behind.

"Adam! Get back in the car!" Beverly yelled from the passenger seat.

"Maybe you should listen to your crazy ass bitch over there," the man said as he sized up Adam.

"What did you just say?" Adam responded, surging with rage as the other three began to surround him.

"You fucking heard me you son of a—" before he could finish Adam punched him square in the face knocking him to the ground. Adam grabbed one of his friends charging after him, then threw them into one another. Adam lost his balance as the third man grabbed him from behind, then punched him several times in the back of his head.

"Adam!" Beverly screamed as she grabbed for her phone to dial 911 only to find there's no service. Adam finally regained his balance, then tossed him into the other two who had rushed toward him. Adam threw a quick jab at one, only to miss, grazing him across the jaw. He managed to throw another blind punch that struck someone in the forehead. A sudden sharp pain radiated throughout his entire right arm from the impact. The other two took advantage of the opportunity by grabbing Adam by his injured arm and shoulder. The driver got back up to his feet and faced Adam as his friends held him from behind.

"I don't know who the fuck you are. But you and your girlfriend will regret playing your little game with us," he said, punching Adam square in the mouth.

Adam struggled to break free from the two, who were still holding him back. One of the men walked over and punched him in the gut, dropping Adam to his knees. Beverly frantically looked around to see how she could help. In the back seat of the car, she found her only answer. She stared back and forth at it, contemplating if she should use it. The driver leaned over Adam with his boot against his chest.

He grabbed Adam by his hair, lifting up his bloodied head, "You're going to pay for this, you little shit!" Adam stared him in the eyes and spat blood into his face.

"You fucking piece of shit!" The driver said as he continued to punch Adam several more times in the face.

"Watch out!" One of his friends yelled as Beverly lunged toward them with the blunt end of the ax. She was stopped short as one of them grabbed her forearm, sending the weapon and herself to the ground. He jerked her arm, then dragged her toward the dirt as she fell to her face.

"Stop! Please, just stop!" She pleaded, sprawled out on the gravel.

"Not yet. I want you to witness us kicking your pathetic boyfriend's ass." He said as he continued to punch him as he laid helpless on the ground. "You want to be a hero, huh? You fucking piece of shit!" He said, slamming Adam's head back to the dirt. One friend kept watch, as the other three continued to kick Adam as he tried to roll over.

"Stop! You're going to kill him!" Beverly cried out.

"Um...guys...hey guys!" They all looked over as a green truck accelerated toward them. The four men slowly backed away from Adam after seeing "Park Ranger" across the hood. Kyle skidded on his brakes only inches away from them. He slammed his door open, resting his rifle over the open window with the barrel fixed on the driver.

"It would be all in your best interest to get the fuck out of my town! Before I decide to use deadly force for assaulting one of my officers," he said, aiming his rifle back and forth between them.

"He started this shit," one of them said in a panic.

"Y'all about to kill this man and his wife in cold blood, and I will not hesitate to enforce the law. I have back-up coming as we speak. So, don't make me repeat myself. I suggest that you leave and never come back to my town ever again." Kyle said in a stern voice as he watched his friends lay helpless on the ground.

The driver wondered why he was not going to arrest them then and there but decided to not call his bluff, "Don't worry, we'll never come back to this fucked-up town again." The driver gave the nod to his friends to get back into his truck. They pulled out, nearly missing Adam as they pealed out in the parking lot, kicking up dirt into their faces.

"You guys, alright?" Kyle said, helping Beverly up off the ground, then checking Adam's injuries as he laid on the ground.

"I've seen better days," Adam said as he got to his feet, wiping the blood away from his mouth, then went over to check on Beverly.

She slapped him squarely across his swollen face, "you could have gotten us both killed, you fucking idiot!" Beverly said, staring into his bloodshot eyes.

"What happened back there? Kyle said as he looked over at the broken chain on the gate.

Adam gathered his thoughts, then explained, "There's some crazy shit happening in those woods, you have no idea, Kyle. Those guys broke in here, did some crazy devil-worshiping shit, then terrorized Beverly last night." He said as he looked over at Beverly, who avoided making eye contact with him.

Kyle looked over at Beverly to see if she objected to his statement but didn't get any response out of her. "I can't believe this shit was going on out there. I'm so sorry you guys had to go through that. You both look really banged up, do you want me to drive you to the local hospital?" He said, placing his hand on Adam's shoulder.

"It's alright, Kyle, we're going to get back on the road and go to the clinic when we get back to Silver Lakes. Beverly walked in front of the car and gave Kyle a nod to thank him for coming to their rescue. She got back into the car and slammed the door behind her.

Kyle pulled Adam to the side and whispered into his ear, "you know you could have gotten both of yourselves killed, right? Consider yourself lucky, Adam, because I only happened to stop by the office to check on a few things. I know you're trying to protect your girl and all. I get it but don't be careless, or all your good intentions will just be in vain." Kyle said as Adam nodded his head, then shook his hand before walking back over to his Jeep.

"You know, Kyle, you have always been there to bail me out of a sticky situation," Adam said with all sincerity as he coughed up blood, then spat it out on the ground. "But things have changed around here, along with our old traditions. Let me know if you ever come down my way, until then good luck with your new family. Thanks again, brother," Adam said as he got back into his Jeep. Kyle watched them leave the campgrounds, then turned back to the open gate toward the woods stretching out to the morning horizon.

Adam and Beverly made their way back onto Interstate 87 heading south-bound without speaking to each other. Well into their journey back home, Beverly finally broke the silence, "what the fuck were you thinking back there?" She said as he stared out at the road with swollen eyes.

"I was only trying to protect you," he said in a calm voice.

"You almost got us both killed!"

"It seemed like a good idea at the time. I knew it was them, and they had to pay for it, " Adam said, turning to her, then back to the road.

"We don't know for certain if it was them, and they could have killed us. You say that you always want to protect me, but I think your anger issues make things a hell of a lot worse. You're not the same man I met back in the city," she said, trying to calm herself.

"I am that same fucking person, Beverly! I just care about you and want to help and protect you. I don't know why that is so hard for you to fucking understand," he said as they drove back down through the long stretch of highway.

"I don't always need you to try and save me, especially when there wasn't any direct danger, just like with what you did to Mr. Kelly the other day. I didn't know if he was responsible, but you went after him like a madman! This needs to stop, or we need to stop!" She said without hesitation as she stared out the window, holding back her tears.

"What are you trying to say, Beverly?" He turned to her, suppressing his rage.

"I can't have this continue if you place yourself or me in any more unnecessary danger. What I mean by this…is our relationship." Adam clutched tighter onto the steering wheel as he turned his head back to the road. Beverly began to tear as she watched the landscape pass by her window.

"I'm sorry and promise I won't act out anymore. You mean everything to me. This trip definitely didn't turn out the way I wanted it to either," Adam said to Beverly, without getting a response.

"I wish it could have turned out different too... Only if it could have been different..." Adam whispered to himself as he opened the center console, looking down at a small box containing a diamond ring. He slammed it shut then drove the rest of the way home in silence, passing by a sign that read, "Saratoga Springs/Silver Lakes—100 miles."

PART II

THE AWAKENING

CHAPTER THIRTEEN

Quarter to one in the afternoon, Adam and Beverly crossed over the town line into Silver Lakes. The autumn leaves were swept into the air before gently dancing back to the ground behind them. The town, where they called home, is one of the lesser-known suburbs near Saratoga Springs. Located on the outskirts of the greater Albany area, northwest of Troy, and halfway between the Adirondacks and New York City. Adam clicked off cruise control as the open highway merged into familiar secondary roads.

"Are you okay, Beverly?" Adam said, turning to her as she stared out toward the small farms with her right cheek against the window. The passenger side-view mirror reflected a restless and emotionless face as he tried to break their silence. "I hope you believe me that I wasn't trying to put you in any danger back there. I only wanted to protect you…It was instinctual…I also don't know what's been going on with you lately, but it's starting to concern me." He paused in mid-thought to wait for any kind of response.

Beverly moved her head away from the window, "Oh, so I'm the one concerning you? I was scared Adam, I was fucking scared for both our lives," she said, eyes fixed on him.

He grabbed her hand, "I was worried too, I only wanted to protect you. I just don't know how to help you with what you're going through." Adam squeezed Beverly's hand without any reciprocation as she quickly pulled it away.

"I think…I need some time to myself to take care of a few things," she said, holding back tears.

"You're talking nonsense now. We can work this out. I can be there for you if you just tell me how, too." Adam said, driving toward the center of town.

"I see the stress that I'm causing you, Adam. I appreciate everything you do for me. But I can't keep putting you or myself through all of this. It's tearing us apart, and I don't want that to happen," she said, lifting a napkin to her eyes.

Adam paused for a moment, perplexed by this, "Are you breaking up with me because of all this?"

She turned her head and muttered, "No, but maybe a small break from each other will give me some time to sort everything out. Not to be cliché, but it's not you. It's me. All this stress is because of what I'm going through. I don't want to drag you or us down because of it."

Adam tightened his grip on the steering wheel, suppressing his anger and frustration. He cleared his throat, "okay, if that's what you want or need. I'll respect your decision," he said in a calm and cold demeanor as they entered the downtown area.

"I'm sorry, Adam. But, I've been thinking this would be best for both of us. Again, I'm very sorry," she said, turning away from him.

Adam glanced back over to her, "well, I still think you should get checked out at the hospital. You most likely had a concussion last night," he said, suggesting to take her.

"I'll be fine, Adam. Just bring me home, please. I have to get ready to see Doctor Spitzer tomorrow," she said as they drove past the medical center.

"Doctor Spitzer," Adam muttered with animosity, trying not to look agitated in front of her. "I honestly think he is filling your head with absolute nonsense with those books he gave you. That's just my two cents on the matter," he interjected as he turned onto her street.

"I knew you wouldn't understand. Doctor Spitzer and his colleague can help me, so I need to trust them," she said as Adam slammed his hand against the steering wheel.

"Trust them! What about trusting me? I'm the one you should trust!" He yelled as he stopped the car abruptly in her driveway.

"I do trust you, Adam. It's not about that. You can't always be there to save me. I need to do this on my own. I hope you find a way to understand. Again, I'm sorry. I really am…," Beverly said, turning to him. Adam continued to stare forward to avoid looking at her. Beverly reached behind her seat for her backpack, then got out of the car. "I'm doing this because I love you," she said without receiving a response, then paused to look at him for one last time.

"I'm so sorry, Adam…," she stood there in silence, wanting to say more but couldn't find the right words and closed the door. Beverly made her way toward her house, fighting back the urge to turn around to see his face. Adam reversed out of the driveway and accelerated down the road, disappearing around the bend. Beverly walked toward her front door and fell to her knees on the doorstep, crying uncontrollably. The fear, loneliness, and despair from her childhood had overcome her once again.

Beverly collected her emotions, then grabbed Adam's spare key from under the mat. She slowly stood, wiping away her tears, and opened the door, dropping her backpack to the side. Tiny sprinted toward the door and greeted her as if she had been gone for eternity. "There you are, sweetheart. I missed you so much. Hopefully, Junie took good care of you while I was gone," she said to him as he jumped on her with his front legs pressed against her stomach, almost knocking her to the floor. She patted him and gently pushed him off, then made her way toward the kitchen as Tiny followed wagging his tail.

"Are you hungry, buddy?" She said, pouring him dog food, then looked around her apartment as to survey it for anything unusual. "I honestly didn't miss this place at all," she said, looking over to the broken TV, which laid across the living room floor. "Looks like I have to explain that one to Junie on Tuesday," she laughed, trying to lighten her mood as she wiped her eyes. She walked back over to shut and lock the front door, then brought her backpack over to the couch.

Beverly watched Tiny devour his food from the living room, "did she not feed you or something?" Beverly smiled, then sat down on the couch, opening her bag. She retrieved the two books inside and placed them methodically side by side onto the coffee table in front of her. She pushed the book regarding sleep paralysis to the side and picked up the other one on lucid dreaming. She glanced over the book's table of contents and introduction, which stated that becoming conscious or lucid in a dream is possible through practice and self-discipline.

She remembered her visions from the woods, recalling all the vivid details, along with how the entire landscape manifested in her dreams. Beverly realized none of it was real but felt awake and aware all at the same time. *Is this what the book is referring too?* She read on in more detail; if you suddenly realize that you were sleeping, you could become cognitive of your dreams and alter them. She remembered her reflection in the water while still trapped in the body of her child-self. *Are my dreams being manifested into reality then?*

Dread fell upon her as she recalled more details of the experience as the image of the dark entity came into her mind. Her eyes watered, along with a runny nose as she turned the pages, battling to suppress her fears on the subject. She flipped through the chapters to the second half of the book, which referenced a type of lucid dreaming called astral projection. Beverly read through the introduction, coming across the term astral traveler, defined as an out of body experience.

With all the numerous nightmares, sleepwalking, and possible lucid dreaming, she couldn't recall ever being outside of her body in any sense of the definition. Beverly laughed to herself, "I may not be all mentally there, but at least I feel physically in touch with reality." She said, continuing to flip through the pictures before coming across an image. "What the hell is that?" She said out loud as Tiny ears perked up, raising his head off her lap.

The book had an artist's rendition of someone asleep on a bed as their spirit body hovered above them. She looked closer at the picture to see a fine silvery thread of energy linking the two together, then slammed the book shut. In her dream, down by the river, she remembered looking toward the dark entity on top of the cliff. Beverly gasped as she realized the same silvery cord had connected her, before quickly being repelled back toward her adult-self sleeping in the chair.

Beverly tossed the book onto the table and brought the palms of her hands to her face. Not in disgust with what she saw but overwhelmed and confused why she was experiencing all these unwanted visions, over and over again. Tiny jumped off the couch as Beverly grew more frustrated. "What the fuck is wrong with me! Why can't I make this all stop!"

She laid across the couch in a fetal position, sobbing to herself before falling asleep from exhaustion. What felt like seconds later, a loud knock rapped against the front door as Tiny ran over barking hysterically. Beverly got off the couch, disoriented, and walked toward the door. "Go away!" She yelled, stepping forward as Tiny snarled and jumped up against the door while the knocking continued. "Shush, Tiny." Beverly noticed a repetitive strobing flash of amber lights coming from the window. What do you want?" She yelled.

"It's the Police. We would like to ask you a few questions?" Her delusion dissipated as she gathered her thoughts to calm herself, then consoled Tiny before opening the door. There was a blond officer, not much younger than herself, standing in her doorway with his radio chattering from his collar mic. Several police cruisers and an ambulance were staged across the street behind him. She rubbed her bloodshot eyes, then noticed yellow tape wrapped around the trees surrounding Mr. Kelly's home.

"Sorry to bother you, Miss. I know its late in the evening. I just have a few questions to ask you," he said, holding a notepad with a pen in his other hand. Beverly glanced down at her watch, noticing several hours had past and nearing nightfall. "We received a 911 call from your neighbor who stated someone was trying to get into his home, and it was going to...well end badly. That is all he kept repeating to our dispatchers before we lost contact."

Beverly stood in disbelief, not knowing how else to interpret this information. He continued, "again, I'm sorry to have bothered you so late, but as of right now, our department is unsure if it is homicide or suicide. I'm currently canvassing the area to check on the neighborhood to see if everyone is safe and if they know or seen anything unusual. Honestly, we haven't had any leads from what occurred tonight. So, that's why I am here. Did you happen to hear or see something tonight, Miss? There was a brief silence as he waited for a response.

"Ma'am?" The officer repeated as Beverly stood there with an absent gaze.

Surprised and puzzled by the news, she watched the lights from the emergency vehicles hypnotically flash in her retinas. She broke out of her trance, then shook her head, "no, Officer. I honestly didn't even know the man nor saw anything suspicious." Beverly explained, trying to keep Tiny's curious head from poking outside.

"I understand, Miss, and appreciate your cooperation. If anything does come up, please don't hesitate to call this number. We'll continue to keep patrol and surveillance over the area throughout the night. Not to add to the hysteria, but I highly recommend that you lock your doors and windows tonight—good thing you have a great guard dog to alert and protect you during the night. German Shepherd's are great family pets too," he said, letting Tiny sniff the back of his hand. "Again, don't you worry one bit. We have this place under control. I can assure you of that," he said as she nodded her head, still in disbelief. "Enjoy the rest of your evening, Miss." The officer said, then turned away and walked back across the street toward the crime scene. She watched him disappear into the amber lights and evening fog.

Beverly snapped out of her own mental fog and went back inside, shutting the door behind her. She fumbled with the locks to secure herself in for the night. Tiny curiously looked up, watching her frantically go throughout the house to check that every window was still locked.

Could Adam have done this? Beverly stopped in the living room and thought with vague uncertainty. *I know how angry he can get. And how he didn't trust Mr. Kelly from the start. Is this his sick way of trying to protect me? Could he have gone completely insane?* She grabbed her phone, which had no missed calls or texts from him. Frantic, she held her finger over Adam's number, hesitating to press the call button. She knew she would regret it if she tried to call him either way.

Even if he was the one responsible or not, she decided it was best to put her phone away. She shivered to the thought, then turned out the lights in the living room. "I just need to get away, buddy. I need to go back home for a bit. Just you and me," she said, looking down at Tiny. As they both ascended the stairs, Beverly looked back over her shoulder at the amber lights flickering through her front window. She continued to her bedroom, hoping the nightmares would not return tonight.

CHAPTER FOURTEEN

That night, Beverly dreamt of standing barefoot near a small tributary on a quiet spring morning. The soil was cold and damp, thriving with the blossoming vegetation next to the river bed. There was a slight chill, accompanied by the warmth of the sunshine radiating behind her. It peaked periodically through the cloudy early-spring gloom, which provided contrast against the woodland landscape. Several residual rain droplets from an earlier storm trickled off the tree branches overhead.

Beverly took several steps toward the slow-moving stream as the fragrance of life had been restored after the long, harsh winter. Her life burdens had momentarily slipped away from her mind, like a long-awaited gentle spring rain. She leaned over the water as her reflection stared back at her. Kneeling by the brook, she cupped her hands together, submerging them in the chilled running water to take a sip. She slowly stood after a comforting hand rested against her shoulder.

Not startled by the unknown presence behind her, Beverly turned to see her mother Judith staring back at her. Her mother wore a beautiful white evening dress with her long wavy blond hair flowing against her back. The sun glistened off her skin with an angelic glow with an aura of pure gold and exuberance. Without saying a word, she produced a vibrant smile and took her daughter's hands into hers.

"Mom?" Beverly said, staring back into her deep blue eyes as a tear ran down from her cheek. "I missed you so much," she said, choked up from how real the experience felt.

"I've missed you very much too, Beverly. There is so much to tell you, but the time is now scarce," she said in a gentle yet concerned voice. She brushed her hand against her daughter's cheek to wipe away her tear, "Don't cry, sweetheart. I'll always be here for you, always know this. But now is the time I need you to be strong for me. Some things in life don't appear exactly as they seem or truly perceived. You will have to find your own inner strength to fight against these fears. Believe in yourself and then, and only then, you will be able to overcome this darkness," she said as she embraced her daughter in her arms.

Beverly leaned over her mother's shoulder, "I don't know how to, Mom! I'm scared," Beverly said as she held her mother tightly, not wanting to let go.

"I'm sorry, I had to leave you so soon, honey. You are strong and will find your way. For now, you need to brave the storm and be there for them. But one day, you'll have to cross the river," Judith told her before letting go. She kissed Beverly on the forehead, then stepped back into the forest. The sunlight reflected across Judith's dress, as her apparition slowly disappeared into the bright light emanating behind her.

"Mom! Don't leave me!" Beverly said, standing alone in the woods. Silence surrounded her except for the flowing river behind her. She dried her tears and stepped forward into the woods, left illuminated with white light.

"Be there for who, Mom? Who are they?" Beverly yelled out as she tried to follow her into the woods. "I'm sorry, mom, and I promise you that I won't be afraid anymore. Just come back to me!" Beverly cried out as she wandered into the woods in a desperate search for her mother. The blinding light encompassed Beverly's surroundings and disoriented her. Her vision was lost, while at the same time, her mind melted into a vacuum before, fading off to nothingness. The rest of her night was dreamless.

Beverly woke that morning at seven to her alarm clock with the same restlessness as with all the previous nights. Tiny had already been quietly waiting by the door to be let out of the bedroom. She went downstairs in her bathrobe, anxious and nauseous as she turned on the coffee maker. Beverly opened the sliding glass patio door to let Tiny out, then prepared breakfast for the both of them. Without having an appetite, she decided to toss a few extra pieces of bacon into Tiny's bowl. She turned on the local radio station with the forecast reporting another unusual warm late-October day, followed by a drastic change to cold weather by sunset.

Beverly grabbed a broom from the closet to clean up the shattered TV glass off the floor. She lifted the television and brought it to the trash dumpsters outside by the curb. When she reached the road, she looked across the street toward the yellow police tape still wrapped around the trees, barricading off the house. Two police cruisers were parked outside Mr. Kelly's home as they continued on with their investigation. She never recalled seeing any other neighbors outside last night or even this morning. As if they hadn't noticed or even cared. Despite being a small, tight-knit community, there was still a sense of isolation.

Beverly thought about Adam's confrontation with Mr. Kelly a few days ago, where he mentioned something about strange things occurring at night. As she closed the trashcan lid, she pondered with the idea if Mr. Kelly saw the same visions she had every night. She wondered if these hallucinations drove him to madness and caused him to commit suicide or even worse if this entity was, in fact, real. A sudden chill rolled down her spine before shrugging off the distant thought as nonsense and pure absurdity.

Then another fleeting thought came to mind. *I can just walk over to the police right now. And tell them I've seen what he may have been referring too. That's right Beverly, just go right over there and tell them all about how the Boogeyman had killed him last night.* The ridiculousness of her thought quickly faded, knowing in a split second they would take her away to the loony bin, white straight-jacket and all. No one could possibly believe that a strange dark supernatural force haunted someone till madness and eventually death.

Beverly noticed one of the detectives dressed in civilian clothes with beige khakis and a badge on his belt. He looked over to her, as he exited Mr. Kelly's home with his camera strung around his neck. She looked away, then turned to walk back inside her house, shutting the door behind her. Beverly stood in front of the door, watching Tiny finish his food as she contemplated about how these events were in some way connected. She doubted if Adam had anything to do with any of this. But kept the thought tucked away in the back of her mind. She felt he was a little too protective and short-tempered at times. But she knew there was no way he was capable of something heinous as cold-blooded murder. *Or could he?*

Beverly questioned if the death of Mr. Kelly was, in fact, self-inflicted. *Wouldn't the police know right away, though?* Or if this was all somehow connected and linked to the same visions. *Maybe, if he had the same nightmarish visitations, tormenting him night after night, he could… or possibly would commit…* She ran the idea over and over in her head, trying to make sense out of it. Beverly understood first hand the feelings of dread and despair. How it could grab hold of you on a much deeper level like a parasite feasting its way through the flesh into the core. As the dark entity feeds on your emotions and fears, slowly driving you insane.

Maybe he experienced the same festering visitations night after night, she thought. *Then to one day eventually snap, taking his own life to put a stop to all his pain and suffering.* Beverly knew what it was like to live with depression. How it would always come in waves like how the sand meets the tide. Some days mirrored the old saying, red sky at night, sailor's delight, where the waves would be gentle and soothing, coasting you along and out to sea.

Other times not so benign, with the second half of the maritime adage, red sky morning, sailors take warning. However, there would never be any real warning. The storm would thrash her mind as if she was holding onto the mast of the ship, with her fingernails dug deep into the splintering wood, hoping to ride it out. Until the bombardment of wave after wave finally sending her head over feet starboard bow into the dark abyss.

The thought of wanting to end it all had always crossed her mind, fleeting, however still there. This last resort had already manifested where she had considered slitting her wrists in the bathtub as the warm water ran cold. Or perhaps, a more humane approach by over-dosing on the Benzos and sleeping pills that her doctor prescribed, to induce respiratory failure as she quietly slept. However, with all these dark thoughts, she still had hope left with the doctor's guidance on the distant horizon like a lost, uncharted land. There's always a chance to make things right. To one day live a long happy and normal life that she desperately desired.

Remembering last night's dream, she mustered the strength to fight whatever this darkness her mother had referred too. Beverly walked over to pet Tiny, then took a shower before gathering her things for her trip to the city. She placed Doctor Spitzer's books into her backpack and locked the front door behind her. Beverly helped Tiny into the back seat of her car, then pulled out of the driveway. She glanced over to her atypical haunted house, avoiding eye contact with the observant and curious detectives standing on Mr. Kelly's front porch. She drove down the road, then disappeared around the corner, embarking on her journey back home.

CHAPTER FIFTEEN

Beverly continued south on the scenic Taconic State Parkway for forty minutes before merging onto the city-bound I-87 highway. She passed a sign for the Bronx as Tiny stuck his head outside the back window, watching the forest scenery slowly transition to an urban landscape. Beverly followed the I-87 until it turned into the Major Deegan Expressway then crossed the Third Avenue Bridge over the Harlem River. She dialed Doctor Spitzer's office over her headset as she got closer to the upper east-side near Central Park. After three hours of driving, she pulled into the Lenox Hill Hospital parking garage and let Tiny out of the back seat. Beverly dropped him off at a pet groomer she knew down the street from the office, then proceeded to her appointment.

She walked the several blocks toward the out-patient center, associated with the hospital, on 5th Avenue facing Central Park. She entered the all to familiar lobby—passed the desk with the half-attentive security guard—and rode the large gold-plated elevator up to the 14th floor to Doctor Spitzer's office. Beverly's stomach turned as she checked in with the receptionist, then took her seat in the waiting area. Beads of sweat formed on her forehead as she clenched tightly onto the armrests of her chair, waiting for the doors to open.

Despite the morning traffic, Beverly made good time coming down for her eleven o'clock appointment with thirty minutes to spare. To preoccupy her mind, she picked up a fashion magazine from the table to pass the time but was distracted by the clock ticking away until her appointment. Uninterested with the topic anyway, she placed the magazine back down on the table then readjusted herself multiple times in the chair as she glanced around the room. To her left, a fidgeting six-year-old child sat next to his mother two seats down from her. Beyond them, there was a tall, handsome middle-aged black man—wearing a pristine all-black suit with a crimson red tie—who sat in the far corner reading a paperback book.

Beverly played with her phone to pass the time and catch up on some work emails, secretly hoping she would receive a message from Adam. There were no new emails in her work inbox or messages on her phone, then placed it back into her purse and watched the clock slowly tick away. After twenty agonizing minutes, the door finally opened with a child in his early-teens emerging as his mother went over to him. Doctor Spitzer came out of his office to talk with her and had his secretary schedule a follow-up appointment.

"Mrs. Epstein, I know you and your children are still going through a tough time after losing your husband. I'm so sorry for your loss. I feel that all your son's nightmares and mood swings are due to grief and depression." Doctor Spitzer explained to her quietly as her eldest son walked back over to his little brother.

"Thank you for the condolences, Doctor. I still feel the sting from the loss too. But this was seven years ago when he was a small child. I was still pregnant with my youngest one after we got the news of the accident. I don't understand why he would still be having such vivid night terrors almost every week now." The mother said to Doctor Spitzer, looking back at her children, as the youngest desperately tried to get his brother's attention. The older brother sat restlessly in the chair next to him with a catatonic expression across his face.

"I understand, but children are more susceptible to grief as they're not able to rationalize the situation when they are young and still impressionable. He may feel that he could have changed the outcome somehow, even though it was clearly out of anyone's control. This event may have certainly led to post-traumatic stress. For now, I will prescribe some anti-depressant, sedatives, and sleeping aids to hopefully help with his sleep problems. Hopefully, in turn, eventually help with his mood disorder and anxiety. Let's see how those work for the next two weeks, then we'll have him come in for a follow-up and to go over any further treatment plans." Doctor Spitzer explained as he handed her the prescriptions.

"Okay, I hope this helps him. Thank you, Doctor." She said to him as Beverly leaned closer in her chair, trying to listen in on their conversation. The tall man in the corner of the room lifted his head from his book, watching the family exit the room.

Doctor Spitzer nodded to Beverly and told his secretary not to schedule any further appointments until this afternoon. "Beverly, I'm glad to see you again. Please step into my office," he said, gesturing to her. Beverly stood from her chair and walked over to shake his hand. The gentleman from across the room placed his book into his suitcase and followed behind her. "Beverly, I would like you to have the pleasure of meeting Doctor Adisa Faraji Imamu, a long-time colleague of mine from New York University." Doctor Spitzer said, introducing them.

"It's a pleasure, Miss Beverly Hollinger. I have heard so much about you," he said with a warming smile and firm handshake.

"Hopefully, all good things," she said, smiling back.

"Very much so, now let us begin, shall we?" Doctor Imamu said with a thick eastern African accent while gesturing for them to proceed into the room. She nodded to his gesture then proceeded into the office as Doctor Spitzer closed the doors behind them.

Beverly walked past his recliner and stared toward the large windows facing Central Park, before sitting on the couch, "Doc, what was that all about? The family outside?" She inquired as they both took a seat in their respective chairs, facing her.

"Beverly, you know I can't talk about confidential information regarding my other patients. But like I mentioned before, you have not been the only patient to experience these symptoms. Yours are just a little bit more severe," he explained to her, then looked over at Doctor Imamu and nodded.

"You see, Beverly, from what I have heard from Doctor Spitzer, is that you've been experiencing vivid nightmares since your childhood. Visions, if you will. Have you ever had a dream where you felt like you were awake or flying?" Doctor Imamu interjected.

"Yes, quite frequently now," she responded, unsure of why he wanted this information.

"I see. Well, these sorts of experiences that you have are called lucid dreams, which can lead to an out of body experience." Doctor Imamu said, leaning in his chair toward her with his hands clasped. "You have a real gift, Beverly. Many cultures, along with my own research, have well documented these experiences. I've spent my entire life and career trying to understand the science behind this phenomenon." Doctor Imamu explained, looking Beverly in the eyes.

"Who are you again?" Beverly said with a confused smirk on her face.

"Sorry for being abrupt with my introduction. I'm a doctor who specializes in neurological functions and a person's mental well-being. I primarily research neuroscience, psychology, and oneirology, the study of sleeping disorders, which all go hand and hand. Don't let my specialties fool you, though. I'm interested in your particular case because you possess something special, Beverly. This is not a disorder that needs to be treated. But a natural talent that should be nurtured and embraced," he said with all seriousness, before leaning back in his chair.

"Are you guys joking with me? I thought this was all just in my head, and were going to prescribe me anti-depressants like the other patients," she said with a concerned voice as she sat on the couch.

"I'm afraid not, Beverly. Those books Doctor Spitzer gave you are from my personal library. I have studied this remarkable phenomenon since I was a child. I grew up in a small village on the island of Zanzibar, located in Tanzania in Eastern Africa. Many of those villagers have also experienced the same things you have been going through. Even multiple people at the same time on one particular night," Imamu said, pulling out his laptop from his bag.

"You mean, all at once?" Beverly said with nervousness in her voice.

"Unfortunately, yes, these mass visions have been recorded on multiple occasions. Zanzibar, in particular, was once an old colonial slave port ruled over by many past empires; Portuguese, British, and Arab Sultans until the bloody revolution in 1964 when we became the sovereign, United Republic of Tanzania. Since our revolution, there had been many reforms in our beliefs to adapt to either Islam or Christianity. However, our people still hold on to their cultural prevalent tribal religions and witchcraft," he said as he opened his laptop.

"Black magic?" She said, looking hesitantly over toward Doctor Spitzer, who appeared receptive of this information.

"You see, Beverly, in our tradition we had Shaman, or witch Doctors if you will, who would spend their entire lives devoted to these practices of good and evil. In the 1970s, after the revolution, there were numerous documented cases of mass sighting attacks as the villagers slept in their beds. Many of these reported attacks would continue around the world to this very day. I can still recall my neighbors, family, and childhood friends discussing these night terrors or what they referred to as visitations in the night." The sleep doctor said, looking down at his computer for a moment.

"Fortunately for me, I've never personally experienced any of these phenomena. This made my curiosity even more incurable as if I was either lucky or not special enough to see what they could see. I've had also been fortunate enough to leave my home town as a young adult to pursue this unsolved mystery and study the scientific explanations behind these events. I attended university in England, with the thought still lingering in the back of my mind that if this was something supernatural," he explained, pulling up photographs from his laptop.

"So, doctor, do you think this is all real...these visitations?" She asked, leaning forward to examine the pictures on his laptop. Beverly studied them intently, astonished that both these credited doctors were validating her insane visions as a reality.

"I do, even to this day. These pictures are of my hometown. I took them during a field internship study, which I conducted for my thesis paper in '95. These sightings were one of the most significant unexplainable outbreaks documented in history. The villagers were afraid to sleep inside their homes at night and eventually got so bad; they decided to gather in the streets to sleep together for protection. The villagers called this dark entity, the Popobawa, which they believed to have been manifested by dark magic rituals on the island of Pemba. The accused Shamans, who practiced in the dark arts, were exiled and even killed for this curse they brought onto their people.

Beverly thought about the stone altar in the middle of the woods as she continued to listen to him. "My academic assignment was to do a full psychological and neurological assessment on a large sample population to see what could have triggered this hysteria," Imamu explained. "To this day, along with the vast scientific knowledge of the human mind I obtained through doctorate school, I could not come to an absolute conclusion with my observations. I hypothesized that this was an emotional excitation, exacerbated by a theological myth."

She glanced through the multiple pictures of villagers crowded in the streets during the night. In another folder, there were old photographs of witch doctors performing rituals on individuals. "This all seems similar to the folklore in the book you had given me." Beverly said, leaning back away from the screen as she ran her hand through her hair in confusion of what she was seeing.

"Exactly, Beverly! My studies have taken me throughout the world, discovering the historical similarities that date back to Rome, and modern times. Everything from folklore, nightly encounters, to even cases of homicidal sleepwalking murderers. Most scientists today regard cases of alien abduction, ghosts, hat-man, and all similar paranormal encounters are linked to sleep paralysis, which stems from our collective imagination like the Mandela effect. But how can they explain this other event then?" Doctor Adisa said, more as a statement than a question as he reached for his laptop.

I'll show you another mass sighting case, which occurred around the same time as the first event in

Zanzibar during the '70s." He said as he selected his video archives on his computer. "This phenomenon was covered up by the U.S. government with the blanketed term Nocturnal Death Syndrome where Moong refugees from the Vietnam war came to America, then started to have unexplainable deaths during their sleep," as he leaned forward and clicked on a video file.

"They displayed much fear to their loved ones before passing," the doctor said before pressing play. The video showed a morgue with multiple deceased corpses lying on the metal slabs in the middle of an autopsy room. Standing next the bodies were United States government officials documenting their medical examiner reports. The clipboard showed the front of one medical record, "*unknown cause of death with unknown medical pathology.*" The footage stopped as the Doctor started another video, with a Shaman slitting a chicken's neck wide-open with a large butcher knife, draining the blood on the floor near his traumatized patient.

Beverly quickly remembered her dream of the dark entity, sacrificing the deer as it squeezed the blood from its heart. The video continued to show the Shaman performing a ritual where he tied a red cloth on the victim's arm, with subtitles that translated, "this will be your barrier as you enter the spiritual realm."

The Shaman began to chant as the person started to seize and convulse on the ground with foam forming around his mouth. The footage went black.

"I've seen enough. Do you think this is some kind of sick joke?" Beverly said, raising her voice as she stood from the couch. "I thought you were trying to help me! Not fucking ridicule me with this nonsense!" She said, choking up as she made her way toward the door.

"Beverly, wait!" Doctor Imamu said, swiftly getting up from his chair. "I'm so sorry to upset you with this information all at once. But understand, this is no joke. Whatever is causing these visions that you're having, I truly believe are supernatural in origin." She stopped before opening the door as he continued. "It feeds on our deepest fears and internal pain as a path of least resistance to create a gateway into our world. I feel this is the root of all the chaos and evil that plagues are species," he said passionately, trying to persuade her to listen to him.

"What do you need me for then?" She said, turning to him disgusted.

"You have a unique ability and gift, which this entity can sense and feel. It's drawn to you, Beverly, because you provide the power it needs to materialize into our universe. I know this may sound crazy, but with my help, we can use your ability to defeat this entity and close the gate. It won't close all the gates in the world where they can manifest through, but it could possibly close the one that haunts you and your loved ones.

Beverly paused for a moment, as he continued. "You just have to trust me on this. I need you to allow me to run some additional tests in my sleep center lab at Bellevue Hospital tomorrow night."

"You need to trust him, Beverly. You need to trust both of us." Doctor Spitzer interjected as he walked over to hand her his card.

"Yeah, let me sleep on it," Beverly responded sarcastically before slamming the door behind her.

"I need her for this experiment, Jeffery," Doctor Imamu said, walking to the window, then looked out toward central park.

"She will come, Adisa. Don't you worry, she will come."

CHAPTER SIXTEEN

Beverly descended the elevator, trying to make sense of it all. She reached the ground floor and exited the building toward the pet groomers shop down the street. She greeted Tiny with a hug, "who looks so handsome?" Beverly said as she paid the groomer and thanked her before taking him for a walk in Central Park. She followed the familiar trails toward the pond in the center of the park as the dead leaves crunched underfoot. She watched the tourist and families walk along the path in the sunny afternoon while reflecting on her childhood and Adam.

She continuously checked her phone, only to find no new messages with the guilt of distancing herself and separating from him finally sunk in. But the one thought she could not live with the most was the fear of possibly being hurt again or hurting him in the process. Beverly looked up toward the cloudless autumn sky, feeling the same loneliness as when she had lived in the city. She turned toward the hospital tower, looming over the park off in the distance, stirring in thought about everything they tried to reveal to her. She sighed, then looked down at Tiny, who was playing carefree in the leave piles.

She reached the pond and took a seat on a park bench to rest for a moment. Off in the distance, a beautiful stone arched bridge reflected a perfect circle across the water. She looked back down to Tiny, then grabbed a handful of dog food out of a zip lock bag from her backpack. Startled by her phone ring, she dropped the kibble next to her feet as Tiny went for them. She fumbled her hands through her bag to retrieve her phone, hoping to see it was Adam but instead saw her friend Kristen calling.

"Hey, Kris!" Beverly answered, trying to sound enthusiastic.

"Hey, hon, what are you up too? Long-time, no talk," Kristen said.

"I know, right? Funny you called, though, *because* I'm actually in the city right now. I had another appointment with my doctor today... now I'm sitting in Central Park like old times," she said, embarrassed with the fact that she still saw her childhood psychiatrist.

"Bev, you still having those nightmares? She responded without hesitation.

"Yeah, sort of…I would've called you to tell you that I was coming down, but figured I was only going to be here for a few hours. Then things changed…," Beverly explained, then paused as Kristen didn't question her any further. "I've kind of been going through a rough time lately, and actually glad that you called. Especially when I need it the most. Are you busy tonight by any chance? Maybe we can catch up, and I could spend the night?" Beverly asked as she looked over toward the water as the gathering clouds and wind obscured the reflection.

"Beverly, I'll always have time to see you, and will be off work in a few hours. Meet me at our favorite pub at six, okay?"

"Okay, hon. I'll see you there!" Beverly placed her phone into her handbag, then took a moment to enjoy the sunshine before walking back to the parking garage. She left a message on her boss's voice-mail, explaining she would have to stay another day in New York due to her family emergency. Beverly helped Tiny back into the car and made her way south toward her Brooklyn hometown.

Beverly entered the downtown area of her old neighborhood and passed by the "Night Owl" theater. Anger swelled inside, eventually overwhelming her as she sped up to pass it by. Beverly took a glance out her window toward the theater's entrance but didn't see any remembrance for the event, only to be replaced by souvenir and roasted peanut vendors. As if the memories were left eroded and forgotten through the sands of time. Only to be a lost and a fleeting memory for the new residents, businesses, and families that moved into the neighborhood over the last decade.

Yet even by the passage of time, she still remembered. Beverly remembered her parents not coming home on that cold and endless night. She remembered being held by her babysitter as she cried through the pain. She remembered being taken away from her home in the middle of the night by police, only never to see her family again. Anger and hatred slowly took over the wheel as she swerved erratically between the lanes of traffic to leave the downtown area as quickly as possible. She took a slight detour down a road that led her to a quiet neighborhood with a cemetery sitting on top of a hill, overlooking the suburbia subdivisions.

She exited the car leaving Tiny in the back seat, who kept poking his head out the window as she walked through the cemetery's rusted-iron gates. She passed the numerous gravestones, which were uniformly adjacent to one another before approaching her parent's headstone one hundred-meters from the entrance. She walked underneath an old oak tree that had already given up its leaves, which were now scattered over the gravesite. Beverly got down on her knees, frantically brushing them away to reveal her parent's names. A poem was visible on their plaque, "*In tragedy, we must have hope. In life, we must learn to cope.*" followed by their names and, "*In loving memory of their daughter,*" with Beverly's name underneath theirs.

She remembered writing the poem shortly after their death and wanted it engraved on their headstone for remembrance. With trembling hands, Beverly wiped away her tears and swallowed her sadness and anger in one large gulp. Knowing all too well when she wrote the poem, she had to keep hope that there was a greater good, despite all the evil and tragedy in this world. She stood and looked across the cemetery to all the other gravestones laid scattered around her.

The sun had set over the tree line, stealing the warmth as an unforgiving cold wind blew over the top of the hillcrest. "I can't be afraid anymore. I need to change all this somehow. There must be a way to stop all this needless suffering in the world.

All my suffering." Beverly said, wiping away the last tear from her cheek before it thickened to her face from the cold. She looked down at her watch and noticed it was a quarter to six.

"Mom and Dad, I love you. I will try to make this right again. We can't continue to live in a world of fear and evil." She said out loud, turning to walk back to her car as darkness fell over the cemetery. On the way back, she tripped over a small tombstone and stumbled before regaining her balance. She looked down to see the name engraved on the small granite memorial, "Sergeant Daniel Potoswki, NYPD 1976-2030."

Beverly's heart sank into her stomach, recognizing the name of the police officer who looked after her that night had passed away this year. "We shall meet again, old friend. I just wish it was under different circumstances. Thank you for everything," she said as she took a flower from nearby shrubbery, then gently laid it across his grave. "Your work will never be in vain. Rest in peace, Sergeant," she said, then walked somberly back to her car, where Tiny waited patiently inside.

Beverly pulled into the parking lot of, "O' Reilly's," local pub and grill. She had a missed call from Kristen

ten minutes ago and assumed she had already gotten there before she did. The wooden sign above the entrance read, "Come on in my friend. Drink, laugh, and be merry, leave behind the burdens that you carry." Beverly laughed to herself, thinking about how often she would come here with friends, to try and forget about her own burdens she buried. She entered the small basement-level bar and recognized the same old familiar patrons watching the Yankees clinch the playoffs.

"Beverly!" Kristen yelled out from across the room, then ran over to greet her with a hug and kiss on the cheek. "I'm so glad you're here! How the hell are you? How's Silver Lakes treating you? How was your long-talked-about getaway with Adam?" Kristen said with a smile, leading her back to the table booth.

"Things could be better," she said awkwardly. "I'm happy we could meet, though," Beverly said as Kristen ordered them each a gin and tonic, as the waiter came around.

"What's up, Bev? Sorry, but first, I have to say you kinda have this homeless girl look going on with ya right now," she said jokingly with a smile. Kristen was dressed in a slick black business-casual blouse with a matching skirt and high heels. Her blond hair was in a loose bun with her make-up done up in contrast to

Beverly, who was wearing an old torn up sweatshirt and dirty jeans from kneeling on the ground in the cemetery.

"I broke up with Adam the other day," Beverly said, looking down as the waiter placed their drinks in front of them.

"You did what? I didn't think of him as being a douche bag, though. I'm sorry I hooked you up with him, I honestly thought it would last longer." She said, staring back at Beverly, who was looking down toward the table, stirring her cocktail aimlessly.

"No, it's not him, it was all me… I've had so much going on with myself, and Adam always wanted to be there for me as if I was helpless. I just don't know how to let him help me. To be honest, I don't even know what I need help with. I didn't want to drag him down with me," Beverly said, lifting her eyes from the glass.

"What kind of issues, Bev? Speak to me, girl," Kristen said as she took a sip from her drink, waiving over to the waiter for another round.

"That's actually why I'm here today. I met with my psychiatrist and his colleague this afternoon because my nightmares have gotten worse, much worse. The doctors want me to do some more tests tomorrow. I just don't know if I should follow through with it. I probably sound crazy right now," Beverly said with a half-smile, taking a small sip from her drink.

"Well, you are my crazy friend, and that's why I love you. But in all seriousness, if they want you to do more tests tomorrow, I recommend that you listen to them. You can stay with me tonight," Kristen offered. She then changed the subject and joked to lighten the mood, "Hey, remember Adam's weird friend, who came down here when you first met? Kyle, the mountain boy, was it? He'll always be far stranger than you ever will be," Kristen said, trying to cheer her up.

"I didn't remember him then, but I was reintroduced to him last weekend when Adam and I went camping. When you get to know him, he is a really great guy who also has a family now. I promised him not to tell you this, but he may or may not have had a crush on you," Beverly said with a smile as she sipped her drink.

"Eww, gross, he was such a creeper back in high school, " Kristen responded with a repulsed look, then laughed. "He used to wear trench coats and army-camo fatigues to class as if he was about to shoot up the place. But, good for him though on the family stuff. Hell, If he could reproduce, then there's hope for the rest of us. I bet he married the yeti of his dreams. Regardless, my point was that you are not crazy. I think you had a rough past and should do whatever the doctor tells you to do."

Beverly's smiled, then nodded, "It feels like yesterday when we used to come to this dive like those regulars over there. I also could never forget the night when I first met Adam here after you secretly invited him and his friends to join us. I'm still happy with the transition up north even though I miss hanging out with you almost every night. Do you miss Silver Lakes at all? Your family?" Beverly asked, looking down at her phone for a moment, not to see any missed messages from Adam.

"Not one frickin bit. I wanted to leave that shit hole well before high school even ended. Not to talk bad about the place you had just moved too, but it just wasn't for me. I used to sneak out with my girlfriends every other weekend and come down to the city to get away whenever I could," she said, laughing but paused to correct herself.

"Again, it was a shit hole for me with my huge ambitions, but I'm sure it's a good place for you to live. Quieter and away from all the crap you were used to down here. Everyone has their threshold of bullshit they can endure before needing a change. Each one of us has something we try to break free and run away from, "

Kristen said to her as Beverly nodded and stared back down at her drink.

"Hell, if I didn't leave Silver Lakes, you wouldn't have known me or had met Adam, good or bad. At least you can say you had the chance to experience it. Personally, I don't feel we should ever remain stagnant," Kristen continued.

"I totally agree with you. However, I do miss the city sometimes. It's just a little too quiet up there at night." Beverly started to laugh, then went back to being serious and leaned in closer. "Maybe not to quiet, though. I almost forgot to mention, there was a mysterious murder or suicide next door to me. The cops were investigating all night long, and this morning before I left. I don't think they know what happened to him either. He was this strange elderly guy from across the street, Mr. Kelly," she whispered from across the table.

"Holy shit, Frank Kelly!" Kristen yelled out, breaking their silent discussion. "He was our town's crazy old librarian. Well, he was in his early sixties at the time, but looked much older for his age, and always preoccupied with this weird satanic folklore nonsense. He would try to tell everybody about it, especially young school children. He would ramble on and on about a pure evil that would come during the night, unless you gave it, what that it wanted. Eventually, with a majority of the town's consensus and complaints against him, the board gave him the ultimatum to either seek psychiatric help or they would have to let him go."

Beverly looked at Kristen stunned as she continued, "Everyone knew he chose his reclusive lifestyle over treatment, so he was forced to resign. I bet that crazy fucker offed himself from all of his delusions that were cycling throughout his head." Kristen said, laughing hysterically as Beverly looked around the room, noticing no one was paying any attention to their small-town gossip.

"Wow, I would have never known that. He always did keep to himself as if he was hiding away a secret. Anyway, I have Tiny with me, so maybe we should get out of here and head back to your place," Beverly insisted on changing the topic and scenery.

"Awe, you brought the little fuzzball with you too? Okay, hon, sounds good to me, this bar is a dump anyways. Why pay for drinks when we can have fun at my... I mean our old house. Let's get out of here, sis." Kristen said, then waived to get the waiter's attention. He walked over as she paid the bill on her company American Express credit card. "There are many perks that come with my job, Bev. If you are ever interested in coming back home, I will hook you up with a nice cozy position. No more waiting tables at cafes or dive bars for us," Kristen said with a smile as she grabbed for her coat. They made their way toward the exit as the bartender poured a frothy pitcher and another round of whiskey shots for the rowdy patrons celebrating at the bar.

CHAPTER SEVENTEEN

Beverly followed Kristen back to their old flat, located on a small quiet street tucked away in Williamsburg, Brooklyn, New York. She got out of the car, then gathered her things as Tiny squeezed passed her and sprinted toward Kristen. "Wow, buddy! You just keep on growing, don't ya. Yes, you do! You look so happy and healthy," Kristen said as Tiny greeted her, balancing on his two hind legs. "Momma has been taking good care of you. More than herself, it seems," she said while petting him.

"Very funny," Beverly said, walking toward them. "I decided to drop Tiny off at the groomers before my appointment this morning," she explained as they made their way to her apartment. Beverly entered the living room and saw how much had changed since she moved out a month ago. "I like what you have done with the place. Do you enjoy sharing it between just the two of you now?" Beverly said as she looked toward her old room, now turned into an office.

I definitely miss ya being here. Erika, on the other hand...I could live without. She's been way messier since you left, and I'm hoping she moves out soon. Unfortunately, she just left for a cruise with her boyfriend yesterday, but I'll definitely give her your regards." Kristen said as Tiny walked nonchalantly past them and jumped on to the couch, making himself at home.

"I wouldn't mind seeing her again, but I agree she was one hot mess." Beverly chuckled, then turned toward the couch, "Tiny! How rude, get off from there," failing to get his attention.

"It's okay, he just misses the days of wandering around here as a little pup. I can still remember the Christmas morning Adam brought him over for you," Kristen said as she took a seat next to him and patted his head. Beverly sighed, rolling her eyes, knowing her dog still needed more training. Kristen told her that there's a bottle of wine and to help herself to anything to eat. They both sat on the couch with Tiny between them, catching up and reflecting on the past. They drank wine and talked long past midnight.

Last year, on a quiet Christmas morning, Beverly unwrapped gifts with Kristen and Erika as the snow fell over their quite New York neighborhood. White powder blanketed the isolated streets below their apartment with frost developing over the windows, as the wind howled and rattled against the glass. The radio DJ cycled through the seasonal favorites as Bobby Helm's "Jingle Bell Rock" played on the radio. A quick knock rapped against their door as they laughed and sipped hot cocoa, not hearing it at first. Beverly answered, knowing the road conditions were atrocious and weren't expecting any visitors, only to find Adam standing in the doorway covered head to toe with snow.

A little black-fur snout popped out from his jacket as she looked up to Adam with a smile from ear to ear, then back down at the puppy trying to desperately free himself. Beverly reached out her arms, which was received by four stick-like legs poking at her as he continuously licked her face. She hugged Adam with her new puppy, scrambling free between them. After placing, the soon to be named Tiny down on the floor, he shook off the flurries, then darted into the house toward Kristen and began tearing apart the Christmas gift wrap scattered next to them. Beverly laughed hysterically, knowing that everything in her life was falling perfectly into place as she embraced Adam under the mistletoe.

Tonight, Beverly reminisced on those memories with a soft smile and tired eyes as Kristen stood up to get ready for bed. She grabbed a few extra pillows and blankets from the closet, then brought her a glass of water with some aspirin. "Thanks for always being there for me. Good night, Kris, we need to do this more often. You should come up to visit me and Ad—" she stopped before saying his name.

Kristen interjected, "I'll definitely come up to visit you soon. We have the holidays approaching, and I'll probably stay with you or my parents. And I'm sure you and Adam will eventually work things out, but you need to focus on yourself right now," Kristen said as she left a key for her on the counter.

"Thank you. You have always been my best friend," Beverly smiled as Kristen placed the covers over her.

"You'll always be mine too, try to get some rest, hon. I left the key for you to lock up, just leave it under the mat before you leave. I'll try to be as quiet as possible while getting ready for work in the morning. Feel free to stay as late as you want. Also, eat anything you can find edible in the fridge. Except for the lasagna...

It may have gone bad." She said and laughed while giving Beverly a hug. "And I'm sure Tiny will protect us tonight," Kristen said, patting him on the head as he slept on the floor.

"Goodnight," Beverly said softly as she closed her eyes, hoping for a good night's rest. Kristen looked over to her and smiled, wishing her goodnight, then went to her bedroom, turning off all the lights behind her and closed the bedroom door.

Beverly tossed and turned while trying to fall asleep, desperate to find a position of comfort on the couch, eventually settling onto her back. The familiar muffled sound of the city streets penetrated through the windows, as party-goers returned home from their nightly outings. The distant ambiance of laughter, yelling, and slamming of car doors created an urban orchestra, which she had surprisingly missed—and found comfort in knowing she was not alone. To be back home with Kristen brought peace to her even though this was where the dark-man began to revisited her after all those years.

Half-asleep, the noise outside faded to a distant echo in the back of her mind. Beverly's body felt lighter and tingled as her consciousness drifted away. There was a sensation of floating in warm ocean water before slowly being submerged underneath the gentle waves.

There wasn't an innate fear of drowning or the need to gasp for air. Only the soothing calmness of the tides taking her in.

With this new liberating experience, her mind imagined the ceiling tear and break apart as it opened to a starlit night sky. There was a sudden separation from her body, as she emerged above her physical shell and floated into the air. She passed through the void in the ceiling and hovered over the street, staring down at the cars below. *Is this all just a dream?* Beverly asked herself, trying to get comfortable with flying, after slowly gaining control of maneuvering herself while suspended in the air. Beverly hovered down the street as her instinct took over, guiding her throughout this nightly journey.

With eyes closed, Beverly soared through the sky as a placental warmth surrounded her. Beverly opened her eyes and found frost crystallizing over the car windows while she was left unaffected by the freezing temperatures. She envisioned the sun in her mind, as it quickly manifested itself over the horizon. The beams of sunlight melted the ice and brightened the sky with a vibrant red and orange sunrise over the building tops. Moisture glistened in the corner of her eye as she continued onward to visit where she used to live as a child.

She flew by her old home, now occupied with a new family, then slowly descended toward the cemetery a few miles away. She felt a strange new vibration, one of a higher frequency. This positive energy radiated throughout her body as she approached her parent's gravestone. Levitating in a prone position a few feet off the ground, she hovered over them like a ghostly visitation. There was another lapse of time when morning quickly turned to midday as the sun sprung over the tree line, rising high into the eastern sky. The wind picked up the lifeless leaves over the ground, sending them on what appeared like predetermined trajectories into the air.

She wiped away her tears as she laid her hand against her mother's tombstone. "I won't be afraid anymore, Mom. I promise you," she said as she ran her fingers across the smooth granite. Beverly turned toward her father's grave and remembered the distant memories of how he would show her how to work on his car and take her to play soccer in Williamsburg park. She smiled, knowing how much of a tomboy she had been during her younger years, but would always still be, daddy's little warrior princess.

As Beverly pressed her hands tighter on the edges of the headstone, an array of vivid images from her childhood passed through her mind. Every sight, touch, taste, and smell overcame her all at once. Images and memories passed through her mind, vanishing as quickly as they appeared. One moment, she saw herself opening Christmas presents with her parents while eating chocolate chip cookies, which she baked for Santa the night before.

Another fleeting memory was of a school field trip with her mother at the Mystic, Connecticut seaport aquarium that came into focus. Beverly saw her younger-self giggle as her mother encouraged her to pet the stingray as it swam to the surface of its tank. The sand-paper-like texture of its skin caught her by surprise as her mother laughed hysterically at her reaction. Then another image transitioned in at full speed of a memory from her 10th birthday party, which didn't fade out like the other visions. She was outside in the backyard, swinging a plastic Wiffle bat at a piñata while blindfolded. Beverly watched her child-self from above and smiled as her father guided her every chaotic swing toward the colorful candy donkey.

Trapped within all these memories, she noticed her shadow float above the ground while suspended between time and space. Out of the corner of her eye, the sun reflected a silvery flash behind her. Beverly turned toward the vibrant light and saw a pulsating reflective silver cord protruding from her back. The cord extended for several more meters and was attached to a large sphere with the same reflective metallic characteristics. She looked into the orb as it showed her past, present, and what appeared to be future in rapid alternating indistinguishable images. Her backyard memory of her childhood-self, family, and friends started to vanish one by one like a disintegrating photograph.

As she tried to fly away from the sphere, there was a sudden jolt, pulling her back toward it. Beverly desperately fought against the resistance and was eventually tugged back into the sphere and absorbed into its liquid surface. Her memories disintegrated as she was brought back into the cemetery in the darkness of night. A sharp chill replaced the warmth she had previously felt throughout her journey. There was condensation from each expiration, which grew with each labored breath she took in. The full moon was suspended in the partially cloud-covered sky, casting an unwelcoming silver glow across the landscape. Beverly stood alone, disoriented, and afraid.

She lost the ability to fly as an unforgiving chill penetrated deep within her mind and soul. In a lethargic state, Beverly glanced behind her to see the cord without its original brilliant glow, now eclipsed by the darkness that had come over her. The sphere had vanished, left with only the silver cord that stretched out into the night sky, disappearing into the grayish clouds beyond. She tried to force herself awake but found herself stuck in this new world as her surroundings distorted around her. Beverly involuntarily embraced the hostile low vibrating energy, which slowly took over her body.

Her mind sank rapidly, as if snared in a muck of spiritual quicksand, perpetually falling into a pit of despair with no spatial awareness of up, down, left or right. The landscape melted away with swirling lights and slowly evaporated into a dark void. Left suspended in the darkness, she heard the distant cries and screams, along with menacing and diabolical laughter that seeped out of the darkened corners of her periphery. The laughter subsided as the cries and screams grew louder like Sirens of the Damned.

Police cars wailed off in the distance as the surrounding darkness manifested into a street corner filled with emergency vehicles. The image became clear to her as people ran frantically out of the theater, falling over each other. Streets ran red with blood as Beverly floated helplessly above as an observer to all the carnage unraveling before her eyes. Paralyzed and suspended in the air, she realized this was the night she buried deep inside.

This new vision quickly faded to inside the theater, as Beverly hopelessly watched people stampede over each other in hysteria, as their screams echoed and penetrated throughout her mind. She shut her eyes but inevitably saw everything through tightly closed eyelids. Sporadic gunfire came from a lone gunman positioned up in the balcony, picking off people as they ran for cover. "It's time, Beverly. You now shall truly see…" A deep droned out voice said into her mind as she tried to force it away,

Police SWAT teams barged through the doors of the left side entrance, using flash-bangs and smoke grenades for cover. They uniformly stormed into the theater, taking synchronized strategic locations behind the orchestra seating. They pinpointed the location of the crazed gunman who sporadically fired shots that rained below, claiming several more lives. He stopped to reload as the SWAT sniper team moved forward into position, firing several precise shots to neutralize the target as he fell over the balcony, landing three stories below. His motionless body laid sprawled over several seats with his neck jerked back with his eyes fixed on Beverly. The gunman's tongue hung out of his mouth with his right eye blown out, now just a deformed blood dripping socket after the precise head shot.

The city police swarmed the building from every entry point to control the perimeter while searching for the reported second gunman who had escaped before the police arrived. Incident command ordered emergency medical personnel inside to triage and treat the remaining victims. Beverly traced her eyes back and forth before spotting her parents, who sat lifeless near the front row. Her mother, Judith, wearing a beautiful white evening dress, had her head tilted forward with a gunshot to the back of her head. Her blond hair was now matted with blood. Her father, Johnathan, leaned lifeless back in his chair as coagulating blood slowly dripped onto the floor after a series of gunshots wounds to his torso.

The menacing voice penetrated her mind, "you see now, Beverly," it said, followed by a disturbing cackle.

"I don't want to see it anymore!" She screamed, struggling to move her body. In front of her, the dark entity walked along the row of seats as the first responders continued to bandage wounds, unaware of his shadowy presence. Sobbing uncontrollably, she forced herself to concentrate on waking up from this nightmarish dreamscape. She regained movement, then turned around to see the silver cord attached to her from before. It began to glow with a vibrant aura as it slowly swayed back in forth exuberantly. She nearly became hypnotized by it, then shook her head to regain focus and reunite with her physical body.

Beverly closed her eyes, then opened them again to see that everything went black except for the silver cord swaying back and forth in her mind. It gave a quick tug while continuing to sway faster and faster. She sighed relief that she was no longer in the theater before letting out a blood-curdling scream as a hand gripped over her shoulders with long ice-cold fingers. The cord yanked harder, pulling her into the dark void. Swirls of light began to surround her as if she had been flung back with unimaginable speeds before slamming into her lifeless body lying on the couch.

She sprung awake, sitting alone, and out of breath. Desperately trying to calm herself and slow down her breathing, she looked around the room to see the light coming through the windows. Beverly slowly oriented herself with her surroundings as she sat there lethargic, looking around her old living room. She got up off the couch to find Tiny wandering the kitchen, then glanced at the clock, surprised to find that it was already one-thirty in the afternoon.

Beverly scrambled to collect her personal belongings and get ready for the day. She paused for a moment to reflect on what she had just experienced and questioned to herself if she should drive back home or meet Doctor Imamu at the sleep center. She needed answers and knew he could explain everything to her.

He could describe what abilities she possessed and how to eventually control them, then hopefully defeat this entity that haunts her dreams.

Beverly stepped into the shower and leaned her head underneath the faucet head. Hot water ran down her trembling body as she tried to remain focused. She knelt on the floor and placed her hands over her head, trying to contemplate what to do next. She didn't want to be afraid of these visions anymore and had to find a way to finally stop them. She wanted to forget everything she witnessed in her dreams, as surreal as the images of her parent's death were, now engraved into her mind forever.

Beverly turned off the water as the steam collected around the bathroom, then wiped her hand over the cloudy mirror revealing a tired and distraught face. She noticed redness over her shoulder and remembered how the entity tried grabbing her before she was pulled back into her body. A tear ran down her restless face as the steam covered back up her reflection. Beverly immediately realized what she had to do now.

Grabbing for a towel, Beverly changed into a spare set of clothes she had brought along with her. She fed Tiny and gathered her belongings, then wrote a note thanking Kristen for always being there for her. She picked up her phone and called her boss to let him know she had to stay an extra day in the city. Paul had disappointment in his voice, but he didn't want to go against his word for giving her any additional days that she would need.

"Beverly, I do have some dire news to share with you, though," he said. "This has nothing to do with your absence. But, I had a call from corporate management yesterday. They told me that they will be closing our division and will have to lay us all off at the end of the year. I know you just started here, and you have a lot going on with your family emergency…but I do need you back here as soon as possible so we can start our end-of-the-year invoicing to close out the accounting books," he continued in a somber voice.

"What? That is horrible! I'm so sorry about this, and I'll be back as soon as possible," she explained to him.

"Thank you for understanding, and sorry I had to add more bad news. I'll see you soon, take care of yourself," he said before hanging up. Beverly took a few minutes to think about what she would have to face after returning home. *Take care of yourself first.* Determined, she knew now what she needed to do to take care of herself. Beverly grabbed her keys and made another phone call to Doctor Spitzer's personal number, which went to voice-mail. She grabbed her bag, put Tiny on his leash, and locked the door behind her, leaving the key under the mat before making her way to her car.

On the way to Manhattan, she passed by the road that led through her old neighborhood and the cemetery. She drove through downtown looking over at the theater, reminding her of the chaos and bloodshed from last night's vision. "This is for you, mom and dad," she said as she merged onto the turnpike, leaving Brooklyn behind, making her way toward the upper east side of the city.

CHAPTER EIGHTEEN

Four in the afternoon, Beverly entered the out-patient hospital's main lobby, then proceeded to the 14th floor. She walked up to the office desk with absolute certainty that she can resolve this. The secretary explained they were no longer accepting any walk-ins and would have to schedule an appointment for next week. "This is urgent! Doctor Spitzer knows I am on my way. I need to see him now," Beverly demanded.

"I'm sorry, Miss, but Doctor Spitzer has already left for the day," Autumn explained in a condescending demeanor.

"That's bullshit," Beverly said as she walked toward his office doors. The secretary leaped up and grabbed her arm to intercept her.

"Get off me, bitch!" Beverly yelled, shoving Autumn away, almost sending her on a one-way ticket to the floor. Beverly opened the double doors to his office and saw him packing up his briefcase.

"I'm sorry, Doctor Spitzer, I tried to stop—" Autumn said, rushing to the door, as he nodded then told her it was okay as if he was expecting the visit. His secretary looked confused and nodded back apologetic, then closed the doors behind them.

Beverly stood there shaking with vacant distant eyes of painful desperation, "Doctor, I'm ready! Tell me what I have to do?" Beverly said as he stopped what he was doing and turned toward her.

"I'm glad to hear your sudden change in heart. I'll call Doctor Imamu and have you meet him at the sleep center later this evening." She nodded her head in agreement without saying another word. "I have to gather my things and print out directions to the facility for you. Meet me in the main lobby, I'll be down in fifteen minutes," he said, grabbing for his briefcase.

"Thank you, Doctor," she said, leaving his office. Beverly noticed the disgruntled secretary staring her down as she waited for the elevator. Beverly looked forward at the door with a hidden smirk across her face.

"Adisa, she came back. Be at the lab in an hour," he told Doctor Imamu over the phone as he continued to collect his things. Doctor Spitzer gave a quick apology to his secretary as he left for the evening and explained how she was an old family friend who was going through some rough times. His secretary didn't acknowledge him as he entered the elevator.

As he met Beverly in the lobby, she turned and said to him, "I only have one problem, Doc," then mentioned the fact she had brought her dog along and needed a place for him to stay while she was at the hospital. He agreed that he would look after Tiny for the night and leave him with his family before meeting her at the hospital. He handed over the directions as he followed her to the car to get Tiny.

"Trust me, my two daughters will love to have him over for the night," he said with a chuckle as he opened the back door. She gave Tiny a hug before parting ways, then got back into her car. Beverly followed the directions to Bellevue Hospital's sleep center, merging onto the expressway, knowing it was not far from her current location. She drove down the FDR highway, which ran parallel to the East River, toward midtown before reaching her destination.

Gnawing anxiety tugged on her insides as she pulled into the parking garage of the hospital. In the back of her mind, she wanted to turn around and go back home. But she knew she couldn't bury her head in the sand anymore and had to face her fears by remaining focused and strong. No matter how crazy her thoughts seemed, and the doctor's explanations were, this was quite possibly the only cure to her problems.

Beverly exited her car, straightened her posture, took a deep breath, and walked with a sense of duty, trying to remain open-minded to all of this. In the back of her mind, she knew how illogical this all was, but at this point in time, she had no other options left on the table. No aces up her sleeve nor a Gypsy fortuneteller prophecy telling her she would live happily ever after. She had to metaphorically jump head first into the deep end of the boundaries between reality and the supernatural. Her world of fading light had quickly plunged into the dark depths of the unknown.

She checked into the front desk and was told by the security guard to follow the signs that led down a ramp to the sleep center. She walked along the well-lit corridor, passing by numerous diagnostic rooms and laboratories, which stretched the entire hallway toward the sleep center's waiting area. She told the secretary sitting at the front desk she had an appointment with Doctor Imamu. The secretary glanced down at her computer for current appointments, then back up at her, perplexed since Doctor Imamu was a researcher and did not deal with patients on a one on one basis.

"Okay, he will be out momentarily, I'll let him know you are here," she said, paging him with the hospital phone. "You can have a seat over there, it probably won't take long," she said, pointing to the empty waiting room. Beverly sat down and took a deep breath as she checked her phone, noticing a text message from Kristen. "*It was great seeing you last night! I'll be up to visit during the holidays. Love ya.*" Beverly responded back with another thank you and a smiley face.

To pass the time, Beverly glanced through some of the brochures on the table regarding parasomnias, one for sleep apnea and depression, the other on sleep paralysis, and rapid eye movement (REM). She took a closer look at the latter, remembering the term used by her doctor. Sleep paralysis, explained in the brochure, was either caused by hypnagogic hallucinations while falling asleep, which could cause audible, visual, and tactile sensations. The other was hypnopompic hallucinations, or upon waking, due to a disruption in rapid eye movement atonia.

It stated there were three stages to REM, which occurred together and were regulated by the neurochemicals, gamma-aminobutyric acid, abbreviated as GABA, and glycine. These intricate stages in the brain's cortical activation for dreaming were for sensory blockade and muscle paralysis. Without this necessary synchronization, it would cause unpleasant visual and audible hallucinations, along with the sensation of levitation and nightmarish encounters. "Yeah, that makes a whole lot of sense," she said out loud

"So, there is an actual scientific explanation to all of this." Beverly said, reading on about REM behavioral disturbance, or RBD, listed below on the brochure. Symptoms were listed as; somnambulism, referred simply as sleepwalking, along with kicking and screaming upon waking or hearing strange noises during the night. The symptoms were also usually reported by a spouse and not by the patient. Studies have linked this to underlying neurological disorders, depression, and sleep apnea.

Beverly sighed, then decided to pick up the latest edition of Time magazine instead, where the front cover showed a picture of the recent London bombings—the title read, "Domestic Terrorism: The Threat of the Modern Era." Repulsed by the article, she laid it back down on the table, disgusted of what the world had turned into. Beverly continued to wait for the doctor for several more minutes as she quietly reflected on her visions.

The receptionist walked over to hand her a clipboard, along with paperwork to fill out. One form for consent, another for demographics and insurance information, then a separate survey to check off any symptoms experienced during sleep. Beverly wrote down her info, then put Adam's number as her emergency contact thinking nothing of it. She included several sentences from her last experiences before crossing them out, finding it harder to remain focused.

Doctor Imamu walked out in a white lab coat, telling his secretary she didn't have to fill out any of those forms and was ready to see her now. Beverly gave back the clipboard to his secretary, who then walked back to her desk, confused. "I'm glad you've changed your mind about all this." He said, greeting her with a smile, then shook her hand before leading her back into the prepping room of the sleep laboratory.

"Of course, I had to come, Doctor. I had the most surreal dream last night. It was the most terrifying experience I've had thus far," she explained as she walked into the room.

"What did you see, Beverly?" He inquired as they stood alone in the room.

"It's hard to explain. But, I think it was one of those out of body experiences you explained to me yesterday. It was calming at first, but I soon felt more in danger and no longer in control. I was able to fly and visit my past so vividly. But halfway through the dream,

I encountered the dark entity again. It showed me the night of when my parents died and left me paralyzed while suspended in the air. It tried to grab and pull me in, but this silver cord yanked me back into my body," she said with hesitation, sounding insane to herself.

He paused for a moment, placing his hand under his chin, which only added to her anxiety and uneasiness on the subject. He finally explained, "There are scientific explanations to everything you've had experienced, and I want you to know that first and foremost. But, I personally believe what you had experienced last night is called astral projection. A separation from your soul and physical self. Where space and time cease to exist. You were in the boundaries of this universe and the spiritual realm. Traveling through these other dimensions of the multi-verse can leave you vulnerable to evil spiritual encounters," he explained as she looked upon him with dumbfounded confusion and disbelief.

"I thought you said this was a gift and I could defeat these entities?" Beverly said as he stared at her for a second and smiled before continuing.

"It's a little more complicated than that, Beverly. Throughout the centuries, the Roman Catholic church condemned and forbidden the practice of astral projection because after the soul leaves the physical body and enters the spiritual realm, it will no longer be protected by the grace of God. It would leave our souls vulnerable in an agnostic state, influenced by other spiritual bodies who possess dark demonic energies in these other dimensions." Doctor Imamu told her as she continued to inquire about how to protect herself during an out of body experience.

"When you reach these new higher dimensional levels of astral traveling, you will encounter different entities of both good and evil. Everything between our materialistic realm and the other dimensions has been referred to as some sort of spiritual ghetto, and the only way to achieve safe passage is by being anointed by the protection of God," he explained to her as if she was not buying into all of this folklore.

"God?"

"Yes, or any Angelical presence which could guide you through the spirit world with their protection," he said with assurance.

"How do you know if any of this is even real? You have never astral projected before. And if there was a God, why would there be multiple universes containing this dark energy?"

He paused for a second then explained, "I know this may sound crazy to you, it did for me too, but with all of my research and reading about every culture on this planet that has the same experiences made me believe we are not alone in this universe. I chose to keep faith that there is more to all of this, even if we cannot see it with our own eyes. I don't want to use the old saying; that God works in mysterious ways, but I feel the universe is much more complicated than our own perceived dimension, where there are checks and balances put in place to maintain an equilibrium."

She looked at Doctor Imamu and decided she had no other choice but to try and believe what he was telling her. "So why is there evil in our world, and the good entities don't help us?" She said, frustrated.

"I believe there have been good entities during the forging of our world, but I also believe that our creator or creators refused to break the rules of the physical universe. They were established to allow us to have free will, so we are not ruled by an authority. However, the dark demonic energies do not follow these rules and will find any way to intervene by finding the path of least resistance, through our very own fears, allowing us to be easily manipulated by their will. I feel this is the root of all the evil in this world," he said with utmost certainty in this statement.

"Okay, then, what do you need me to do?" Beverly said as she looked over at a window, revealing a large room filled with medical equipment that surrounded a bed in the middle.

"Of course, let's get started, shall we?" He instructed her to change into the hospital gown behind the curtain while sending in a female technician to help her get prepared for the polysomnography. "For scientific research, I will need to perform multiple tests to study your progress as you sleep. I'll need to hook you up to an electroencephalogram to study your different brain waves, an electromyograph to study skeletal-muscular movement, along with an electrooculogram, to study your eye movements during REM sleep. I'll also place an electrocardiogram to monitor you for any arrhythmias that could be caused due to stress," he explained to her.

"Oh, okay, is that it?"

"I know it's a lot, but it's imperative to monitor everything for medical research and to ensure you remain stable throughout this entire process. I'll have an emergency physician-on-call if anything happens to go wrong…"

"If anything goes wrong? It's only sleeping, Doctor."

"Don't worry, it's only protocol," he smiled hesitantly. "You don't have to fear a thing, Beverly. Use the bathroom if you need too before we start the experiment, also change into the hospital gown, and leave a urine sample in the cup. My technician will be over in a few minutes," he said, walking back to his medical station.

Beverly went behind the curtain and took off her clothes, feeling the cold ambient temperature against her skin as she pulled over the hospital gown, tying the straps around her back. She tried to calm her nerves by recalling a memory she had with her father when she was eight-years-old. Her mind went back to a small amusement water park off the coast of Wildwood, New Jersey. The rides were primarily meant for small children, but there was one slide she was deathly afraid to go down. It stood forty-feet into the air as it swirled and curved multiple times, then descended into the pool below. Every summer, she would glance up toward the top as it defiantly stood like a giant before her.

It wasn't until one day her father noticed the fearful curiosity in her eyes. He tried to encourage her that there was nothing to be afraid of. He would tell her she was a big girl now and could swim very-well on her own and that everything would be fine. He took her hand, not to force her, but to encourage and comfort her, allowing Beverly to conquer her fears of the towering water slide, which she desperately wanted to go down. She would see all the big kids having a great time, screaming with joy as they splashed down into the pool below.

Every summer and every year that went by, she would try to muster up her fears to go down it by herself, but it wasn't until her father took her by the hand. He promised to go down with her as she laid on his lap. She knew there was no turning back at this point, but felt at ease as her father was there to show her there was nothing to fear.

"Okay, Peanut, on your count!" He said with enthusiasm. "One, two…" then paused before yelling three as he pushed off with her screaming, safely secured in his lap. They splashed down into the pool as she quickly swam back up to the surface, spitting out water and wiping her eyes dry. Beverly laughed uncontrollably on how silly her fears were and wanted to go down it again by herself this time. She got out of the pool and gave her dad a hug, then ran up the stairs as he smiled from below.

Julia, the female technician, entered the room and explained all the procedures as she connected electrodes to her head, chest, and limbs—followed by taking her blood pressure, connecting a pulse oximeter to her finger, and placing capnography cannula prongs into her nose. "We just have to start an IV to draw blood, and in case we need to give you any medications.

"Protocol, right? Beverly said as she held out her arm and clenched.

"Of course," Julia said, smiled, then inserted the IV in the right antecubital vein of Beverly's left arm. The technician gave her a thick blanket and escorted her into the large room. There was a single bed in the middle, surrounded by medical equipment and blinking monitors. She kept thinking about the water slide as she climbed into the bed. Beverly knew her fears would not allow her to achieve real greatness, which she desperately sought after. She focused on how she could control her dreams and felt a new sense of strength and calmness flow through her.

"Everything will go smooth and according to plan tonight. I only ask of you is to remain focused and reach the higher dimensions. Legend has it there are scrolls referred to as the Akashic records. It is believed that they hold the secrets of the universe and were written through a cosmic intelligence from a higher plane of existence if that makes any sense. If you can find them, they may be what we are looking for," Doctor Imamu said as he prepared the monitoring equipment.

"What we're looking for?" She said, raising an eyebrow while lying in bed as he retook her vitals.

"Beverly, they would help you, but at the same time could possibly hold all the information to our entire perceivable universe. Any knowledge obtained from these records would be a great benefit for humanity, there are only a few who had claimed to have tapped into this rich source of knowledge, which led to great breakthroughs in their fields, backing up their claims." The doctor explained to reassure her.

"I don't want to be some sort of laboratory rat for you," Beverly said, having second thoughts about this.

"You need to trust him, Beverly." Doctor Spitzer said as he entered the room, walking toward the bed. "You need to trust both of us. We'll be able to help you, while at the same time, you could provide us a great deal of knowledge that would help humanity as a whole." He said as she slightly nodded her head in agreement.

"Okay, let's do this then. I'm getting exhausted listening to you guys anyway."

"Sounds good, Beverly. We'll be in the other room monitoring you for the night. Sweet dreams, our little astral traveler," Doctor Spitzer joked as the technician walked in to finish prepping her for the night.

"Is Tiny okay?" Beverly said before he walked out of the room.

"Yes, both of my daughters adore him very much, you have a really wonderful dog. Get some rest, Beverly. I shall see you in the morning," Doctor Spitzer said as he exited. The lights went out, and the room went pitch-black. Her hand vanished in front of her face as she laid awake on the bed with racing thoughts.

Both doctors and the lab technician watched her through the one-way mirrored window. On the other end of the glass was only darkness, except for a few lights from the medical equipment surrounding her. "Lights, camera, action!" The technician said as she turned on the live video feed of the room, showing multiple angles in night vision. She turned on the polysomnography, which monitored her muscle and brain activity, along with measuring her eye movement through closed eyelids.

"Can you hear me, Beverly?" The Doctor Imamu said over the PA system into the room. She gave a thumbs-up for acknowledgment. "Good, we'll be monitoring everything live from within here. If there's any kind of emergency or if you need to talk to me, use the intercom push-button bed remote by your side. I don't expect that you'd need to use it, but it's there as a security blanket if you need it. Just so you know, you'll be locked in until sunrise, so rest peacefully tonight. Remember what we've had talked about."

"I'm all systems go Houston ground control," Beverly responded before the PA system clicked off, leaving her in complete silence.

"I'll take over from here," Doctor Imamu said to them as he took a sip from his freshly brewed coffee.

"Do you think she can really pull this off?"

"I honestly do, Jeff…I really do."

"Okay, let me know if anything happens, and I'll be back over as quickly as possible." Doctor Spitzer said as he grabbed his overcoat, preparing to leave. Adisa nodded his head toward his technician to dismiss her for the night, then took over the monitoring station.

They both left the room as Doctor Imamu looked back over to Beverly through the window as she fidgeted, trying to get comfortable.

"I believe in you, Beverly. I know you can find what I've been searching for my entire career." He said to himself as he leaned back in his chair, watching over the equipment readouts with no signs of any changes. He closed his eyes, reflecting on his own childhood and his family's stories of the Popobawa and how he made a pact with himself to solve this mystery and free the curse, which plagued his village and all of mankind. He opened his eyes, sipped his coffee, and watched Beverly through the night vision video feed as she tossed and turned in bed, staring back at him. Doctor Imamu reclined back in his chair, resting his tired eyes, then eventually fell asleep as she laid awake in the darkness.

Beverly tried to get comfortable as her eyes readjusted and grew accustomed to the dark. Still, the eerie silence reminded her of her condo back home. She felt the anxiety fester inside, but fought against those thoughts while trying to remain focused and free her mind from anything negative. She continued to remember the water slide and how this was just another silly fear she had to overcome.

The comforting memories of her mother and the dream she had by the river occupied her thoughts, telling her subconsciously not to fear the unknown. Beverly laid there in a meditative state, hoping her parents were watching over her, as her mind and consciousness slowly slipped away, falling into a deeper sleep.

CHAPTER NINETEEN

Beverly Hollinger emerged out of her body like a cocooned chrysalis going through morphogenesis. She levitated above her dormant body, which laid lifeless on the bed below. Floating toward the ceiling like a lost specter, she passed through the various medical floors before breaking free from the building into the night sky. All her worries and struggles had slipped away, now replaced with the sensation of flight. She soared over the city at incredible speeds while looking down at the busy streets below. The cold air was deflected by the warmth encapsulated within her aura as she flew out toward the horizon.

Beverly's spiritual body descended, diving straight toward the East River before she corrected her flight with absolute precision. She parted the waters below before her reascent into the sky. There was an overwhelming sense of blissful surrealism as she continued to soar across the city landscape, observing all the hapless individuals below. She coasted near the ground, undetected, as she explored Central Park.

Beverly came across the bench she sat at the other day, still in disbelief of this entire experience. Up ahead was the arched bridge with the full moon reflecting a perfect circle in the water with exquisite beauty like a gateway into another world.

Off in the distance, a subtle hoot came from an owl perched up in one of the willow oak trees. The owl's cry radiated into Beverly's mind, drawing her attention toward it. The brown owl sat on a branch, watching over her as she floated suspended in the air. The owl ruffled his feathers and flapped its wings before hooting another soothing cry to her.

"It's like you can see me," Beverly said out loud, then laughed to herself. She floated toward the owl, noticing his wide, wild black eyes which had intense shades of magenta, yellow, blue, and red, all blending together. Upon a closer look, they were spiral galaxies and nebulae of the universe swirling within his pupils. She stared into his hypnotizing eyes, then heard someone call out her name.

"Beverly," it repeated directly into her thoughts. Caught off guard by this, she looked around not to see anyone following her. "I'm your spirit guide, Beverly." It said to her as she turned back toward the owl as it stared at her while flapping its wings.

"No fucking way!" She said out loud while looking upon the owl as it revealed its wingspan, before departing from its branch and taking flight.

"Follow me, Beverly of New York. I'll show you everything, but you'll have to trust me," she heard in her mind as the owl unfurled its wingspan, then took off into the night sky. She felt comfort in trusting this new entity and knew deep down that it was for her best interests to pursue after him. Beverly turned her head, watching the Earth become smaller as she ascended further into the heavens. The same silver cord from last night, stretched out behind her into the thin atmosphere as she approached the boundaries of the stratosphere and the vacuum of space.

"Where are you taking me? I won't be able to breathe soon!" She said in a panic, but the entity soothed her worries by projecting high-frequency vibrational thoughts into her.

"You don't need to breathe, Beverly. Trust in me, and I shall set you free."

She followed her spirit guide, escaping low Earth's orbit, then turned around to take in all the majestic beauty of her homeworld suspended in space and time. Half of the world was blanketed in darkness, as the other half was illuminated by the vibrant Sun burning off in the distance. Beverly took a moment to comprehend all this before turning back to catch up with her guide. She reached the magnificent rings of Saturn in a matter of minutes, as the owl stopped to wait for her.

"Beautiful, isn't it?" He said to her as she turned around, no longer able to distinguish any other planetary bodies. "The icy rings of this world are magnificent, along with its many moons teaming with life underneath its frozen surface. See that pale blue dot over there? That is Earth. That large star over there. That is your Sun," he said as she stared back, engrossed with all of its beauty, as her silver cord stretched on throughout the darkness of space.

"Makes you feel small, doesn't it? In the grander scheme of things, of course. However, the universe that you visibly see is not the true definitive end. Come with me, and I'll show you more." The owl said as he began to warp space-time, distorting reality around them. The stars started to drip and swirl at high speeds into the darkness, as the observable universe broke down, sending her through a vortex of tunneling light.

Within an instant, Beverly was transported to another world, which appeared much different than her own. Her surroundings weren't anything from her known universe, as everything seemed to glow with an aura, similar to the dream she had of her mother. Her senses were heightened to a new state of awareness un-familiar to her. As if her memories, dreams, thoughts, and future were all rolled into one existence.

A world of towering mountains throughout the landscape as waterfalls flowed with intensity. They drained into the vacuum of space, then redistributed as beautiful rain showers over the enchanting forests below. The eternal sunlight encapsulated the entire landscape without casting a single shadow over this new pristine world. Beverly turned around to find her silver cord still attached to the same metallic orb from the other night as it reflected images of multiple spiraling universes.

"We're almost there," the mysterious guide said to her. They flew toward the side of a large mountain with a temple near its peak.

Beverly tried to take in all the beauty as she gracefully flew after him, before descending and landing softly onto the large stone platform at the entrance to the mountain. The towering marble pillars and statues were far superior and beyond the architecture of any human capabilities and achievements. Beverly walked around the temple grounds as if she was back in her physical body. She examined the statues of giants, none proportional to any man she had ever seen, as she ran her hands across the magnificent and ancient architecture.

A bright light emanated out of her periphery, blinding her momentarily. The owl whom she had followed morphed into pure white light energy, with such intensity, she had to pull away to protect her eyes. As the blinding light faded, she turned back to see a tall humanoid figure wearing gold and silver reflective armor, which fractionated beams of light throughout the temple.

"Who, or what are you?" Beverly said, astonished.

"My name is Ezekiel, I am your spirit guide. I belong to a higher order of species referred to as the Guardians. Mankind may have referred to us as angels.

"Jesus Christ, you got to be shitting me," Beverly said as she looked upon him with all his exuberance. "I'm going to hell for saying that, right?" She said, then laughed, but stopped herself to remain some composure.

"There's much more to the universe than what your species has pondered in their mythology. This is not my true form, but only what you would be able to comprehend with your own senses and knowledge. We can transform into anything we desire as long as it serves us purpose." He explained as several male and female humanoid beings manifested in the temple shrine.

"So, what do you want from me? Why did you bring me here?" Beverly said, no longer fearful of the truth, which she had continuously been seeking.

"Your God, you refer too, is as infinite as the energy and consciousness that surrounds your universe, and the infinite number of universes around it. We are entities of pure energy that came from that same original source of creation to serve as messengers, guardians, and protectors of all living and non-living matter. We are the byproduct from the origins of time and space," he explained to her.

"Well, if that is so, and you're the protectors and all. Why do you allow all of the evil bull crap and chaos in our world to occur?" She skeptically questioned.

"Life had sprung long before your world existed and is regulated by the laws of nature of their respective universe, which we swore not to break or intervene. We exist in a higher realm. Only a spiritually sentient and sapient being, such as yourself, can access this higher frequency through practice or through death. Your species, along with many others whom originate in your physical universe, could access the higher dimensions, but it comes with a risk," he pointed out to her.

"What are those risks? And you haven't answered my question. I still don't know what you want from me?" Beverly demanded, still confused by all of this.

"In this realm, only entities with energy of a higher frequency can be protected, and then and only then, they could reach the higher dimensions to prosper within their mind and consciousness. However, like with all matter. There resides a repelling dark or anti-matter to create an equal balance. Entities full of hatred and anger radiate lower energy frequencies, leaving them to dwell amongst the physical dimensions."

He continued, "These spiritual bodies no longer flourish and eventually will feed off the energy of lower dimensional beings, such as the ones from your universe. An individual focused solely on power, greed, and ego will always prey on fear and try to reap those benefits. Quick gratification will never nourish the soul and ultimately lead to internal pain and suffering." Beverly stood speechless as he explained the dynamics of the universe and spirit world to her.

"You have a special gift, Beverly. You have the ability to reach the higher realms before death, which leaves your truest form vulnerable to these dark entities of whom I speak of. They cannot fully manifest themselves into your universe but can manipulate your species' thoughts and actions. If a person does not have the ability or willpower to suppress their own fears, they will one day also be drawn to these lower frequencies. They can, and will physically harm you or the ones you love if your fear allows them too. They feed off negative energy and emotions as they strive to manipulate mankind, only if that your species continues to allow for it."

"Well, you guys will protect me. That's what angels do, right?" Beverly said, troubled by this explanation.

"We can only help you in the higher dimensions. However, since you can project your mind and energy into the other lower spiritual realms, it would leave you vulnerable to these entities. Your physical body cannot be possessed, but your consciousness has opened a gateway for them. They won't stop until you offer them a sacrifice in return. These beings are powerful, and were once part of our race until they sold their souls for complete control and defiance. We swiftly defeated their rebellion and banished them from all higher dimensions. Now their spiritual energies are left to roam and scavenge the lower realms to stay alive," he said to her as she stared into his emotionless eyes.

"So, you cannot help me, is what you're telling me?" Beverly said as he unfolded white feathered wings as his aura glowed brighter.

"What I'm telling you, is that we have a responsibility to protect spiritual bodies that are not bound to their physical dimensions. The meaning in life is that you have free will over most other living organisms. The beauty in life is that you have the ability to make a stand and make a difference in your own life and the lives of others. The spirit will always live on and prosper if they value self-sacrifice and altruism."

He continued, "The silver cord attached to you is the link between your physical body and your spiritual one. Only you can sever it, break the golden bowl by shattering the pitcher against the spring. Then the wheels will break, turning to ash over the ground, finally setting your soul free. Only the good and righteous souls with the purest of intentions can break the chains which binds them to their universe," he said.

"Oh, I see…crystal clear. Also, by the way, asking for my inquisitive friend back home…What are the Akashic records?"

"They're nothing for you to worry about right now. I've explained everything that you need to know," he said, placing a small dagger into her hand.

"What is this for?"

"You can always call upon it in the spiritual realm. Use it to protect yourself on your journey home and use it to define your own destiny." Ezekiel said as Beverly's mother emerged from the corner of the temple. "Mom?" Beverly said, running over to give her a hug. Her father stood next to her with a smile as she turned to him, "Is this just another dream?" Beverly said as she turned to give her dad a hug.

"No, honey, we need you to be brave and go back and protect the ones you love," her mother said as Beverly felt a tug on her silver cord.

"Mom, Dad?" She yelled as the cord tugged harder, throwing her off balance. "Ezekiel?"

"Good luck, Beverly." Her guide said as the cord gave one final yank, sending her backward off the platform toward the metallic sphere in the sky. She flew past the mountainous terrain and waterfalls, then through the spherical orb. The world around her disintegrated into fragments of light. Beverly materialized into the orbit of Saturn, back into her familiar four-dimensional universe.

Beverly laid suspended in time and space, desperately trying to become oriented to her original universe. She found herself still tethered to the silver cord, which stretched out for millions of miles, toward the small pale blue dot glimmering amongst the stars. Focused on returning home and to her physical body, Beverly felt the cord tug harder in the direction of her world.

Barreling back to Earth at astronomical speeds, she remembered her parents presence and how real it was to hold them once again. Beverly thought to herself how wonderful it would be to live among the stars with them in that beautiful world. She approached Earth's elliptical orbit as the silver cord suddenly seized, sending Beverly forward, spinning along its axis.

A low penetrating voice emerged out of the darkness of space, "I can make sure you stay here among the stars with me forever," as the vibration came closer. Beverly tried to orient herself as she plummeted uncontrollably above Earth's orbit. As soon as it stabilized and regained control, the entity pummeled her. "Missed me yet, darling?" it said into her mind as she struggled to break free from its grip.

With one free arm, she struck it repeatedly in the head. They dangled weightlessly over Earth and spun parallel along its orbit with an awkward dance for control. She felt the cord continue to recoil as she struggled to break free from its locking grip. They continued to spin over the atmosphere with the tether latching on tighter beneath her.

"I won't stop until I get what I want from you," the entity said as its clawed hands dug into her back.

In the vacuum of space, her screams were silenced as it slowly leaned in closer to her. The being opened its wide jaws of sharp jagged teeth near her head. Her aura slowly dissipated, as the energy siphoned into the dark void of its mouth. She remembered what Ezekiel told her as her strength dwindled away. She visualized the dagger in her free hand, which manifested itself with a glowing light. Beverly jabbed it directly into the entity's neck, breaking free of it consuming her energy, but not of its grip.

"Not today, you son of a bitch!" She yelled, regaining control, then focused on returning to her body. The silver cord gave one final yank, tumbling them toward the planet at supersonic speeds.

Doctor Imamu sprang awake to the system alarms with the electrocardiogram displaying Beverly's heart rate increasing to 160 beats per minute, as the other sensors showed increased skeletal muscle activity as she laid twitching in bed. Her EEG brain readouts went from slow synchronized delta and theta waves to chaotic gamma and beta waves, indicating to him that she was under distress while returning to a wakeful state. He looked over at the video monitor, surprised to find her still asleep as she twitched violently in bed.

"I've never seen anything like this before." Doctor Imamu said as he continued to monitor the readings, which showed she was fully conscious while still asleep. He pushed the button for the intercom. "Beverly, this is Doctor Imamu, can you hear me?" He repeated again, without any response. Her heart rate continued to climb on the ECG, as he wiped the sweat off from his brow.

Beverly plummeted through the sky, as the demonic entity held tightly onto her, as the cord pulled her toward her physical body. She fell through the ceiling of the medical center, down toward the basement level, into the room where her body rested. "Beverly, what they had told you was a lie; I will show you the truth," the supernatural being said to her, as she continued to struggle to break free from its grip.

"Go to hell!" She yelled in its face, finally freeing her arm again.

"Oh, sweet Beverly. I promise to take you there," it whispered into her ear with a menacing voice. The entity let go and reached its claws into her stomach as she screamed in agony. "You can't win, Beverly," it said as she focused all of her energy on manifesting the dagger.

Doctor Imamu watched her body convulse as the florescent lights in the room flickered rapidly. They glowed with an intense light before exploding with glass shrapnel screaming across the room. The video monitors all went to static as the medical equipment malfunctioned, sending sparks of electricity across every panel. Doctor Imamu ordered a code blue and summoned the on-call emergency physician.

The entity looked around the room, noticing the doctor trying to get in, then used its mind to slam the door shut back on him. Beverly took advantage of this distraction and summoned the dagger once again, then with one swift movement, she rammed the blade straight into the entity's chest. Finally freeing her of its grip.

As the demon fell backward, she regained her strength and gave one last solid jab, sending the blade back into its chest. The emergency physician and doctor Imamu finally gained entry into the lab, watching her seize in the darkness as equipment sent sparks into the air.

"You can't destroy me, Beverly. Once the seal has been broken, it cannot be undone. I shall return to take what is mine," the entity said as its body slowly dissipated into smaller fragments.

"I'm not fucking afraid of you!" Beverly screamed as its energy dissolved into smaller particles, then vaporized, evaporating from the room. The silver cord gave one final yank, pulling Beverly back into her body, while still in an unresponsive state. The emergency doctor accessed the medication code box and drew up two milligrams of Ativan in a syringe, then administered it through her IV. Her seizure subsided as other personnel entered the room and lifted her onto the gurney.

"I'm sorry, Beverly." Doctor Imamu said to her as they took her unconscious and flaccid body out of the room toward the emergency department. One nurse strapped a non-rebreather oxygen mask over her mouth and nose while monitoring her pulse oximetry and heart rate on the portable ECG monitor.

Beverly slowly regained consciousness as they rolled her down the long corridors. She stared at the florescent lights on the ceiling with several emergency department personnel by her side, discussing diagnostic plans to treat her. She grimaced and screamed out with the agonizing pain as she held her lower abdomen.

"Beverly, my name is Doctor Snyder, I'm the attending emergency medical physician at Bellevue hospital. We'll take good care of you, just hang in there," he said to her as they rolled the stretcher into the emergency department. She slipped in and out of consciousness from the pain and medication side effects. The doctor quickly assessed her carotid pulse, breathing, and pupil reactivity as other nurses and resident doctors assisted at the bedside. After several diagnostic tests, they rushed her to the operating room.

Beverly found herself standing alone in a dark jail holding cell, facing iron bars illuminated by the moonlight coming from the small window behind her. Water dripped from a leaking pipe on the ceiling above, then splashed in the puddle on the floor next to her feet. The drops echoed throughout the silent corridors in synchronization with each expired breath of condensation. She rubbed her arms and shoulders to provide warmth from the unbearable chill. Beverly felt warm fluid on her hospital gown as she touched her tender abdomen. She raised her hands into the moonlight to find copious amounts of blood running down her palms and fingertips.

Diabolic laughter cackled from the cell across from hers, revealing nothing but blackness and iron bars. "Who's there?" Beverly said in a soft, hesitant voice. The uncontrollable laughter continued, reminding her of last night's vision from the theater. "Guards! Guards, please help me!" Beverly screamed until her throat was raw as she held her abdomen. The metal door at the other end of the corridor opened, then slammed shut, followed by two sets of footsteps and rattling keys. The laughter ceased when the lights slowly glowed to a steady yellow dim, revealing an empty cell across from hers.

Beverly pressed herself against the bars to get a glimpse down the hall as one guard walked over without haste. "Help me, I'm bleeding and shouldn't be here," she said, trying not to cry. The guard kept a steady casual pace as a man in a suit followed behind him. "You gotta get me out of here, see look," she said, drawing attention to her bloodied hands and hospital gown. The guard stood in front of Beverly's cell without acknowledging her, then slowly reached for the side of his hip.

"Wait, what are you doing? Did you hear me? I need your help," Beverly said, confused and frightened as he reached for his metal baton. The guard raised it, then slammed it against the bar near her face. She let go and backed up several feet, trembling and crying. "What the fuck are you doing? Somebody, please help me!" Beverly yelled as she fell to her knees and covered her face, hoping this nightmare would end.

"That'll be all. I'll take it from here," the man in the suit said as he walked over to them. Beverly cowered in the corner of the room, then slowly lifted her head after hearing the familiar voice.

"Thank God you're here, Doctor Spitzer. You can straighten this all—," she said, trailing off, surprised to find a younger version of him standing next to the prison warden. "Doc, it's me, Beverly. Where the hell am I?

"Ah yes, Beverly Hollinger. I remember you very well, they brought you in not to long ago, and we spoke in depth of your crimes and pleas of insanity. Your delusional psychotic fits of rage and hallucinations. Not to mention your chronic emotional and mental instabilities. I am completely aware of that little string of murders you committed. But, it wasn't your fault, right?. It was the voices in your head from the boogeyman telling you to do it." Doctor Spitzer said as the guard chuckled next to him.

"Delusions? Murders? What the fuck are you talking about? Get me the fuck out of here now, I'm bleeding to death!" Beverly yelled, then looked down to see that the blood was gone and now wearing a standard-issue orange jumpsuit.

"Don't worry, Beverly. We'll have you shipped out in the morning to the insane asylum and schedule that lobotomy soon. Get some rest, okay?" Doctor Spitzer said with a smirk, as he walked off with the guard and turned off the lights, slamming the metal door shut behind them.

Beverly screamed in the darkness while banging on the bars, then turned and slid her back down along them. She sat, facing the window as moonlight streamed along the floor as a voice emerged out of the darkness from behind her. "Come to me, Beverly. I can set you free," it said, as Beverly turned to find a pair of red eyes behind his bars. She quickly got up and ran toward the back corner of her cell.

"No, this can't be happening. I defeated you." Beverly said, slowly side-stepping toward the barred window.

"Think again, I'll see you soon," it said as the eyes vanished into the darkness.

Bright light flooded through her window and illuminated the entire cell and corridor, blinding yet comforting. Beverly envisioned herself back at the temple with her parents and Ezekiel as all other negative memories were temporarily wiped clean. She felt all her burdens suddenly lifted as a powerful voice ringed throughout her head. "Go forth, and not be afraid. Don't succumb to the negative energy and cherish the time you have left with the ones you love. Your destiny is of your own choosing. The greatest prison of all is in one's mind, so embrace the light and set yourself free," the entity projected into her thoughts as the cell began to break apart with immense light. The walls were finally toppled.

After several hours of operating, Beverly slowly woke in the post-op care room, groggy and nauseous, without any recollection of her dream. She looked up and noticed Doctor Imamu talking with the surgeon from across the room. "Beverly, you're awake," he said, turning to her. He walked over as she looked around the unfamiliar room. "I'm glad to see that you're doing okay. How do you feel?" Doctor Imamu said to her.

"A little sore. What happened?" Beverly said, lethargic from the anesthesia.

"Well, it seems you had a seizure during your sleep study, and we then soon discovered that your appendix had burst. They performed an emergency appendectomy surgery this morning to remove it," the surgeon explained to her.

"How is that possible? I never had any issues before," she said, then remembered the abdominal pain from last week but left it unmentioned.

"Well, the appendix could have been acute without any kind of warning. And regarding the seizures, we're not sure yet. We pulled up your records at another hospital to find there wasn't any history of epilepsy. We're currently trying to rule out eclampsia, but you're not exhibiting any other symptoms for it," he explained to her.

"Eclampsia, what is that?"

"It's a condition that could cause seizures in a pregnant patient, especially after being exposed to flashing lights that occurred in the lab last night." Doctor Imamu explained.

"Pregnant?"

"I hate to break the news to you in this way…But you're in your second trimester, Beverly," he told her somberly.

"What? I can't be!"

"I'll give you information for a great obstetrician in your area that you can follow up with as soon as you get back home. I'll also order for a follow-up EEG with a neurologist to rule out any other seizure activity. Take care of yourself and feel better," Adisa said as he shook her hand, then made his way to the door.

"Doctor, I never knew…," she said, ashamed of herself.

"It happens, Beverly. You may have someone else to explain this, too, besides me. We'll catch up soon about what you saw last night. Feel better and get some rest. Also, by the way, we used the emergency contact that you wrote down. So, you have a visitor, and he seems extremely worried, I'll send him in," he said before exiting the room.

Adam walked in the room with flowers in his hand and a smile across his face. "Adam, is that really you?" Beverly said, sitting up in bed, still lethargic from the anesthesia.

"They must have really given you some heavy-duty drugs," he said jokingly to make her smile. He came to her bedside, then gave her a hug and kiss as he handed her the flowers.

"Adam, I am so sorry," she said and began to cry.

"What's wrong, sweetheart?"

"I don't deserve any of this. I don't deserve you. I regret turning you away. I've been going through hell after our break up," she said, holding him.

"Don't feel sorry, I was really upset, too, but I knew I needed to give you some space until you figured this all out," Adam said as he tried to not hug her too hard since she just got out of surgery.

"All I figured out was that I missed you so much and need you in my life. I love you so much," Beverly said, squeezing him tighter.

"I love you too," Adam said as he sat next to her in the hospital bed.

"Adam, I need to tell you something," Beverly said, choking up over her own tears.

"What is it, honey?" He asked as he held her hand, then kissed it.

"I know I haven't been the best girlfriend to you, and I've been a real pain in the ass, acting very emotional and stressed over having all these stupid nightmares," she said.

"A real pain in the arse, I know," he smiled.

"In all seriousness, though. I've literally hit rock bottom without you by my side. I've been stressed over my past, present, and future. On top of all of that, I'm about to be laid-off at the end of the year with my job. I'm a real winner, I know," she tried to laugh, but it hurt physically and emotionally.

"You're a winner to me! Also, these nightmares will pass, and I'll help find you a new job," he said to console her.

"Well, that's not everything. I also just found out, literally a second ago that you'll be a father soon," she said nonchalantly, not knowing what his reaction would be.

"Wait! What? That's wonderful news!" Adam proclaimed as he gave her a kiss, then rubbed her belly.

"I honestly didn't know until now. Are you upset with me?"

"Why would I be upset? You just made me the happiest man ever. I'll have a child with the woman I love! Don't worry about the job. I'll move in to take care of you and take on a second job if I have too. Only if that is what you want, of course?" He said, trying to not force the decision on her.

"Of course, honey. That sounds perfect, but I don't want you to have to work to death to provide for me, I'm still independent, remember?" She said with a laugh, grimacing from the pain.

"Oh, I'm fully aware," he said, laughing along with her.

"This feels wonderful. I feel the past is behind me now and ready to embrace the future with you," she said with a smile, then gave him a long passionate kiss.

"Hmm, Hmm…Hope I'm not interrupting a special moment here." Doctor Spitzer said as he knocked on the door as Tiny tried to barge into the room as he held him back with his leash.

"My buddy!" She said as Doctor Spitzer released the leash as Tiny ran full speed, jumping on to the bed in between her and Adam. Tiny tried to continuously lick Beverly's face, then snuggled his snout against her neck as he wagged his tail with excitement.

"Easy there, Tiny. I just got out of surgery," she laughed, hugging him tight as he frantically broke free to lick her face again.

"I see that I'm easily replaced over here." Adam joked as he patted Tiny on his back.

"Doctor Spitzer, I want to introduce you to my extraordinary family. This is Adam, and you're already well acquainted with this little furball over here," she said as she continued to hold Tiny.

"Very nice to meet you, Adam. You have a real special woman that loves you. I'll let you guys be, to catch up and rest." The doctor said as he shook Adam's hand.

"Before you go. I just want to thank you again for everything, Doctor Spitzer," Beverly said, then smile.

"My pleasure. But, please call me Jeff, we're like family now, too," he said, smiling back.

"I appreciate everything you and Doctor Imamu did to help me. I feel like I conquered my fears and finally ready to move on with my life," she said as she held Adam's hand.

"I'm glad you feel better. If you ever need anything, just give me a call. Get some solid rest for once, will ya,"

Doctor Spitzer said with a laugh as he exited the room.

"I feel like the happiest woman in the entire universe right now. Scratch that, the entire multiverse," Beverly said, reclining back in the bed as she held Adam as Tiny snuggled against them.

"I'm happy for the both of us. I will always be there for you, Beverly. I will always chase after you, through all the darkness. Always know that," Adam said as he laid there with Beverly in his arms.

"I know, and always will. That is why I love you so much," Beverly said as they held each other before falling back to sleep. Restful and dreamless.

PART III

THE REBIRTH

CHAPTER TWENTY

Six months later, in late April, the new spring had thawed the final remnants of the harsh cold winter. The melted ice and snow-runoff was now only a faded memory for the small town in upstate New York. Life began to spawn from its long hibernation as the recent rainfall slowly restored the flora from the earth. An afternoon in the mid-sixties was a time of rejoicing after the barrage of Northeasters that struck the region during the early new year. In like a lion, out like a lamb is how the ole New England adage went.

During a warm and pleasant weekend, Adam took over grilling duties for Beverly and his family. The smell of fresh bison burgers and German bratwursts filled the backyard as he grabbed a cold locally-brewed lager from the cooler. Adam took an unopened warm beer sitting on the table and poured half of it over the brats as they simmered in the aluminum tray. He looked over his shoulder to quietly watch his mother and Beverly talk amongst themselves—discussing gardening and the new baby—across from each other at the picnic table.

Adam smiled, then turned his attention back toward the grill.

"You know I like mine medium-rare, right?" His father said, followed by a hardy laugh. Jacob placed one hand over his son's shoulder, shaking him playfully.

"I know, Pop. You're next, right after I finish theirs," Adam said.

"Aren't you going to offer your old man a beer?" Jacob said as Adam fished through the ice and produced one from the cooler. Jacob took it, popped the tab, and gulped half of it down, "Now, that's refreshing. I haven't had a drink all winter long since your mother had me cut back. Scolding me that I'm too old and need to watch my diabetes. Heck, I don't have to explain, you know how she is…But today is a celebration, so I can splurge a little, right?"

His father paused for a moment, then finally said a phrase Adam hadn't heard in a long time, "I'm proud of you, Son. You have yourself a wonderful woman over there. Just like how your mother has been to me," Jacob said as he patted him over the shoulder. "You'll be a great father, my son. I know you're stressed to high heaven over everything, but it will all become second nature in due time," he explained as he checked on the food over Adam's shoulder.

"Thanks, Dad. I know I shouldn't worry, but it's probably instinctual to feel a little nervous bringing another life into this world," he said to him as he looked over to Beverly.

"Just know that your mother and I will be there to help you guys every step of the way," he said to reassure him.

Elizabeth turned to them with her usual, I'm the boss so-don't-question-me face, and shouted, "Guys, we're getting hungry over here. Adam, your wife needs her iron," his mother said straight-faced as Beverly hesitantly laughed along. "How much more time on those burgers?"

"They're coming off the grill right now, I just need to toast the buns first. Bring out your potato salad," Adam yelled back over to his mom from across the backyard.

The Groves' property is located in the high valley of Silver Lakes and expansive as all the other homes within the area. Their four-acres overlook the valley toward the east with endless woods of leafless trees along their property. The southeastern portion stretched behind their rustic, single-story, simple four-room home. They had two gardens, one was Elizabeth's prized flower bed in the backyard near the gazebo, which she only tended too all spring and summer. The other, a vegetable crop, that his father seasonally sowed to avoid the increasing cost at the local farmer's markets.

"You're going to love my dishes, darling. I'll share with you all of my secrets. You can learn a lot while trying to feed those animals over there," she said and smiled as she slowly stood with aching arthritis.

"Can I help you with anything? I want to contribute to this amazing picnic," Beverly said, not expecting to be waited on.

"We have everything under control, dear. You can cook for us when we come over to see our new grandchild," Elizabeth said as she walked back into the house. Adam placed the plates down onto the table, then gave Beverly a kiss. His mother returned with a large bowl of red skin potato salad as Adam walked back toward the barbecue to serve the food. They gathered around the table as the evening approached with a steady and unusual warm early-spring breeze.

"I must say, I love your new dress, Beverly," Elizabeth said as she passed her the potato salad. Beverly wore a loose-fitting light-blue dress with white trim that went down below her knees.

"Thank you, it's been hard trying to find clothes that actually fit these days," she said with a laugh, scooping the potatoes onto her plate.

"I bet, but you still look great! When I had Adam, I swore I had a bowling ball inside of me," she said.

His father interjected, "he got that from me," as everybody laughed and continued to eat their food.

"Do you guys have any names picked out yet? You are due sometime next month, right?" Elizabeth said, even though she already knew and anticipated the due date of May 23rd.

"Yeah, three weeks from today actually," she said with a smile as she rubbed her belly. "Well, I had some suggestions for a name which I thought were nice. If it had been a girl, I was thinking, Luna. But since we know now we're having a boy I wanted to name him after my father, Jonathan. We also agreed on Adam's first choice, Seth, for his middle name," she said as Elizabeth nodded in approval.

"Jonathan Seth Grove, I can already picture myself calling him by his full name when he gets into mischief playing in my garden. Knowing these guys here, I bet he will be a great handful too," she said, then took a sip from the freshly squeezed lemonade.

"You're scaring her honey, you make it sound as if it was hell to deal with us," he said, getting everybody to laugh. Beverly suddenly became quiet after hearing the word hell, remembering the experience she had in the sleep center six months ago. She tried to forget everything from that night but still had specific triggers that made her feel uneasy.

"I bet your father was a great man. He and your mother raised a great young woman," Elizabeth said to her as she grabbed Beverly's hand to snap her out of her thoughts.

"They were, and thank you. I can feel them watching over me and my new blessed family," she said with a smile, trying to forget about her darker suppressed memories.

"They're watching over us today. It saddens me how we still live in a world of such evil and tragedies. But I want you to know you're like the daughter I never had, and it's a privilege to have you apart of our family now." Elizabeth said with a sincere smile as she squeezed Beverly's hand with a loving gesture.

"I really appreciate that and thank you all for having me a part of your amazing family. I've loved Adam since we first met. You have raised a wonderful man who has always been by my side through thick and thin." Beverly said as Elizabeth wiped the tears from her eyes and smiled. Adam leaned over and gave Beverly a kiss.

"You definitely bring out the best in our boy. And I promise you that Jacob and I will always be there for you guys no matter what, and be the best grandparents you could ever ask for." Elizabeth said, getting emotional herself, which was not often.

"What she said…But, you guys may get tired of us always trying to intrude to see baby Jonathan," Jacob chimed in to lighten the mood.

"Thank you both for everything. I'm sure I won't ever get tired of the intrusion. My life was a lonely one before Adam. We're family now," Beverly said as Jacob raised his cup.

"I'll cheers to that!" He proclaimed as everybody raised their plastic cups in laughter. They continued to talk and finish their dinner until the sun went down over the tree line, followed by a beautiful sunset of reddish-orange to conclude their evening.

As night fell, the all-too-familiar chill of winter came as they brought everything inside to wind down for the evening. Adam tried to help his mother with the dishes but encouraged him to go with his father into the den so she could talk one-on-one with her daughter-in-law. Adam didn't protest and left the room with his father, who offered him a glass of scotch and a cigar. They walked to the enclosed den off to the side of the house.

"Are you sure you don't need any help?" Beverly said as she stood next to her by the sink.

"I'm positive, Beverly. It's practically all paper plates, which will just go in the trash. You can hand me that container over there, though," pointing toward the opened cabinet.

"This one?" Beverly said to confirm, then handed it to her.

"You can take home the leftovers. I know Adam doesn't know how to cook, and I will definitely make sure he learns quick," Elizabeth said with all seriousness. "I can remember the time like it was yesterday when he almost burned the house down. He was twelve at the time and tried to make me pancakes for my birthday," she said as they both broke out with laughter.

"I know you'll take great care of him, and will be a terrific mother soon enough," she said as Beverly thanked her with modesty. "You probably already know this, but he is crazy about you. Well before you moved up here," she said to Beverly as she washed the bowl in the sink.

"He's always been very affectionate towards me," Beverly said with a smile.

"He'd be embarrassed with me saying this. But, Adam would literally talk about you even after shortly meeting you for the first time. He would go on and on about how he met this amazing girl from New York City," she laughed and turned off the sink, drying her hands with a dishrag.

"Really? Awe, that's so cute," Beverly said, blushing.

"Honestly, at first I was a little concerned with the idea of him wanting to date a city girl since I'm very old fashioned and had never left Silver Lakes myself. I always figured anybody who wasn't from around here and especially from a fast pace lifestyle wouldn't be able or have the time, to truly care about my boy. But, you changed my stubborn views. You're an amazing woman, and I can see how much you care about him, and I'm so relieved and appreciative of the fact. It's every mother's worse nightmare where their kids get involved with someone, you know, just isn't right for them. But I know with certainty you are both perfect for each other," she said with a smile.

"I feel really blessed right now to be a part of your family's generosity and being able to be with your amazing son to raise a family," Beverly said as she welcomed a hug and a kiss on the cheek from her mother-in-law.

Adam sat on the couch next to the leather recliner, where his father leaned back, puffing on a cigar. "With all these warm feelings aside, I hope you're willing to do everything you can to provide for your family. It is a huge responsibility, my son," he said as he took a sip from his scotch on the rocks.

"I know that dad, I've been taking on extra side jobs from the guys down at the mechanic shop on East Main street. With summer coming, my carpentry and landscaping gigs should become more frequent, too," Adam said as he took a drag from his cigar and coughed.

"You're skilled at what you do. Hell, you learned from the master carpenter over here," he said with a laugh. "But remember this is a small town, and winters are harsh here. Business isn't as it was when you were a kid. Back then, I would have to turn people away left and right, now it's far in between from that," he said as he leaned forward in his chair.

"What are you trying to say?" Adam said as he choked down his scotch whiskey.

"I remember you telling me about a conversation you had with Beverly a few months ago after she was laid off. She mentioned that her friend could get her a job in the city with good pay. Kristen, was it? I remember her, one of Jack Citdel's four daughters, she always seemed trustworthy. With all honesty, and all due respect, I always thought you would hook up with her back in the day." he said, chuckling to himself.

"Dad! Don't ever say something like that, she was only a friend. Beverly and I have both considered the options of relocating, but we both came to the same conclusion. The best decision would be to remain here so my child can be close to his grandparents and attend a good school system," he explained.

"I understand, Son, but know that we are getting older too, we can only be there for you guys with dinners and babysitting, but can't offer much more than that. I can't even promise you the house after we're gone. I had to take out a second mortgage and loan for my business to just stay afloat. What I'm saying is that moving to the city can broaden both of your horizons. This small town doesn't offer anything anymore," he said as he stood to pour himself another drink. "Men like us are used to being able to build, create, and provide with our hands. The new era now is with computers and automatized machines. You can find a job in sales in a heartbeat down there," he said as he puffed on his cigar.

"You don't think I can provide for my family?" Adam said agitated.

"No, all I'm saying is that there isn't much for you or your family here. I think if Beverly took a city job with Kristen, it would open up more opportunities for you, my son. Just think about it some more is all I ask," he pleaded with him.

"I don't ever want Beverly to go back there. She is happier here. We're both happier here! You may be having some difficult times, but you're nearing retirement soon. I'll continue to work everyday until my hands are raw if I have too! I don't expect anything from you nor ever asked you for your money. I know I can provide for my family perfectly fine, and we'll live the rest of our days in Silver Lakes," he proclaimed, fighting against his own frustrations and doubts.

"I understand your enthusiasm, Son, but I feel you are making the wrong decision to stay here. It's time for you to leave the nest and experience the rest of the world too. Don't let your wife or family feel stuck here like the rest of us have."

"I'm the head of my family, and my decision to stay is final! I will provide the bread with these hands until my death!" Adam said to finish the conversation on the subject matter. Jacob Grove took another sip from his glass as Adam stood from his chair and walked out on him.

Beverly sat across from Elizabeth at the table, continuing to talk as they enjoyed their tea and fresh blueberry pie that Elizabeth baked earlier this morning. "Beverly, I know it must've been a stressful experience growing up as a young adult without your parents. Especially living in the city without any sort of support. Moving up here all alone had must also been a frightening experience, too. How did you cope with it all? If you don't mind if I get personal, that's what mothers-in-law are there for, right?" Elizabeth chuckled as she slowly cut into the pie with her fork, then took a bite without breaking eye contact with Beverly.

"Well, it was tough growing up in the orphanages and learning how to make it on my own for sure. But, I met a few great people along the way. It wasn't until the day I met Adam, who had shown me there was more to life. I was more than happy to relocate up here to be closer to him." Beverly said as she scooped whipped cream on her slice of pie.

"It must've been a huge transition for you to move to Silver Lakes. We don't even have our own movie theater," she said with a laugh.

"Yeah, it's much quieter here, but I like it, though. Perfect for raising a family," she said as she took a bite of her pie.

"Good to hear it. But don't you miss the excitement of the city life at all?" Elizabeth continued to inquire.

"Not at all. Adam and I discussed to maybe move down to the city since our mutual friend Kristen offered me a well-paying job at her firm," Beverly explained as she blew on her hot tea.

"That'd be nice, but wouldn't it bring back bad memories? I'm also happy that Adam has moved in to take care of you too. Plus, you have us right across town."

"It's been great, and he's been accommodating for sure, even though I still have to do all of the cooking," Beverly said with a laugh. "But he started to build a baby crib from the ground up, which is pretty amazing," Beverly said, ignoring her first question.

"I know he'll continue to be amazing. But with all honesty, I think the idea of moving away would not suit your family. Having you near us would be the best for both of you and your child. Can I ask you a personal question?"

"Of course, you can," Beverly agreed cautiously.

"Well, I wanted to ask about how you were doing, overall?"

"Good, of course, I have a wonderful and caring husband, and the obstetrician that I see regularly tells me I'll have a healthy baby boy soon, so what more can I ask for?" Beverly said, then smiled.

"What I meant was your nightmares?" Elizabeth said, leaving the conversation in a brief lapse of silence as Beverly's fork scratched the plate, missing the slice of pie.

"I didn't know you knew about those," she said hesitantly and ashamed.

"it's a small-town, Beverly, besides Adam only brought it up once or twice but nothing in detail... He only mentioned you had some bad dreams on occasion, understandably due to your past, of course. I just want to make sure that you're okay," she said to sound empathetic but inappropriately curious.

"Good, I guess, I haven't had any bad dreams since my last visit to New York. I've been good for the past six months, maybe because your son and I are happy," she said with an uncomfortable laugh.

"You were seeing a psychiatrist, right?" Elizabeth continued to press the subject further.

"Beverly, don't answer that!" Adam said, overhearing the conversation as he made his way back into the kitchen.

"What's wrong, son? I'm just making friendly conversation with my daughter-in-law," she said innocently.

"No, you and Dad always have your ulterior motives, playing the role of the perfect family. I should have known you would try and pry us for more information after your hospitality. Beverly, grab your coat, we're going home." Adam said to her as she got up without questioning his decision.

"You are acting absurd, Son, come sit down with me so we can talk some more."

"We had enough of your guy's advice for the night, and it's best we make our way home, it's getting late as it is," he said as his father stepped into the kitchen.

"Thank you for the lovely dinner," Beverly said as Adam took her by the hand as they made their way to the door.

"I don't know why he gets so offended sometimes," his father said as he watched them leave in a hurry.

The screen door slammed behind them as they walked down the porch toward the driveway. "What was that all about?" Beverly asked as Adam started the engine and pulled out of the driveway.

He turned to her, "I saw you were getting uncomfortable with my mom's questions."

"She didn't mean anything by it, she was probably just curious. It's okay, I need to be open about these things anyway. I always kept everything to myself and feel if I want to get over my past, I need to start talking about it," she said with sincere optimism.

"Not like that, though, it seemed more like an interrogation. Trust me from personal experience, my mom likes to overstep her boundaries and pry into everyone else's lives," he explained, then continued. "Maybe my dad was right. Maybe we should leave this small town behind and move to the city to raise our child."

"I thought you loved it here, and I also like it here too. Plus, the school system sucks in the urban areas, and we would also need your parents to babysit from time to time." Beverly turned to him, then finally said, "I don't want to keep running away, Adam. I know deep down we can make it work here. I'll find a job soon, and you're obviously multi-talented with all your trades," she explained as he paused for a moment to think and recall his own experiences he had grew accustomed too.

"Sometimes, I feel everyone in this town has nothing else better to do then try to know everyone's secrets."

"Secrets?" Beverly interjected, "we have nothing to hide. I have nothing to hide!" She said, confused and annoyed with his statement.

"You know what I mean, hon. If we chose to move to the city, there would be more opportunities for both of us. Silver Lakes is just a stagnant pool of the ignorantly bliss. I'm starting to feel that staying here is not the best for our family anymore." Adam argued as he finally understood what his father had tried to explain to him.

"Let's discuss it after we have our son and sort it out then, okay?" Beverly said as they drove down a long dark stretch of road. "I hope we didn't upset them for leaving so abruptly like that. Deep down, your parents are caring people. We all have different personalities. They're just more open and direct, which I'm not used too. People in the city mainly kept to themselves or try to portray some other image far from the truth. I like the people's honesty up here, and there is also the fact that—Adam watch out!" She yelled as he slammed on his brakes. Her seat belt locked and pressed into her chest as they came to a complete stop with his hood inches away from a deer that wandered out onto the road.

"That was a close one. Are you okay? You also don't have to worry about deer in the city, that's for sure," he said. The deer stood in his halogen headlights as Beverly stared back into its fixed glaring eyes, remembering the night in woods. "Beverly? You alright?" Adam said as she sat next to him in a trance. A brief flashback of the dark entity passed through her mind. For a split moment, she was back at the alter, witnessing the entity feast on its sacrifice. Beverly snapped out of the vision after Adam grabbed her by the shoulder. The deer turned away and galloped back into the woods. "You okay, Bev?"

"Yeah, it just caught me off guard that's all," she said, trying to not make anything out of it.

They continued to drive home as the full moon glowed in the night sky. They pulled into the driveway as Adam got out first to open the door for Beverly, then they made their way into the house. Tiny jumped on Beverly as she walked in. "What did I tell you about jumping on her like that, she's pregnant you idiot," Adam said, scolding him.

"He's just happy for us to be home, Adam. There's no need to call him a dumb," Beverly said, walking over to the kitchen, then looked down at the bills stacking up on the counter. "I think I'll go to bed early tonight. I'm pretty tired from today," she said, heading toward the stairs.

"Okay, I'll stay down here and work on the crib some more. Can I have a kiss goodnight?" He said before she walked away.

"Of course you can. Sorry, I'm just exhausted," Beverly said as Adam kissed her goodnight, then watched her go upstairs as Tiny followed behind her.

Adam went back over to the living room, which laid scattered with pieces of wood, then opened his toolbox near the unfinished crib. He sat down on the couch, looking over the project for a moment, then went back to what he does best, getting lost in his work. Since he didn't have any clients the next day, Adam stayed up into the late hours building the frame. He decided to bring it down to the shop in a few days to sand it and paint it before adding the fabric and cushioning. He shook his stiff hands out of exhaustion, then laid back on the couch, resting his eyes for a bit before eventually falling asleep.

In the early hours of the morning, Adam heard a slight tap against the window. He slowly rose from the couch, looked at his watch, then over toward the window. In a mental fog, he heard the tapping again and realized it wasn't a dream or his imagination. Adam made his way toward the front door and looked out the window, finding nothing out of the ordinary. Adam started to walk away until he heard it again, as knuckles gently tapped against the glass. He took a closer look out the window and found no signs of life anywhere.

Adam glanced over toward Mr. Kelly's house, which remained coldly vacant with the streets illuminated by the moonlight, as it made its journey across the early morning sky. "That's strange," he said, noticing someone standing across the street, before suddenly vanishing behind the oak trees in the front yard. Adam thought it was only his imagination and walked away from the window. As he turned, the tapping continued but now against the door with a deep voice calling out his name, as if only a whisper inside of his head.

"Adam," it called out to him, making his skin crawl with horripilation. The tapping ceased as he walked back to the window, looking out, only to not see anything.

"I must be exhausted, I just need to go back to bed," he said out loud as he turned away before hearing his name one more time.

Agitated, he turned around and shouted, "What? Who is it?" As soon as Adam turned, there was a loud bang against the door with the handle shaking violently back and forth.

"Let me in!" The slamming and handle ceased as Adam walked over to the door in a trance. "That's it, Adam. Let me in, and I'll show you the truth." A voice repeated in his head as he twisted the deadbolt, then slowly turned the handle to push the door open. He stepped out into the cold night air, which snapped him back to reality. Confused on why he was outside, he looked around to not see anything, then immediately went back inside, locking the door behind him. He proceeded to the couch half-awake and quickly fell back to sleep.

Adam laid on his right side, facing the wooden stand where the new television stood. Multiple voices originated around the room as he concentrated on it before it singled in on a location directly in front of him. The low vibrations of indistinguishable garbled voices unified into an intense demonic presence and penetrated deep into his mind.

Adam's body convulsed on the couch, jarring him into a paralyzed subconsciousness. His eyes were fixed in a trance as he stared toward the coffee table to find a pitch-black lanky figure, sitting with his legs tucked inward toward its chest.

"Rise and shine, Adam. I have something important to tell you." The entity projected into his mind as Adam remained paralyzed with fear. "Your sweet, oh so sweet, little Beverly is not to be trusted. During your absence, she was seeing someone else." The entity told him as Adam moaned helplessly on the couch, unable to move.

"That's right, Adam. Another man, a suitor, defiled your soon-to-be wife well before your love turned you away as a distraction to hide her own infidelities. The child she carries is not of your kin. You need to take care of this, so shame doesn't fall upon you and your family's name. No one will ever know about your vengeful deeds. Everyone would suspect it was suicide. I can assure you of that. You know what you need to do now," The entity told him, then vanished into a black mist before being absorbed into the walls.

Adam regained control of his body, but not of his own mind. He slowly rose from the couch and sat, staring at the empty table. Anger boiled through his body as he looked over to the unfinished crib. His hands trembled with rage as he slowly stood before making his way over to the kitchen. "She lied to me. That fucking bitch lied to me! She has always been deceitful from day one," he mumbled to himself as he took an eight-inch butcher's knife from the wooden holder and held it up toward his face. Adam ran his fingers along the knife's blunt spine, then twisted his wrist as the steel showed a distorted reflection of his grinning face.

Adam walked upstairs with the blade tightly gripped in his hands. "Her and that bastard child must go," he rambled as he approached the half-opened bedroom door. He peered in with a lethargic lunatic gaze to find her asleep in bed with the blankets down by her waist. Adam pushed the door open without waking her, then walked to the bedside, where he stood staring down at her with a possessed rage. As the knife closed in on her neck, Beverly stirred in bed before rolling over to her left side, facing away from him.

"Do it, Adam. Do it now, and set yourself free from this lie," the entity said with a thirsty grin as he stood in the far corner of the room with blood-red eyes.

Beverly moved her arm toward her face and said softly, "Adam, is that you, sweetie. Come to bed, my love," she said before falling back asleep. Adam looked down at her, then over to the entity from across the room.

"Do it now, Adam! Free yourself from this infidelity," It said as Adam looked back down at Beverly wide-eyed.

"I know what I must do now." Adam said to himself as he raised the knife in his hands with the blade angled below his grip. Her soft neck would effortlessly split open, spewing copious amount of blood as it bubbled with the escaping air from the trachea, drowning her within a silent sleepy haze. *No regrets*. With one clean swipe, Adam ran the blade across the top of his left palm as blood pooled in his hand. The pain snapped him back to reality as Beverly opened her eyes and turned to face him. Adam quickly hid the knife behind his back and smiled while biting his lower lip.

"Adam, what are you doing? Why are you standing there? Come to bed, honey," she said, still half-asleep.

"I was just...checking in on you. I thought I heard you talking in your sleep, that's all," Adam said, biting his lip to hold back the pain screaming from his hand. "I'm going back downstairs to work on the crib some more," he said as she ignored him, then turned over to fall back asleep. Adam brought his left hand to his mouth and sucked his wound, noticing they were alone in the room. Adam slowly backed out of the bedroom and closed the door behind him.

He rushed back downstairs, nursing his laceration, and ran his hand over the sink to wash the blood away, then held pressure until the bleeding finally stopped. He washed the knife off with soap, then placed it back in its holder before wrapping his wound with paper towels. Adam stumbled over toward the couch in a stupor as he cradled his injured hand with his left arm, vaguely remembering what had just occurred before drifting back to sleep.

"Adam…Adam?…Adam!" Beverly said, concerned as he mumbled in his sleep as she prepared breakfast. He woke on the couch in a state of panic, looking around the room as if he had fallen asleep at a watch-post during a Vietnam ambush. He turned to Beverly with a blank stare as she stood over the stove, looking back at him.

"You okay? Bad dream? She asked, laughing.

"Yeah…I mean no…I honestly don't really remember. I must've fallen asleep working on the crib late last night," he said, sitting up and rubbing his eyes. "You're up early," he said to her, trying to change the subject.

"It's ten in the morning and wanted to make us breakfast. I was trying to be quiet, but it looked like you were having a bad dream," Beverly said, then smiled.

"Shouldn't I be the one making you breakfast in bed?" Adam said, stumbling off the couch.

"Not after the story your mom told me last night." Beverly began to laugh hysterically.

"Very funny, Bev. I'm sure my mother had plenty to share." He mumbled as he walked over to her as he tried to orient his unsteady movements.

"The crib looks amazing! I appreciate you staying up late to finish it," Beverly said as she prepared him a plate of scrambled eggs with bacon and toast.

"Thank you, I'm going to take it down to the shop on Monday to finish it," he said as he kissed her, then sat to eat breakfast with her.

"I kept seeing you twitch and talk in your sleep. What startled you in your dreams?" Beverly said half-joking, half-serious.

"Honestly, I don't really remember, nothing crazy, though, " he told her as he inhaled his breakfast quicker than Tiny, who sat beneath him.

"Why is there a cut on your hand?" Beverly said, grabbing his wrist and pulling it closer to examine it.

"Oh yeah, that. I accidentally cut myself with the trimming saw last night. It won't need stitches," he said, vaguely remembering the events from last night.

"Oh, okay. As long as your fine. What are your plans for today? She said, noticing he seemed to be in a rush and not himself.

"Not sure yet, babe. I was thinking maybe we could take a trip downtown to check out the Spring festival carnival they're having all weekend long. How does that sound?" He offered.

"That sounds wonderful! I'll start getting ready, maybe we can go to a few shops to look at baby clothes together, grab lunch, then head over from there," she said, enthusiastic over the idea.

"Okay, babe, I'll take care of the dishes while you get ready. Let's try to leave in an hour or so if that's enough time?" Adam said as he drank from his coffee mug with a trembling grip as if he had survived the ambush of guerrilla warfare.

"Perfect, I'll start getting ready now!" She said and kissed him before heading upstairs to get changed for the day.

Adam sat at the counter, staring over toward the crib, not remembering finishing it last night. He turned toward the front door and window as the only memories of his dreams resonated back in his mind in the form of a splitting headache. Uncertain of what had happened last night, he gulped down his coffee, and slammed the mug onto the counter, startling Tiny who rested in the kitchen below his feet. He got up to clean the dishes and pushed the thoughts away from his mind. It was a new day. He had hoped.

CHAPTER TWENTY-ONE

Beams of sunlight scattered through grey clouds as Adam and Beverly walked down the sidewalk, holding hands in the typical gloomy April afternoon. They continued to window shop after a satisfying brunch at the local bistro cafe. Adam walked along her right side before stopping to reach down to pluck several small flowers and place them between her ear and flowing brown hair. Beverly kissed him, then smiled as she noticed the other families making their way toward the market place. Several children ran between the yellow road closure cross-guards, which were placed several days ago for the festival.

Beverly was lost within a blissful daydream, envisioning how her son would one day follow suit among the other children in the near future. She turned to Adam without having to say a word, as they both knew deep down Silver Lakes was the perfect place to raise their family. She recalled the tough city life and felt this small town provided a great atmosphere and a sense of comfort for herself and her family. Beverly understood all her hardships would one day be lessened living here, and everything would eventually turn out okay if they stayed.

Local farmer markets and craft stands lined the sides of the street as they walked toward the town green. The fresh aroma of homemade blueberry pies and bread—baked by an older woman this morning—enticed them over to her booth to try a few samples. They passed by an older man, wearing torn-up jeans and a white t-shirt stained with multiple colors, as he vigorously painted the street corner scenery. He stood there deep in thought as he made careful brush strokes, trying to capture memories from the day. Beverly wondered how he could possibly remember all the people passing by as if they were stored images or fleeting ghosts and somehow resurrect them onto his canvas with utmost precision.

The gentle notes of a classical guitar suite filled the air, as a young musician in his late-twenties played a rendition of Antonio Vivaldi's first-movement in front of a café. Patrons' enjoyed their coffees and croissants as they conversed amongst themselves. Indistinguishable small-talk regarding their families, summer dream vacations, and places they had wished to visit before settling down.

Burdens of more weighted discussions were droned out by the musical melodies and town square ambiance.

Several children ran passed them, toward the town green carnival several feet ahead. "Honestly, I can't remember the last time I was down here for one of these festivals. I'm glad I could revisit it and share these memories with you," Adam said as he tenderly took her by the hand.

"I'm really enjoying everything today and know that our son would love this too," Beverly said as he smiled. Adam tugged on her hand as if he wanted her to run into the amusement park like the other children. Beverly laughed as they made a short sprint into the town green toward the admission table. Adam paid for the small roller coaster and Ferris wheel tickets, then led her over to the fried Oreo stand.

"Bev, you have to try these!" Adam said, then laughed as she took a bite, which left a faint chocolate ring along her lips.

"Mmm...delicious!" Beverly mumbled with her mouth full. Adam gave her a kiss, then wiped away the chocolate around her mouth.

"Do you like roller coasters?" He asked as they made their way toward the first ride.

"Well, I guess I do, but these makeshift ones are a little scary. I remember reading stories of where they would malfunction on occasion," Beverly said and embarrassed as she told him the story about the water park as a child. Adam reassured her there hadn't been any incidents he could recall as he held her hand standing in line.

"I bet it's not as scary as that water slide," he joked as they waited their turn. Several kids screamed with joy overhead as the coaster did several laps around the tracts.

"Tickets please," the acne-faced teenager attendant said. Adam handed them over, then helped Beverly into the front of the coaster, as the attendant secured the bars in front of them.

"Are you ready for this?" Adam said as he squeezed her hand. Before she could answer, the coaster jolted forward then slowly ascended thirty feet, suspended in the air with anticipation.

"Believe it or not, this is actually my first time on a roller coaster," Beverly said as they plummeted down the tracks, picking up speed as it navigated around the twists and turns. Beverly screamed and squeezed Adam's hand tight. The coaster inverted in a ninety-degree angle before ascending to the top, providing a view of the entire downtown area. Mesmerized by the view, she looked out toward the horizon to see the forest and lakes, which formed a secure barrier around their town.

Every nerve and muscle in her body fired and tensed as the coaster rolled forward, gliding gracefully around every turn, before dropping down again. Beverly felt the sudden urge to finally embrace the freedom of letting it all go. She released Adam's hand, then raised her arms into the air as the coaster went into free fall down the tracks. Beverly screamed for joy, looking over to Adam, who was leaning back in his seat, clutching onto the padded bar in front of him.

She smiled as they went around for another pass, going up, then back down again. She held her hands up with every twist and turn before making it back to the top, revealing the beautiful landscape around them. The attendant reversed the switch and had the coaster fall backward, retracing their route before coming to a slow, graceful-stop where they started.

"That was freaking amazing!" Beverly said as Adam, unsteady on his feet, helped her out and off of the platform as people boarded from the other side.

"Yeah, I know. I wasn't expecting that at all. I never remember it being that fast when I was kid," he said as the color returned to his face. "Let's go check out the other rides for a bit," he said, walking past a few game stands as carnies verbally fought for their attention.

"Step right up! Make a basket and win a prize!" An older disheveled scruffy man with sunken cheeks and bloodshot eyes shouted over toward them as they passed by his booth.

"Hey, you there, pretty boy. Step over here and show off your skills to win a prize for your beautiful lady," he shouted to get Adam's attention.

Beverly chuckled, then poked him to go over. "Looks like you have been challenged to try and impress me," Beverly said as Adam smirked, then walked over to accept the carnie's invitation.

"You look like the purebred athletic type, I bet you can make a basket with only one try. With five dollars, you can have three chances to win any one of these grand prizes on display," the man said as Adam pulled out an Abe Lincoln from his wallet.

"I hope this isn't rigged," Adam said as he cautiously handed over the money.

"Please, my dear boy. I'm a hundred percent legitimate," he said, pointing over to a young teenager who recently walked away with a prize.

"Okay then, I got this, Bev," Adam said confidently, as his first throw went soaring twelve feet down the lane missing the net entirely.

"Not a good start to impress your girl, my boy," the carnie said, bellowing with laughter as his gut shook in every direction. Adam took another ball from his hand with discontent.

"Does this game frequently consist of all your half-assed comments too?" Adam said as he threw the second attempt out of frustration, watching the ball bounce off the rim before rolling back down the lane toward him.

"This is easy stuff kid, I usually give everyone two shots, but somehow I knew you'd need a third." the carnie said with a shit-eating grin across his face. Beverly looked over to Adam to see how well he would control his temper. Adam clenched the last ball, trying to remain focused and concentrated on taking dead aim as he launched the ball from his hand. It gracefully floated through the air and passed through the hoop without grazing the backboard or rim.

"Nothing but net!" Adam said straight-faced.

"I have to be honest, which ya'll. That other kid over there didn't win that prize here," he said, turning to him, then over to Beverly. "Okay, having said that. What'd it be, young lady?" The carnie said as Beverly jumped up and down, clapping her hands, then pointed over to the large teddy bear. The man handed it over to her as she turned toward Adam ecstatic, then gave him a hug and kiss with the giant stuffed bear between them.

"My game isn't rigged, but it's definitely not easy to win. You're my first winner for the weekend," he said with a hesitant laugh.

"What can I say. I'm very competitive when the pressure is on," Adam said as he took Beverly's hand, kissed it, then walked her to the Ferris Wheel.

"Thank you so much, Adam! I knew you can do it! Despite that guy running his mouth, of course," she said, laughing and smiled as they got in line for the next ride.

"I remembered your advice to keep cool and not get frustrated. I'll have to say, it really works," Adam said as the attendant took their tickets.

"I'm glad you actually listened to me for a change." She said with a laugh. "Our baby will absolutely love this bear," she said and placed it next to her side as she sat close to Adam. Then with a sudden jerk, they were lifted up into the air.

The Ferris Wheel went around in a few slow rotations, then stopped while they were at the top, towering over the roller coaster and entire town. The trees were in bloom with small green, white, and yellow buds from the coming of Spring. But, like with the old saying April showers bring May flowers, the clouds darkened the sky, obscuring the sun. With clouds suspended in the air, raindrops began to fall. Below, market stands were quickly closing from the approaching storm. Vendors rushed to throw large tarps over the tables and loaded their vans with unsold merchandise. As the storm approached, the attendants began off-loading passengers one by one from the other rides.

Beverly and Adam were brought back to the ground and helped off the Ferris wheel. Adam took off his jacket and draped it over her as they hurried back to the car. They ran past the basketball booth, noticing he had already closed his stand with gray tarps staked to the ground. The rain fell harder as they ran through the town green's muddy grass back onto the sidewalks of the street corner, as merchants were near finished loading their vans for the day.

The guitarist no longer serenaded the cafe patrons, as the outdoor seating was moved back inside. Rumblesof distant thunder replaced the classical suites, which previously filled the streets. The aroma of blueberry pies was washed out of the air by the downpour of rain.

The artist had already left, taking the serene afternoon landscape along with him. Leaving behind the mystery, if he had finished his vision for himself or sold it to a family, who wanted to capture the memory of the day. Or, took the painting home with him to add to his collection of other unfinished work. A few children followed shortly behind their parents, as they splashed around in the puddles before getting scolded to hurry up.

Thunder crackled in the sky as Beverly and Adam rushed back toward their car, passing by the shops and bistro. "Almost there," he said as they reached the parking lot and opened the door for Beverly, who placed the teddy bear and jacket inside but didn't get in. She turned to Adam as the rain continued to come down over them. "What are you doing? Aren't you going to get in the car?" He said.

Beverly stared back with a silly smile on her face as her wavy hair was soaked with the water dripping from her head. "I had an amazing time today, and I love you," she said as she started to passionately kiss him in the rain.

"I love you, too," Adam said as they kissed and held each other as the storm passed over them. The rain finally let up, as the sun briefly emerged from behind the clouds. Beverly looked up toward the sky as the rain gently fell over them, then looked back to Adam.

"No matter how horrible the storm, the sun will always come back and continue to shine," she said while holding him, soaking wet.

"That's true, but the storm isn't over yet," he said, laughing.

"It is for me, Adam. It is for me..." Beverly said with a smile as water continued to run down her face.

"I love you, Beverly. Let's get back home, though," he told her as he wiped the water away from her eyes and gave her another kiss before helping her into the car. He got in and pulled out of the parking lot as the rain increased steadily after the eye of the storm passed, darkening the skies with the rumble of thunder off in the distance.

They got back to the house and took off their muddy shoes, as Tiny looked to them in confusion, on why they were soaking wet, and remained at a distance to observe them. "I'll run us a hot bath," Beverly said as she quickly went upstairs.

"Okay, hon, I will make us some hot chocolate in the meantime." He said as Tiny jumped onto the couch and stared over at him in the kitchen. "Sorry, bud, it's mommy and daddy time tonight," Adam said as he went upstairs, turning off the lights behind him. They undressed and sat in the tub together. Beverly's memories of being alone had faded away, like the harshness of the winter forgotten by the first warm day of Spring.

Adam held her in silence as they sipped their hot chocolate. Beverly reflected on last Christmas when Kristen came to visit during the holidays and celebrated her recent baby shower. She also Reflected on when she gave the announcement of her wedding, which would come after she gave birth toward the end of summer.

She recalled sending out invitations and thank you letters to Doctor Spitzer and Doctor Imamu, expressing the great gratitude she had for them for being symptom-free ever since that night. She recalled briefly without despair of the old visions six-months ago and felt it was her way of conquering her fears and finally letting go of the past. She finished her hot chocolate and enjoyed their time together in the bath, before making their way to the bedroom to make love for the rest of the evening.

CHAPTER TWENTY-TWO

Two weeks later, in early May, Adam rushed home, barging through the front doors. "I have a surprise for you, but I need to bring it upstairs first, so close your eyes for a moment!" Adam said excitedly as she covered her eyes with a smile across her face.

"Okay, I can't wait for it, babe," she said as he brought the crib inside the house, which he had finished sanding, staining, and painting at the workshop the week before. He stumbled inside without any finesse, banging it against the door frame as he tried to discreetly bring it upstairs. Beverly withheld taking her hands away from her face and giggled, "What are you doing over there?" She asked as Tiny curiously watched him bring it inside.

"No, peeking!" Adam said as he struggled to carry it up the stairs.

"I'm not!" Beverly said with a smile as he stumbled down the hall into her bedroom.

"Okay, I'm ready for you to come up now," he shouted from the bedroom. Beverly went upstairs to find Adam standing next to a large object veiled underneath a bed sheet. "Okay, hon, you can pull the sheet now," he said, anticipating the excitement on her face. Beverly yanked the sheet to the floor, revealing the crib painted pearl white and royal blue fabric with plush cushions on the inside of the bed.

"It's amazing, Adam! Thank you for being everything and more to me. You're so talented!" She said, running her hand along the edges of the crib and soft plush fabric cushions. "You are absolutely amazing!" Beverly said, giving him a hug and a kiss. They both turned back to look at it, admiring all the detail he had put into his work. "This is perfect for him. I can't wait until the day we finally bring him home with us," she said, trying to not get choked up.

"I know, Beverly...I know," Adam said as he placed his arm around her as they continued to admire the crib in the corner of their room.

"It's missing one thing, though," she said as she went to her closet and grabbed a small teddy bear amongst the clutter, brushed it off, then placed it in the crib. "There, he has my old teddy with him and yours of course, too," she said, staring toward the carnival prize sitting in the corner of the room. Adam kissed her as they held each other's hands before walking back downstairs to prepare dinner for the evening.

"Adam, you could easily make more of these cribs to sell and market," she mentioned over dinner.

"I know, hon. There's a lot of things I could do to make some extra money, especially when the jobs get light around here. Also, my father will be retiring soon. Hopefully, I'll be able to continue with his clients that he had worked with throughout his career. Summer is also right around the corner and should bring a lot of outdoor projects for me to do. During the Fall, I'll have tree cutting and landscaping, and throughout the winter, I'll plow snow and work on making these side projects to sell. I want to save up enough money so I could lease a larger workspace down at my friend's warehouse." Adam said, expressing his goals to her.

"I know that the city has more career opportunities for you. But as you know, I like to work with my hands, and since I don't have any professional licensing, it would be easier to find work up here and neighboring towns. I will do what I need, too, so you would never have to work again," he explained as he finished his dinner.

"I agree, and we'll be fine living here with a single

income. I know you want me to be a full-time mother and all, but I also want to get back to work again soon, too," she explained.

"I understand, honey. We'll find something soon, or we could make it into a family business. We'll continue with our plan instead of leaving. Plus, we both feel this is a better place to raise our child," he continued.

"It is," Beverly said as she felt a kick inside her belly. "Looks like he also agrees too," she laughed, placing Adam's hand over her lower abdomen to feel his son inside her womb.

"Only a matter of time now," Adam said with a smile as he cleared the counter. Beverly walked over to the couch and noticed the two books Doctor Imamu had sent to her were unexpectedly laid on top of the other magazines on the table.

"Where did these come from?" Beverly said, curious and surprised to see them resurface again since she had put them away six months ago, forgotten until now.

"Oh, those books? I was just bored one night and wanted to look through them to understand a little bit more about what you had experienced," Adam explained, thinking nothing of it.

She picked up the book, "whatever I had experienced is over now and was all just in my head. I finally faced my fears, and that's what finally put a stop to it. I forgot to send them back to him, and will mail them back next week," Beverly said as she tossed it down on the table.

"It's very fascinating stuff, though…Oh, I also forgot to tell you the details of my dream that I had a few weeks ago," Adam said as she paused, staring back at him with a stunned look on her face.

"What dream?"

"The one I had when I was sleeping on the couch a few weeks ago. I remember it now. There was this tapping at the front window, and something whispered my name, then it started banging on the door, trying to get in. That's when I woke up," he said as he finished the dishes, making nothing out of the conversation.

"Wait! What? Why didn't you tell me this before?" Beverly said, trembling and angered.

"Relax, I only started to remember it the other day while finishing the crib. The dream reminded me of the same things you were going through and just wanted to read a bit more on the subject. To see if there was a reason why I had a similar experience." he said with a quick hesitant laugh as he walked over to her.

"This isn't funny, Adam. I hope this isn't one of your stupid jokes," she said, not amused with the conversation.

"I'm not joking with you. If I knew this would upset you, I wouldn't have said anything. You mentioned about the books, which made me think of it. I'm sorry if I upset you," Adam said to her as she stood in the living room lost in thought. "Everything, okay?" Adam said to her as she remembered what the entity told her six months ago. *I promise to take you there, Beverly. You can't win...you can't defeat me...*

Memories flashed in her mind from several weeks ago when the deer crossed in front of their car, followed by the vision of her parents standing near the altar in the Adirondacks. Beverly envisioned the demon standing by the fire as it scattered the entrails of its sacrifice before devouring the heart in its mouth of endless teeth. She remembered what Adam's father said at the picnic, *you make it sound like it was hell...*then repeating in her mind, *you can't defeat me...I promise to take you there...I'll take what is mine......you can't win...you can't defeat me...sever the cord and set your soul free...*every memory flooded back into her mind, like a broken faucet.

"Beverly?" Adam said as he laid his hand over her shoulder, which startled and snapped her back to reality.

"Yes, of course, why?" She said to him softly as if in a somnambulist trance.

"You were just acting a little odd for a moment there," he said as she stared forward, away from him.

"Yeah, I am okay, I'm going to take Tiny for a quick walk, I'll be back later," Beverly said, grabbing for Tiny's leash off the door hook, not wanting to continue the conversation.

"Okay then, I'll be upstairs getting ready for bed, I'm exhausted tonight," he said with no response as she led Tiny out the front door leaving it open behind her. Adam shrugged it off as nothing, closed the door, then went upstairs for the evening.

The street lamps flickered on as Beverly walked along the moonlit street as Tiny continued ahead of her, sniffing out for a place to relieve himself. The night's temperatures dropped to near freezing as winter desperately tried to still cling itself across the landscape.

A light frost covered the new grass blades and shrubbery that were desperate to grow. Her expiration plumed from her mouth with each breath as she shuttered from the chill before continuing down the road. Tiny tugged on his leash, forcing her closer toward the woods at the end of her cul-de-sac.

"Come on, you stupid dog, I'm freezing my ass out here. It's not time to go play chase the critters in the woods," she said as Tiny continued to pull harder, forcing her to regain her balance. "Come on, I'm not kidding around here!" Beverly said, standing near the edge of the dense woods, which continued to stretch on for several miles before fading to darkness. "Adam was right, you need better discipline. No more treats for you if you don't come back here right this second!" She yelled as Tiny continued to tug more intensely, then began to snarl and bark toward the woods.

Overwhelmed with dread, Beverly stood frozen in fear, not knowing what to do. Tiny continued to bark as he tugged on the leash, trying to break free from her grip. She felt the tension in the leash as Tiny fought back against the resistance. "Come on, Tiny!" Beverly screamed as she took the leash with both hands, giving it one final forceful yank as the tension snapped, sending the collar into the air, followed by a shrill yelp.

Beverly lost her balance and fell backward onto the ground, then looked up to see Tiny barking hysterically into the darkness. Before she could get up, he sprinted off at full speed. "Tiny!" She yelled out to him, then quickly got to her feet and ran toward the edge of the woods. After losing sight of him, she mustered up all her courage to follow him into the unknown. Disoriented by the darkness and by him barking off in the distance, she stumbled over the uneven landscape, trying to catch up.

Beverly continued to run after him, tripping over shrubbery, rocks, and fallen tree branches scattered along the ground. Cold dampness filled her shoes and socks as it became saturated with the muddy water as she crossed over a creek bed. Tiny's muffled barks echoed all around, sending more hopelessness and disorientation during her pursuit. The street lights were quickly replaced with the entrapment of the woods circling in around her.

"Come on, buddy! This isn't funny! Come back here right now!" Beverly yelled out in exhaustion and frustration as she leaned against a tree to catch her breath while holding her abdomen.

His barks were clear and close as she continued to follow the echos, hoping she would stumble right behind him in the pitch-black as the moon remained hidden behind the thick cloud cover. The continuous barking placed her into a trance and state of desperation as she tried to seek it out, forgetting about the time and how far she had already traveled into the woods. As soon as she felt she was getting closer to him, the barking would cease. Then there was one final loud yelp that came directly ahead of her, followed by permanent silence.

"Tiny?" She said as her voice and body trembled to go further, aching, and afraid.

Beverly followed her instincts into the darkness. She reached a small clearing where silver moonlight broke through the canopy and cloud cover, illuminating the landscape around her. She ventured forward to another small creek and stood looking toward the other side at a tree where a large shadow covered the portion of its trunk. She proceeded to walk hesitantly over to it and found a dark viscous fluid along the base of a tree.

As Beverly got closer to examine it, she found pieces of scattered fur and blood along the trunk and over the ground as if something was dragged away violently. "Tiny?" Beverly whispered, not wanting to jump to conclusions. She felt the heartbreak and anger seep through to her core as she yelled hysterically in the middle of the woods. Out of breath, she tried to calm herself as the silence fell upon her.

Branches snapped loudly off in the distance. "Tiny?" Beverly whimpered, knowing deep down, she was not alone.

In the clearing on the other side of the embankment, a dark figure appeared, standing completely erect near a small tree. She rubbed the tears away from her eyes as she continued to look onward in fear, as a shadowy figure stared back at her. It was still too far away to make out any details, that if it was a person or just the shadow cast from the moonlight off the other trees. She shook her head to assume it is her imagination, then traced her eyes across the clearing in search of her German Shepherd.

Out of fear and curiosity, she drew her attention back toward the shadow figure. Only to notice it was now in a different location from before, questioning if it was her imagination. She took a step back and laughed hysterically to herself. "This isn't real. None of this is. I'm dreaming all of this. Tiny is probably sleeping at the foot of my bed as I lay next to Adam."

Then off in the distance, a pair of red eyes shimmered in the darkness. Beverly stepped backward onto a large branch, which broke underfoot, sending a crackling snap echoing throughout the woods. Fearing for her life, she gave up on the search to quickly turn and run, twisting her ankle in the process. As she tried to regain her footing, the pain intensified and radiated throughout her leg to drill in the reality that this wasn't a dream.

"I'm so sorry, Tiny baby. I'll come back in the morning to look for you, mommy needs to go home right now..." Beverly muttered while groaning in agony from the pain and confusion. She periodically glanced behind her to see the dark figure hypnotically shift back and forth among the trees. Her adrenaline rush, accompanied by her fears, made the journey bearable as she tried to retrace her path back home.

She stumbled through the woods with her injured ankle over the inclined surface blanketed with fog. Branches continued to snap and pop off in the forest as she forced herself to not turn around to see if it was following behind. The pain intensified to a holy glory of swears as she made her way through and over the obstacles in the middle of the night. In the distance, she could see the faint lights emanating through the trees ahead. With relief knowing that the street was not too much further, she tripped headfirst onto the ground as footsteps approached closer from behind.

Beverly turned herself over as she cradled her arms over her belly, with a maternal instinct to protect her baby in the womb. She took a second to look around the landscape to see if she was still being followed, but the darkness of night and fog obscured her surroundings. Branches and twigs crackled and popped off in the distance as it slowly approached from all directions. She pushed herself up to her knees, then back to her feet, and continued to hobble back toward the street lights several feet ahead of her.

Beverly came to the end of the road and picked up Tiny's leash on the ground as she wiped away her tears, then quickly looked back to the woods to see burning red eyes off in the distance. She turned forward and sprinted on her limp foot after reaching the concrete. The street lights began to flicker off, one by one, as she ran down the street toward her home. She fell onto her lawn in exhaustion and crawled toward the front door before getting back to her feet again. Before closing the door, she turned to see the street lights flicker off and on in a strobe-effect as a shadowy figure emerged from the forest. She slammed the door shut and locked it behind her.

Beverly stared out the window only to not find anything coming after her as the street lights turned back on. "None of this is real, I'll find Tiny in the morning." She told herself as she walked across the living room floor, leaving muddy footprints as her pajamas were torn and covered with dirt, sweat, and blood. Beverly kicked off her shoes and grabbed a bag of frozen peas from the freezer, then went upstairs to the bathroom. She looked over to her bedroom to find Adam sound asleep and unaware of her absence.

She quietly grabbed a change of clothes and ran a hot bath. She got into the tub and soaked in the warmth of the water as she continued to shiver from the cold night air. She placed the bag of peas on her ankle to reduce the swelling and grimaced from the pain. She tried to think about what had just happened if it was all in her head and hoping it was just another bad dream. She thought of Tiny and wondered if the blood on the ground was his or if he was still wandering out there, alone and scared as much as she was.

She broke down and cried as she laid there alone in the tub, fearing this wasn't in her head anymore, and whatever she had faced before was back and couldn't be stopped. She held her belly and remembered the night the entity attacked her in bed and what he told her the night when she thought she had finally defeated it. *Once the seal has been broken, it cannot be undone. I shall return to take what is mine.* Not only does she fear for her own safety, but of her entire family now. She stepped out of the tub as the water slowly drained, leaving behind dirt and soil that accumulated near the drain.

She dried herself off and changed into clean clothes, then made her way to her bedroom. She left the hallway lights on as she closed and locked her bedroom door behind her. Beverly walked toward her bedroom window, looking outward, not seeing anything unusual. She climbed into bed next to Adam, trying not to disturb him. I'll wait until tomorrow to tell him what had happened. She turned away from him, feeling the same loneliness she had felt from her childhood as she quietly cried herself to sleep from exhaustion.

The night fell silent as she continued to periodically wake up, rollover, and fall back asleep. A presence slowly stirred her awake. Beverly's eyes widened in fear as the dark figure was in the corner of her room as she laid there paralyzed once again. Beverly screamed for Adam to wake up, but came out as moans as the figure stepped from out of the shadows. It didn't come toward her but instead over to the crib near the foot of the bed.

She helplessly watched as the being looked over the empty crib, staring down into it with its intense red eyes. The entity reached with its long slender hands down into the crib to grab for what would soon be inside. She felt severe pain in her abdomen, as it continued to reach inside the crib. It looked back over to her as it retracted its long arms, then walked over toward the foot of the bed. Beverly desperately tried to move, hoping to wake Adam, but without success as she continued to lay still as the entity leaned over them.

It first glanced toward Adam, who quietly slept, then turned its attention back over to Beverly as it walked alongside the bed, before inching itself closer to her. It leaned its beastly face toward her as its mouth opened, revealing rows of teeth with an unbearable stench of rotting, burnt flesh. Beverly closed her eyes as it stroked her hair with its long, cold fingers.

Frost began to form over the windows as it leaned closer, "Adam can't help you, Beverly. No one can help you now. The time has finally come. I shall return to take what belongs to me," it said into her mind, before walking away from her. She cried to herself as it vanished into the darkness of the corner of the room, then disappeared into the shadows where it once originated. She laid there in agony and fear, waiting for the morning sun to slowly rise through the bedroom. The light of day seemed so far away on that long night.

CHAPTER TWENTY-THREE

Beverly woke with full-control of her body as she screamed in agonizing pain, which jarred Adam up from his deep slumber. She sat straight up in the bed, hysterical with Adam looking over in confusion.

"Where were you?" Beverly shouted.

"I was sleeping, what are you talking about?" Adam said, sitting up in bed as Beverly continued to tremble with fear.

"I don't know anymore! I lost Tiny last night in the woods while taking him for a walk. It was right before you mentioned the visions you had two weeks ago. What you saw is back again," rejecting Adam's hand as he tried to console her.

"I don't understand. You took him for a walk without saying anything. Then I went upstairs and fell asleep," he said, frustrated and irritable.

"He just ran away from me. He wouldn't listen, and I couldn't stop him. He just ran and ran, like he was after something. I chased after him in the woods to only find his blood and fur. Then that thing…that fucking thing…had returned and chased me home…it came into our fucking bedroom. And you…and you, Adam…didn't fucking even know it!" Beverly said, sounding delusional.

"It could have all just been a bad dream. I'm sure that Tiny is okay and resting downstairs," Adam said as he tried to get her to go back to sleep.

"No! Tiny is fucking gone…gone forever… Sayonara. Dead! And now that thing wants our baby!" Beverly yelled, getting out of bed.

"Honey, this is all just in your head. Its all folklore and silly nightmares. There's no way something attacked Tiny, then broke into our home without me noticing it." Adam said, trying to reason with her.

"No! It was real, and it was his blood. I know what I saw out there. I don't care if you don't believe me."

"It just keeps getting harder and harder for me to believe. I just don't think whatever you saw was Tiny. I'll call my friend later this morning, and we will go out to look for him," he said, getting out of bed to use the bathroom.

"Okay, but I'm coming with you," she said defiantly.

"You need to relax, hon. Things will be okay," Adam said as he watched Beverly start to clutch her abdomen and grimace in pain.

"What's wrong? Are you okay?" As he walked to the other side of the bed, noticing her bruised, swollen ankle.

"I've felt this pain before. This pain...This pain doesn't feel like any of the false contractions I've had before. It started again last night as it came into our room," she said. "Our baby. Oh god! I think my baby is coming," she said as she sat on the edge of the bed, experiencing intense contractions.

"Holy Shit!" Adam shouted as he put on his shoes and grabbed for their coats. "You think this is the real deal?" He said as Beverly grabbed him by the shirt collar, bringing him closer as sweat poured from her face.

"Does it look like I'm fucking faking?" Beverly yelled, releasing her grip in pain. She laid back in bed, holding her distended belly as Adam tried to brush away the sleepy haze from his head.

"We need to get to the hospital now," Adam said as he helped her over his shoulder, then walked her out of the room and downstairs. "Breathe Beverly, just breathe for me," he said, trying to reassure her as she clutched on to him and the handrail. Adam noticed Tiny was nowhere downstairs as he helped her to the front door, making their way to his Jeep.

It was a quarter past six in the morning, as Adam pulled out of the driveway, making his way down the street toward the center of town to the local medical center. "I think my water just broke," she said as he rushed her to the hospital.

"Hang in there, honey. We're almost there," Adam said as he pulled swiftly into the parking lot, repeatedly honking his horn to get the attention of the security guards near the entrance. "I need a wheelchair, STAT!" Adam yelled out the window as one of the newer security guards ran inside, beckoning his request, as the others walked over, used to false alarms from panicked families.

"What's wrong?" The t all a nd l anky guard said, looking into the car window at Beverly.

"My wife is in labor!" Adam yelled over to them as he rolled down the passenger window. They noticed her distress and tried to open the door as the rookie guard rolled up with the wheelchair.

"Unlock the door, sir," the guard said as he pulled on the handle.

"Yeah, sorry," Adam said as he unlocked the door for them to help her into the chair, then brought her into triage. One of the valets took Adam's keys as he rushed into the hospital behind them. The triage nurse assessed Beverly's contractions, which were two minutes in duration and three minutes apart. The nurse paged the attending emergency medical doctor to alert him of a possible pending childbirth. The doctor emerged from the closed double doors—to examine her out in triage so he could decide if he would deliver in the ED or send her to labor and delivery.

Adam stood there silent and listened as the doctor inquired about her due date, risk factors, and number of pregnancies. He also asked if there had been any bleeding or fluid discharge along with her contractions. Beverly mentioned that her water had already broke. He assessed her within a matter of seconds, which felt

like an eternity for Adam as he waited helplessly by her
side.

"Call up to Doctor Wassermann, the obstetrician
from the labor and delivery floor, and tell him we
have a twenty-six-year-old female in active labor, and
she'll be coming from triage." The emergency
doctor said as the nurse made the call, then turned
to Adam to explain they will bring her directly up to
the floor. The emergency physician wished her well
as the hospital security guard, and another emergency
nurse escorted them to the near-by elevator, taking
them to the fifth floor in the hospital.

"Why isn't she going to the ER? Adam asked as
they got into the elevator.

"The emergency doctor assessment concluded
she was not in imminent delivery and would receive
more care from the specialists on our labor and
delivery floor than in the emergency room. I'm an
experienced nurse and have an obstetrician kit with
me just in case if I need to deliver her baby," she
explained to reassure him more so than Beverly was
concerned. They exited the elevator to the labor and
delivery wing and checked in as Beverly continued to
have contractions.

"Can we hurry this registration stuff up, please?" Adam impatiently stated as he looked over to his wife in pain.

"Hello, I'm the head obstetrician, and we'll take great care of her," Doctor Jeremiah Wassermann said, introducing himself as he walked over to greet them. "We'll bring Beverly to her room and conduct a thorough assessment and will perform an ultrasound immediately. When we deliver your child today, I will need you to remain calm in the room. Do you understand this?"

"I understand," Adam said as the technician brought her to her room and helped her into a hospital gown. One nurse quickly performed the ultrasound of her uterus as the other nurse placed her on the electrocardiogram monitor after taking Beverly's vitals. Adam waited in the corner when Doctor Wassermann entered the room with his chart and examined the nurse's findings. The doctor knew her labor would soon be imminent. First, he needed consent for pain relief, but Beverly refused any medications to help reduce pain or induce labor.

"It is okay if you want a natural birth, but if the pain gets too intense, do not hesitate to ask for anything," he said as her contractions continued.

"Just get him the hell out of me!" Beverly yelled as she sweated profusely.

"That's it, Beverly, just keep pushing. We'll take it from here," a middle-aged nurse said to her in a calm southern accent, as if she had been in her position before. "I'm trying over here!" Beverly said, then yelled for Adam as he stumbled over to hold her hand as she continued to push.

Beverly gripped Adam's hand like a tight vice, squeezing it to a pale white, matching the color of her face. She continued to scream and focus on her contractions, then took a quick look around the room. Beverly saw Adam's terrified face, along with a team of doctors and nurses by her feet. She noticed someone slowly entering the room, with his presence not drawing anyone else's attention. The tall man had long flowing golden blond hair with eyes of vibrant emerald green as he walked amongst the staff.

The unexpected visitor didn't wear hospital scrubs or a doctor's coat, but a cloak made of a pearl white and golden fabric. He walked in silently and observant of the room before making eye contact with her. She stared back into his eyes, making it easier to focus on pushing through the continuous labor pains. A sense of comfort washed over her as she slowed her breathing and began to push with ease.

"That's it, Beverly! We're almost there," the nurse said as Beverly paid no attention and faded out all the other distractions in the room. Adam's voice and everyone else around her sounded muffled as if she was submerged underwater.

The figure's aura radiated a vibrant golden light as he walked over to her without anyone noticing him. Without speaking, he brushed his hand over Beverly's abdomen sending an unexpected warming sensation throughout her body, making her more relaxed. Unsure why no one else had noticed this person who had entered the room, Beverly felt a sense of comfort by this stranger. As if in a trance, she continued to watch him as he stepped away from the bed, taking a few steps toward Adam, who appeared to be under more stress than she was in.

The mysterious man laid his hand over Adam's shoulders, bringing him at ease as he held Beverly's hand, which relaxed and now more joyous than the previous struggle. Sliding his hand away from Adam, the man walked behind the hospital bed, disappearing from view. Beverly pushed with ease through her contractions, turning her head behind her. She remembered the night six months ago at the sleep center. Her visions came clear to her all at once.

"That's it, Beverly. She's fully dilated. Push, Beverly! Push!" The doctor said as she turned her head back around.

"Don't be afraid, Beverly. Don't be afraid to let go," the cloaked man whispered into her ear. Golden light filled the entire room then dissipated, taking the entity along with it. She snapped back to reality and found no one standing there except for Adam, who had kept holding her hand.

"We have crowning! Keep pushing, Beverly. We're almost there!" The doctor proclaimed as he helped the new baby boy into the world. The senior nurse suctioned his nostrils, then mouth to clear his airway. The doctor guided his shoulders out with ease, cradling her baby in his arms with several sterile towels. Beverly's attention was immediately drawn to the cries of her newborn baby, as the staff clamped the umbilical cord in two separate places after it stopped pulsating.

"Would you like the honors, Dad?" The doctor said, allowing Adam to cut the cord between the two clamps. Doctor Wassermann performed an Apgar test to determine his vitals, then wiped off the excess fluid from his small cold and shriveled body. He handed him to the nurse, who then wrapped him in heated blankets while placing a blue beanie over his head.

"Is that baby Johnathan?" Beverly said with a laugh of exhaustion.

"Yes, it is! He is very beautiful," the nurse said with a smile as she handed him over to her. Beverly held her child for the first time as Adam stood over them with a grin across his face.

"He's so precious," Beverly said with tears of joy as she held him in her arms. Johnathan stopped crying as he looked up to her with his blue eyes. The nurse rechecked her vitals as the doctor waited in the room to deliver the afterbirth.

"Congratulations to both of you, Mr. and Mrs. Grove. Once we deliver the placenta, I'll then administer your child's vitamin K shot and take a heel-stick blood sample.

"What are those for? Is our child okay?" Adam inquired anxiously.

"These are all normal procedures after childbirth. The shot is to increase Vitamin K deficiencies found in all newborns. The blood sample allows us to find other deficiencies or any hormonal issues, such as hypothyroidism," he explained to them as the nurse performed another Apgar test to ensure adequate cardiopulmonary perfusion. "Nothing to worry about, you have a healthy baby boy, we always run these tests as routine screening," he said, making them at ease. Twenty minutes later, Beverly delivered her placenta as she continued to slowly bleed.

"It's okay if you want to start breastfeeding, it will help stop the bleeding," the nurse explained as the doctor controlled the hemorrhage with sterile pads.

"I just want to thank you again, Doctor. I also wanted to apologize about before. I'm obviously new to this. Sorry, if I tried to rush you guys back there," Adam said with an embarrassed expression.

"No hard feelings, it happens. I deal with frantic parents all the time," Wassermann said with a smile as he removed his face shield, gown, and gloves, then walked over to wash his hands in the sink. Adam followed over to give him a handshake thanking him again. "I'll leave you guys alone to become more acquainted with your baby and check up on you three later," he said with a smile. Beverly reciprocated back, then looked back down at Johnathan with utmost fulfillment. The nurse showed them the call bell button on the remote before she exited, leaving Beverly alone with her family.

"Isn't he so precious?" Beverly said to Adam as he leaned toward them to give him a kiss on his little head, then kissed Beverly.

"He sure is! I'm the happiest guy in the world right now. I can't wait till he is at home and see how he likes his new crib." Beverly laughed as tears of joy and happiness ran down her cheek as she held him tighter in her arms. She felt the warmth of his body radiating through hers.

"Adam, I'm sorry about before. I know I was acting out of hand, blaming you for not being there. The truth is, you have always been there, and I am very sorry if I took all my stress out on you," Beverly said, looking over to him.

"I appreciate that, hon. Just know that I'll always love you and will be there for the both of you." Adam said as he brushed his hand against his son's back.

"I know you will be a terrific father for our son. That's why I have to tell you…" she paused for a moment. "If anything would ever happen to me…I want you to be able to carry on and be there for our son. Can you make that promise for me?" Beverly said with a tired expression on her face.

"What on earth would happen to you? You are talking nonsense," Adam said with a hesitant laugh to brighten the mood.

"Just promise me, okay?" Beverly said as she kissed her child on the top of his head.

"I will, and I promise you. But nothing will ever happen to you, Beverly. We will make it through all our hardships together," he said to her.

"Would you like to hold him?" Beverly said with a smile.

"Of course, I would love too!" Adam said as he clumsily took his son away from Beverly's arms. Adam's son began to cry, "Shoosh, their little guy, daddy's here," Adam said as he sat in the chair with him in his arms, rocking him back and forth. His baby settled down, then fell asleep as Beverly was about to do the same. She looked over to them with a smile before closing her eyes.

CHAPTER TWENTY-FOUR

Beverly woke above her body as Adam held their child in the chair next to her. She glanced around the room, then over toward the window to find an owl perched on the ledge looking in. Beverly stared into its large hypnotizing eyes as if to see into the heart of the universe. She floated toward the window as her own umbilical cord, made of light, followed behind to link her physical body, which laid motionless on the bed.

"Don't be afraid, Beverly. Life is beautiful and continuous as long as you embrace the light. Fear will only lead to darkness and consume everything you know and love," the entity projected into her mind as she passed through the closed window. The owl flapped its wings and took flight, disappearing into the sunlight. "Remember, the physical realm is not the end," it spoke to her as she desperately flew after her spirit guide only to lose sight of him in the sunlight.

"Wait! What am I supposed to do?" Beverly cried out, lost, and afraid as she ascended into the cloudless sky.

She approached the stratosphere, as the sky quickly turned from pale blue to black. The stars were vivid and vibrant as she continued searching for Ezekiel. Beverly turned to see the Earth slowly rotate as it was suspended in time and space with her silver cord stretching down toward the surface. In the distance, the sunlight illuminated the planet, eclipsing the other half in darkness. Dread and hopelessness overcame her as she floated helplessly above the world without any signs of her spirit guide.

The stars spun rapidly around her, then melted from the sky, along with her conceived reality of the universe accelerating away at extraordinary speeds. Left disoriented in the void of darkness, a low vibration radiated throughout her core. Followed by a new, strange sensation as if she had floated toward a black hole that was trying to rip her apart by spaghettification, as it continued to penetrate her body and mind.

A stone spiral staircase materialized underneath her feet as she suddenly lost the ability to fly. An endless dark sky periodically illuminated her surroundings with flashes of light from the grey clouds above. From where she stood, there wasn't a top or bottom to the staircase, only endless spirals of stone steps along with storm clouds violently igniting from above. The emanating low vibrations ran through her body, sending a chill of impending doom, loneliness, and despair. Her cord now felt like a ball and chain of all her lifelong burdens as she ascended the endless staircase.

Out of desperation, Beverly continued to climb as the lightening intensified the higher she climbed. Through her periphery, an entity came hurling through the center of the staircase from the skies above. The figure resembled Ezekiel, *maybe he came back to rescue me*, she thought, but noticed the entity was stripped of his armor and had black featherless wings covering its body. It dove headfirst with folded wings, as it crashed straight into her, knocking her off the steps. She plummeted as the dark entity held on tighter as she continued to fall between the double helix spiral staircase.

The descent was quick and disorienting as she felt the sharp pain of its claws piercing into her flesh. Beverly regained control of her senses, then looked up to see the dark angel staring back at her. The supernatural being unfurled its black wings to slow their descent toward the perpetual darkness below. She tried to break free as it lowered her to the bottom while flapping its disfigured wings. The entity suddenly released her as she fell the short distance toward the ground, followed by a splash of chilling water.

Beverly regained her footing, shaking, and trembling, while trying to orient herself in the darkness. She stood in knee depth ice-cold water of this endless world while sensing the presence of the creature lurking off in the distance. The staircase had dissipated as the storm clouds remained ominous in the sky, revealing the hellish landscape with fire raining from above. The flaming embers crashed into the waters below, igniting the surface with violent explosions, which continued to burn over the surface.

The fire scattered across the endless lake, illuminating the fear in her face as the storm continued to drop flaming embers from above. She could sense the low vibrations in the water as flapping wings approached her from a distance. "Adam, Ezekiel, Mom, Dad, someone, please help me!" Beverly pleaded, hoping to fly away and escape, but felt chained and imprisoned to this new hellish world. The entity coasted along the surface, parting the water with small waves as it glided toward her. Beverly tried to run but felt the fear and darkness grip her tighter as she sank further into the quicksand.

Distant moans and cries rose from out of the darkness as souls suffered in the waters below, trying to gasp for salvation. The dark angel stood several feet in front of her with vibrant green eyes and long wavy black hair. His body had a muscular build, similar to Ezekiel, which was covered in a torn cloth tunic instead of the typical armor worn by the Guardians. He retracted his wings behind him, which had several white feathers tattered along the black scaly skin. He possessed the same similarities of the others at the temple, but only stripped away, well before the rise of humanity and their observable universe.

"See, Beverly. I'm not all that frightening in my true form," he said as he waded through the fire-covered water toward her.

"This is not your real form! Ezekiel told me the truth about your kind, now let me go!" Beverly said, trying to free herself.

"Ezekiel?" He laughed. "Had it ever dawned on you, maybe he was not telling you the whole truth. I can show you more than he could ever do," he said, finally facing her.

"What truth. This hell? You have shown me enough!" Beverly yelled as he caressed her face with his hand.

"Come now. This is only the depths of the spirit world where lost souls reside. I'm an entity that transcends the universe and heavens. You can one day be as powerful as me. I just only have one request before I set your soul free. You act as a gatekeeper into the physical realm, and you have something I want," he said as Beverly tensed as he brushed his hand across her face, trying to look her in the eyes.

"I already know what you're after. You want my child's soul. I'll never allow you to take him from me!" Beverly yelled as she pushed his arm away and turned her head, repulsed by his presence.

"If you don't adhere to my simple request, I will slowly drag you and your entire family down to the depths of this world for eternity. I'm offering you a bargain here so that you and your beloved Adam can live out the rest of your lives in peace. To one day possess the same power I have after you die," he said as he grabbed her chin and leaned in closer, looking directly into her eyes.

"I would never agree for you to take my baby away from me! Go to hell, you piece of shit!" Beverly screamed, then spat into his face.

"Oh, so now you have become the brave and fearless, Beverly, which I've never had the opportunity to truly meet. Don't give me a reason to reintroduce myself to you. Unfortunately, you have no other choice, and I will take all your souls with me. You'll live the rest of your lives out in misery until the day I come in the night, after your final breath, to claim your souls forever. And then, and only then, you will return to this tomb of despair." He threatened as his eyes burned to an intense red.

She pushed him away and regained her footing to finally move freely in the water. "You have tormented me all my life, killed my parents, then my dog, and now you're trying to bargain with me to take my baby away from me! I'm not fucking afraid of you!" She screamed as he stepped backward, surprised by her defiant resistance against his powers.

"You're not afraid of me? Oh, you will be. You were right, this is not my true form," he said and hysterically laughed as his human manifestation broke apart, molting from its shell. The human disguise fell underneath the water like shedding reptilian skin, as the hideous beast from her nightmares, revealed itself to her. She tried to not show any fear by staring back at him while slowly regaining her footing underneath the water.

"You even said yourself, I am the gatekeeper to the physical realm. You're powerless without me. You're one pathetic piece of shit, no wonder why you were cast out of the higher realms to live in this world of despair." Beverly said as she tried to summon the dagger from her last encounter without any luck. The supernatural being stepped forward and grabbed her by the neck as she continued to struggle to break free.

"How valiant of you, but nothing can save you and your family now," it spoke into her mind, then slowly opened its mouth, revealing the rows of sharp teeth. "I shall feast on your soul and flesh, then of your child's pure energy," the entity projected into her mind as she tried to break free. "But first let me show you…" it said, pulling her head underwater.

Images of her childhood, present, and future life flashed before her eyes as she was submerged while struggling to break free. She envisioned nightmares of Adam and her son as they grew older with or without her. She experienced within one second all their pain and suffering as the entity grew stronger. He pulled her up for a moment as she continued to fight back, kicking and screaming. "You see now what I'm capable of? Maybe not quite yet," it said as he placed her head back underneath the surface. Rapid images of war, death, pandemics, famine, and evil, continued to plague her species entire existence long into the future. He pulled her head up from the cold black water with her hair sticking along her face.

"I can create this or prevent this. Your species has always been powerless. It desperately clings onto the belief of an all-powerful deity to straighten out your pathetic existence. Well, here I am. I'm your new God now, and I expect my sacrifice of gratitude," it said as she gasped for air as if she was back in her physical body. The entity lifted Beverly and threw her to the side as she struggled to get to her feet. "I'll ask you one more time. All I need is your child's soul, and I'll set you free. If not, I will torment him until he becomes the next mass murderer. You know, like the one who killed your parents," the demon cackled as he sank his claws into her side, lifting her up into the air.

Beverly summoned all of her strength and concentration as the dagger manifested into her free hand. "Haven't we been down this road before, Beverly? You know you can't defeat me, I'll just keep returning when you least expect it," it laughed as he clutched tighter, opening its mouth to consume her energy.

"Maybe so, but I know who can. I will deprive you of what you want, and watch you slowly die by their sword," Beverly said with the last bit of strength she had left.

"Your species has always intrigued me with their meaningless heroics." It said to her before depleting the rest of her energy.

"Don't ever underestimate what the human spirit and a pissed off mother can do. Rot in fucking hell, you son of a bitch!" Beverly brought the dagger behind her back and severed the silver cord with one solid tug.

"No!!" The demon yelled, dropping Beverly to her knees in the water. The cord recoiled away from her, vanishing into the dark void. She knelt while staring up into the sky, without noticing any change. She held her breath as the entity looked around to find they were still alone. "You have sacrificed yourself for your child. How precious, but I have other ways of getting what I want. All you did was sacrifice yourself to me with no glorious cause," he laughed as she closed her eyes and helpless on her knees.

Back in the hospital, Beverly's electrocardiogram went from normal sinus rhythm to asystole, chiming the machine's alarms. Adam woke as his son cried in his arms. He heard over the intercom PA system, "Code Blue, Room 524! Code Blue. 524!"

"Beverly...Beverly!" Adam looked over toward Beverly, who laid unresponsive in bed. He saw a flat line across the screen of her ECG monitor. Adam jumped from his chair as the hospital team rushed into the room with a medication crash-cart. He held onto his son, as a nurse checked for a carotid pulse, then started to do chest compressions.

Doctor Wassermann rushed in to take control of the situation, ordering epinephrine through her IV as they continued CPR. "What's going on, Doctor?" Adam said as his son cried in his arms.

"I don't know yet, your wife went into spontaneous cardiac arrest. We need to work quickly. It'll be best for you to leave the room so we can try and reverse it," the doctor said as he oversaw the resuscitation.

"I need to stay, I won't get in the way I promise," Adam said to him as the doctor nodded with approval as he ordered Vasopressin to be administered. They placed the ECG pads only to find a non-shockable rhythm. The doctor went to the head of the bed, then lowered it to perform endotracheal intubation to secure her airway. Adam turned away and continued to console his baby.

"I'm sorry, Adam. But, one of the technicians will have to escort you out. We'll need to focus on the reversible treatments that caused this," the doctor said as he looked back down to Beverly.

"I understand, Doctor. Please save my wife! Adam said as he was escorted out of the room.

The fiery brimstone rained down over the endless landscape as Beverly scrambled back to her feet. The impacts exploded, sending water twenty meters into the air, followed by turbulent waves in the lake of fire. "Not what you were expecting?" Beverly said as she stood, watching the entity look around in confusion. "Did I upset the balance?" She said sarcastically as the constant bombardment of fire and rock ruptured the ground below. The water drained through the fissures and cracks as the rocky surface violently tore apart. The landscape was now of ragged stones as the crevices broke away, as water spilled from the edges, draining into the darkness.

"You can't defeat me, silly girl," the dark angel said.

"I know I can't, but I certainly know who can. We all have to face our fears one day, right?" Beverly said with a grin as the ground crumbled underneath them, leaving trenches and vast mountains forming off in the distance. "I know what you fear most. And now they will come to rescue me. When the cord is severed, the golden bowl is broken, and the pitcher shatters against the spring, and only then, will set my soul free," she proclaimed as the grey skies parted, shining golden rays of light down upon the landscape.

"You'll never stand in the way of a mother and her child! I knew my sacrifice will benefit my family and all of mankind. Your time has come to receive your judgment."

"You'll well never defeat me or my kind," he said, opening his wings, then lifted himself off the ground and dove toward Beverly. He clutched deep into her flesh with burning red eyes while staring into her soul. Intense pain radiated through her as the demon dug his claws deep into her sides. "They don't care about you, Beverly. No one will ever care about you. I shall take you with me into the depths of hell!" He said as he opened his mouth, ready to devour her soul.

Beverly screamed out her last breath as the universe collapsed around her as a fiery portal opened beneath them. She no longer could fight back as she awaited her eternal demise, glancing up one last time to the stars, which slowly reappeared into the heavens as Earth floated off in the distance. Her silver cord flailed back and forth, no longer attached to her spiritual body. The

entity slowly descended into the fiery portal below.
"Your soul belongs to me now!" The demon said as it
opened his mouth wider, absorbing her energy as it
took her with him.

The emergency team continued resuscitation efforts
without success and prepared to cease their efforts
before Doctor Wassermann, gave the order to continue
as he went to talk to Adam. He turned toward his
staff with an expression of frustration and heartbreak
on his face. "I'm a physician who is used to bringing
life into this world, not departing from it." The doctor
said, wiping his brow as he stepped out of the room.
He turned toward Adam, who had been waiting in the
hallway with his baby, hoping for better news.

"Adam, we've been trying the best that we can,
but unfortunately, there aren't any clinical signs of
improvement. She hasn't had any changes in her heart
rhythm that we could treat. Her heart just stopped, and
we're running out of ideas how to get it going again,"
he said in a somber voice.

"What! How can this be? She was talking to me
an hour ago before she fell asleep." He rushed passed

Doctor Wassermann back into the room. A nurse took their baby to the nursery as Adam remained bedside, looking over Beverly as she laid lifeless as they continued compressions. "Beverly, if you can hear me? I need you to keep fighting for me, …for all of us! I love you so much, Beverly!" Adam yelled to her as he placed his hand across her forehead and gave her a kiss before holding her limp hand.

"Adam, there's nothing else we can do, I am truly sorry," the doctor said as he looked over to him.

"She is strong! Beverly will make it, just keep trying!" Adam yelled as the doctor respected his wishes and had his staff continue with another round of epinephrine and chest compressions. Adam held Beverly's hand, "I love you, we all love you, just come back home, sweetie." Adam said in desperation as he fell to his knees, crying at her bedside.

Beverly no longer struggled, as the beast descended into the hellish portal as it clutched onto her. She heard Adam's distant cries and voice penetrated through her head, as sorrow radiated through her, while being carried away against her will. She looked back toward Earth as her lifeless cord slowly retracted into the atmosphere. She prayed for forgiveness as the entity laughed at her futile faith.

Beverly, in a dream-like state, glanced around at the shimmering stars as the pit opened up beneath her. She slipped in between the dimensions of the physical and spiritual realm, slowly losing consciousness as her body felt as if it would soon be torn apart in the black hole's event horizon. She looked up toward the stars as space and time no longer ceased to exist. Several lights zoomed past overhead, bringing back memories of the shooting stars from her camp trip in the Adirondacks. The stars grew brighter, shining beams of light toward her as she slipped in and out of consciousness.

"There's no escape," the being said as the light grew more intense around them. Giant tentacles emerged from the fiery pit below to constricted around them. Beverly heard in her subconsciousness of Adam's voice calling out to her. Beverly heard her mother's distant voice, telling her to fight back.

Beverly woke from her trance, "I won't be afraid anymore." Without hesitation, she summoned the dagger in her hand, which glowed with a blinding light, then rammed it into the neck of the beast, releasing its grip and setting her free. The lights in the ether gradually encapsulated them, as they floated suspended over the fiery portal. Guardians appeared off in the distance and quickly descended from the heavens above.

"Beverly, your time has come!" The beast said as it lunged after her, but was intercepted by several glowing entities which manifested around them. Beverly saw angel-like soldiers armed with swords between her and the beast. A blinding light of pure energy illuminated in front of her.

"Ezekiel!" Beverly cried out. She looked back to Earth as her silver cord descended beneath the clouds toward her physical body.

"I'm not surprised you would show up to try and save this pathetic soul," the dark entity said, as he turned back into his human form.

"We have an obligation to protect all life. She has a pure soul, and I cannot allow for you to take her," Ezekiel said as he drew his sword.

"It's sad how it shall come down to this, we were brothers, and now, you feel it's your duty to protect this pathetic girl," he said, locking eyes with Ezekiel.

"You've chosen your path, and I have chosen mine. I preserve life while you seek to destroy it. I cannot allow you to take her soul. I'll make sure you have no control in the spiritual realm as we have cast out your kind before." Ezekiel said as the other guardians surrounded him over the portal.

"So be it, brother. You can't defeat me, and I shall drag you all back to the hell that you created for me!" He said, engaging with the other guardians, before quickly changing back to his beastly form. Ezekiel dodged his first charge as he slashed his flank with his sword, which shimmered with glowing light, spewing purple dark-matter energy into space.

The other two guardians repeatedly stabbed the beast as he fell closer toward the portal before consuming him. The dark entity was engulfed into the fiery pit, as the dimensional portal closed the gateway, before vanishing into a singularity. Time and space was restored back to equilibrium.

CHAPTER TWENTY-FIVE

Beverly woke in a large open field, near a narrow river as tall weeds blew back in forth in the breeze. A large mountain peek stood off toward the far horizon. The tree next to her casted no visible shadow as the sun warmed her skin. A radiating light encapsulated Beverly, blinding her momentarily. She looked toward a cloaked man who appeared in front of her with an aura of pure white energy. The man reached out his hand for her to join him.

"Ezekiel, you came back to save me," Beverly said, trying to regain her strength.

"I had to come. You sacrificed yourself for your family, and it was my duty to protect you. You were anointed by a higher power when your soul was set free."

"Did I make a mistake?" Beverly said, sobbing while thinking about Adam and her newborn son."

Ezekiel stared into her tearful eyes, "You did what

you had too, so you could protect the ones you love. There is evil in this universe, and you gave the ultimate sacrifice to try and defeat it," he said sincerely. "Your higher vibrations summoned us, and you no longer have to be afraid anymore. Your spirit will always live on," he said as he laid his hand on her forehead, revealing visions of her parents living on after death. Remember, evil will always persist in your world, but you can now live in harmony with your parents and one day be reunited with your own family." Ezekiel said to her as she turned toward a blinding light glowing ahead of them. Beverly took his hand and crossed the river and into the light…

The doctor finally called off resuscitation efforts, as the staff stopped performing chest compressions. "Adam, I'm sorry, but there's nothing left we can do. She is gone," he said as Adam fell to his knees and took her limp hand into his. He sat there for several agonizing minutes before taking a ring out of his pocket, then slid it onto her finger. "Till death do us part," Adam said as he stood back up, then leaned over to kiss her. "Life just isn't fair. I hope you finally find peace my darling," Adam began to emotionally breakdown by her side as the nurse tried to comfort him.

"Fuck it all!" Adam yelled, turning to her with tears of rage in his eyes. "Bring me my son." Adam said in a monotone voice.

"Of course," she responded and exited the room as the doctor walked over to him.

"I'm so sorry, Adam. We did everything that we could. A mother could die during childbirth without any signs or symptoms. We can do an autopsy to find out the cause of her postpartum death?" He said with hesitation.

"No, that won't be necessary. I don't want anyone disturbing her body. I want to give her the final rest she deserves. Doctor, can I ask you a question?"

"Yes, Adam, of course."

"Have you ever loved someone more than your own life? Have you ever loved someone where they always brought out the best in you? Where you would change your stubborn ways and would do anything to make it work. Have you ever loved someone so much that you would move heaven and Earth for them?"

"Yes, I have, Adam. I met my wife thirty years ago and had three beautiful daughters with her. Unfortunately, this world isn't fair. I had also lost the woman whom I loved through thick and thin, to cancer eight years ago. Her memories live on through our children, though. Every day that I spend with my daughters reminds me of her. Cherish every moment you have with your son and know she will always be with the both of you in spirit. Again, I'm so sorry for your loss, Adam."

"Thank you, Doctor," Adam said. He turned to Beverly resting in her permanent slumber, reflecting on everything she had done for him. All the memories they shared from day one, good and bad. He remembered what she had always represented to him. Love and affection, which he felt he took for granted at times. Something he will always have to live with till his dying age.

During the first week of June, friends and family gathered in the Brooklyn cemetery where her parents resided. The late morning fog lifted as the sun peaked through the overcast over the hilltops. The dew glistened off the new grass as trees sprouted their first leaves. Magnolia flowers bloomed along the shrubbery of the iron gates. A priest and undertaker stood by an open grave as everyone took their respected places around the casket and six-foot hole in the ground.

The young pasture held a Gideons bible, prepared to give his sermon. "We're all gathered here today, under the grace of God, to remember and mourn the life of a wonderful woman, wife, and mother, Beverly Hollinger-Grove. I would like to read to you all a passage from Psalm:23. Please join me in prayer and repeat after me. The Lord is my shepherd; I shall not want. He makes me lie down in green pastures. He leads me beside still waters. He restores my soul. He leads me in paths of righteousness for his name's sake. Even though I walk through the valley of the shadow of death, I will fear no evil, for you are with me, amen," the pastor looked up to the bowed heads chanting amen in front of him.

"Thank you all for coming to join us in the remembrance of dear Beverly. We are all children of God as our spiritual bodies reside in our temporary corporeal vessels of flesh and bone. We're all blessed with the free will to choose any path in life we desire. The most fulling path we can follow is the one of good faith towards our family, friends, and neighbors by giving personal sacrifices to help the greater good of mankind. Beverly was just that, as she committed her life for greatness for the ones around her. When we leave here today and go back to our lives and daily routines. Remember, just one thing, all we simply need to do is love thy neighbor, sow the fruits of our labors and turn away from temptation. We will all one day rejoice in the presence of the Lord and be reunited with Beverly and the ones we love, amen…Adam, if you have any final words." The pastor stepped aside as Adam walked somberly toward her casket and rested his hand on it for a moment.

"Thank you, everyone, for coming today," clearing his throat as he looked over to his mother, who held his son in her arms. "My beloved wife, mother of my child, and best friend gave me the greatest joys in life. Several days ago, on the same day that our son was born, she turned to me and had me promise something to her. As if she knew her time was running out." Adam said as he wiped tears away from his bloodshot eyes before continuing.

"I had to promise to carry on and take care of our son if anything would ever happen to her. I thought she was just tired and emotionally protective. Little did I know that would be the last time I would ever speak to her again." Adam said as he tried to hold back his tears and frustrations. "Of course, I made that promise and will always continue to uphold it. Beverly shaped me into a better man than I ever could've been without her. She was the perfect woman for me in every way. I can still remember the first day we met…" he paused to recollect his thoughts.

On a long, seemingly endless summer night in Brooklyn, Adam and his friends arrived at the location where Kristen arranged to meet. Kyle and Eric greeted Kristen at the door—then followed her to the bar as she introduced them and Adam to Beverly, who sat quietly by herself, not expecting any company. Beverly's light blue eyes met Adams as she smiled back at him. Kristen playfully nudged Beverly as she whispered into her ear that he was single. Beverly laughed and nervously sipped her drink.

Kristen warmed them up by sharing stories of how Adam was a history nerd in class, even though no one took him seriously since he was also the captain of the lacrosse team and star receiver on the football team. Beverly sporadically brought up her love for ancient Hellenistic Greek culture with the hope of one day visiting all the islands. She became quiet after revealing too much of her passions. He smiled, then slid his chair closer to her and asked if she preferred the Mycenaean or Minoans. Beverly smiled and almost came to tears with laughter that he actually knew their history. Their conversations bounced between topics, some serious, some light, with playful banter throughout the evening.

After the last call, as everyone made their way outside, Beverly stood underneath the light post, illuminating her velvet dress as Adam took her hand. She stood there, smiling back, not knowing what to say as he leaned forward to kiss her. They embraced each other as the street traffic began to wind down for the evening. Kristen stood patiently by her car with a smile on her face as Adam's friends discussed sports with the bar's security guard around the corner. Beverly and Adam parted ways after saying goodbye, promising to one day see each other again.

"That very night, I made my first promise to her, which I will never break and follow through with. That promise was that I would see her again." Adam said as Kristen looked back at him with a tear running down her cheek. "I was never able to put myself in her shoes or understand completely what she was going through. Her life journey was a difficult one, and I hope she gets the final rest that she deserves. In this cemetery and over that very hill, her parent's gravestones still stand engraved with a poem she had written for them seventeen years ago—In tragedy, we must have hope. In life, we must learn to cope."

Adam took a moment to look up at the overcast skies before continuing, "today, I will try sweetheart... I promise you that I will try my best..."   Adam   said, looking   back   down   at   the ground weeping.

"I want to thank everyone who came out today to grieve and celebrate the life of my one and only true soul mate. When you go home today, I urge you to enjoy every moment you have with the ones who love and care for you and reciprocate that same love back. We're all in this world together for a limited amount of time, so there's no reason to hold onto anger and past regrets. In the words of my beautiful wife, In tragedy, we must have hope, and in life, we must cope. In remembrance of her, we must have the same strength that she had shown me. We must continue to fight. That is all, thank you…," Adam concluded as he placed his hand on her casket for the last time before stepping away in silence.

The late spring rain fell over them, as family and friends tossed a handful of soil over the top of Beverly's casket as it was lowered into the ground. They gathered underneath a nearby gazebo as the rain began to fall harder, while watching the undertaker restore the earth above her. The priest made the sign of the holy trinity over her grave, then walked over to bless Adam before making his way back to the hearse.

The rain slowly gave way to overcast, with a momentary break in the clouds as the sun shined down upon them.

Adam tensed as his father's hand rested against his shoulder. "I am sorry, son. I don't know how else to put it into words and comfort you in a time like this. Just know that your mother and I will always be there for you and Johnathan. We'll get through this together." Jacob said, trying to comfort him.

His father continued, "I have property that I've never told you about, far north from here. It has been a source of the lumber that I used for my business a long time ago. I'm too old to do anything with it, and you will inherit all of it starting today. It is in your hands if you choose to sell it or continue the family business." Adam nodded and took his son from his mother's arms and held him close.

"Thank you, Father," Adam said, then looked down at his child, "I'm so sorry you will never get to know your mother. But you are special, my son, just as she was special. You are a miracle to me and to all of us," Adam said as he kissed him on his forehead.

"Adam, you can stay with us tonight, if you want too?" His mother offered as he walked down the gazebo steps toward the car.

"I'll be staying at our house tonight to sort this all out. Thank you, though." Adam said as he gave his mother a kiss on the cheek, then said goodbye to them.

"Also, let me know if you ever need anything," Kristen said, walking over to give him a hug and kiss on the cheek before parting ways. Adam stood quietly looking back at the undertaker shoveling the last bit of dirt over the grave as he held his son in his arms. The sun was eclipsed by the clouds, followed by a caressing breeze and gentle rain. Adam treaded through the muddy grass and secured his child in the car seat in the back of his jeep. He took one last look toward the cemetery before getting back into his car to make his way back to Silver Lakes.

Three weeks later, before dawn, Adam sat on the couch downstairs, as his son slept in his crib in Beverly's room. He picked up the book on lucid dreaming and flipped through the pages toward the end where it mentioned astral projection. He took a sip from his coffee, then continued reading about the higher dimensions which were reserved for only the purest of spiritual beings. He noticed a diagram of a body resting in bed, connected to its spiritual form form with a cord linking the two together. Labeled below the picture, was a description of the astral cord connecting the physical body of the astral traveler.

One passage read that dark entities in the lower dimensional realms absorb the energy of the living when there was a path of least resistance, either brought on by emotional turmoil or mental anguish. The minds of the living can become susceptible to the will of these entities as they try and harvest their energy or have them serve as a vessel for their own bidding. Adam went to the last page of the chapter, where it explained that the astral traveler who enters the non-corporeal realm could only be protected once they have severed their own cord. Leaving behind their physical body to fully embrace their spiritual one, to close the gate of the lower dimensions, and be anointed by the protection of God.

"This can't be happening. This is all bullshit! Did she sacrifice herself?" Adam said to himself as he slammed the book shut, then threw it across the table. He got up from the couch and looked around the living room over to the new TV on its stand. He could envision the shattered pieces across the floor. He remembered all the nights of how terrified she was to simply go to sleep. Adam looked over to the kitchen where Tiny's food bowl once was, as he started to believe that this was all actually real.

He turned back to the TV stand, piecing it all mentally together, as his own vision of the dark entity sitting atop of it flooded back into his mind. Clarity finally came to his racing thoughts as he remembered how it was trying to persuade him to kill. *Kill who?* He thought, then it struck him like a storm without a distant warning. *It wanted me to kill her! The bedroom.* "Oh god, It wants my child!"

Adam rushed upstairs, tripping over his own steps as he ran toward the bedroom door, slamming it open. The glow of early morning sunlight illuminated the room, as he caught a glimpse of the dark shadowy figure towering over his son's crib. Long slender fingers slipping over his child's sleeping body before turning to Adam with a devilish grin across his face. But in reality, there was no one else in the room except for him and his child. Adam kept thinking to himself as he slowly doubted his own sanity before grabbing his son out of his crib. Adam sweated profusely as he held his crying child in his arms. He squatted to the floor, with his back against the door, sobbing uncontrollably.

After an hour of daybreak, Adam got back to his feet and made his way downstairs. He placed his son into his car seat and heated up a formula bottle for him, then rushed back upstairs to gather his things.

"We are going for a ride, my son," Adam said to him as he came downstairs and picked up Beverly's books before hurrying out the front door. "There's only one person I can count on right now." He said as he got into his car and made his way back down to New York City.

CHAPTER TWENTY-SIX

Adam walked into the office lobby of the 14th floor, pushing a stroller bassinet toward the secretary desk. "Do you have an appointment today, sir?" Autumn asked, turning her head to see the schedule displayed on her computer screen.

"Yes...I mean no...well, I mean the doctor will know who I am...," Adam finally said to her.

"You need an appointment and a referral, sir. We do not accept walk-ups, it's office policy," she said impatiently.

"Yes, I have a referral," he said, looking down at his son. "You know what? I can wait here all day until the doctor is free and he will recognize me. I just need to see him. Can you just do me that one favor?" Adam said as he reached down to give his son a pacifier.

"What is your name, sir?"

"Adam Grove. You can look under the name Hollinger, though."

The secretary took a second as the name sounded familiar to her. She pulled up the records of Beverly Hollinger in her system. The numerous visits from 2024 up till late last year populated her screen. Is she your…?"

"Yes. Beverly's my wife," Adam responded.

"I do remember her. But there is no record of you in our systems. How is she, by the way?"

"She is no longer with us… I need to see Doctor Spitzer, so if you could please pass along that message, that would be great, thanks." Adam said as the secretary looked over at him, then down at his son in the stroller.

"I'm so sorry, I'll see what I can do. Have a seat over there for the time being, sir," she said, trying not to get choked up.

"I'll do that, thanks." Twenty minutes had past when the double doors opened with a frantic middle-aged man exiting as the doctor escorted him to the secretary's desk for a follow-up. Jeff Spitzer spoke briefly with Autumn as she pointed across the room to where Adam sat. The doctor looked over surprised, then gestured for him to follow him into his office.

"How are you, Adam?" Doctor Spitzer said as he closed the doubled doors behind them.

"Well, I'm here today on behalf of my lovely wife Beverly," he said as he pushed his son's stroller toward the couch next to the recliner.

"I'm so sorry for your loss, Adam. I heard the news of her passing from Doctor Imamu, who attended the wake." Spitzer said, turning to face him.

"Why didn't you come?" Adam asked, making direct eye contact with him.

"I just couldn't go through it again. Come, Adam, take a walk with me." Doctor Spitzer gestured as they walked toward the window overlooking Central Park.

The leaves were a lush green blending in with the landscape and tree canopies below. The city's residents made their way along the parkways and city streets on their daily commutes. A random streaming consciousness that continued like clockwork day by day, year after year. A consciousness, that was synchronized with its environment, yet still detached from true existence. Life continued without the hinders from the past in a linear continuum. Adam and Doctor Spitzer looked out the window with their reflections fading against the sunlight.

"Why, Doctor? Why, the unpredictable evil? The pain, the loss…why, Beverly?" Adam asked, turning to him.

"No one will ever have the answers to those questions, Adam. We just have to keep moving forward. There's a cognitive dissonance, or logical disconnect if you will, from reality and beliefs. Seeking logic and knowledge has led us to this world of what you see below us. However, in the wonder of all our technological triumphs, we still don't have a freaking clue or even the answers to life's simplest and most important questions. We all have a hunger that is still left unsatisfied. In fact, we're the ones who are lost in this dream world that we call existence," Doctor Spitzer said with his hands behind his back.

"Why is that, Doc? What the hell is the point to all of this then?" Adam responded back, looking dimly into the doctor's eyes. "Why all the suffering? Why all the bloodshed? Why all the evil?"

"Living is the meaning to all of this. We cannot control the world around us, but we'll have to try and do our best to make it the best possible experience for ourselves and to everyone we share his small planet with. Our world is only a mirror looking back at us. Society is only a mere reflection of all of our combined accomplishments and deepest fears . The light lost deep within the darkness…"

"Doctor Imamu and I both felt something special within Beverly. A strength that couldn't be questioned," he continued. "I knew this when I first met her as a small child. Where she was beyond all of this. Her spirit was destined for greater things than what this world could offer her. I felt that on a deeper level but did not know how to express that to her. My entire career was to find the answers to life and how to mind works. What I found was that she was the answer to life." Spitzer said as he turned around to look at Jonathan sleeping in his bassinet. "She will always leave behind a legacy through the sacrifices she has made."

"Her sacrifice?" Adam said, not wanting to believe it as he turned toward his son.

"Beverly was strong, and she would want you to find your own inner strength during this time of grieving. You need to carry on, Adam, and continue her legacy by raising your child. I honestly believe that she isn't truly gone, though. She lives amongst all of us now. And hopefully, one day, you'll all be reunited. That is not my professional opinion, only my personal one. Take care of yourself and your son, Adam." Doctor Spitzer said, giving him a handshake and hug. "Carry on for all of us." Adam nodded, then walked back to the stroller and exited the office.

Adam walked into Central Park, rolling his son's stroller next to a park bench near a pond. He took a seat and watched the families and joggers crisscross along—their possibly predetermined pathways and trails—near the waterfront. Adam leaned over to grab sunscreen for his son from out of his backpack, then noticed some dry kibble on the ground. He looked back up and wiped a tear from his cheek as he stared forward at a beautiful bridge off in the distance, reflecting a perfect circle over the water's surface.

The skies were blue, the trees were full of leaves, and the sun warmed the air as the seasons continued on like clockwork. He took his son out of the stroller and cradled him in his arms. "I'll try my best to provide you with the life that your mother never had. I want you to always know that I'm here for you, my son. And know your mother loved you deeply and will always be proud of you no matter what path you take. Always choose to take the higher and righteous one."

"She is still alive, somewhere. I can feel it, Adam said to him, then stared out toward the reflection over the water.

Several feet ahead from where they sat, was an old oak tree with its branches spread outward. On top of one branch sat an owl staring down at them. Adam looked up at it and thought how out of the ordinary it was to see an owl during the day in Central Park.

Their eyes locked for a moment as he took comfort by this. The owl continued to hoot from above and flapped its wings before taking flight. It soared upward into the air and circled around them several times before going toward the reflection of the perfect circle in the water. The owl passed underneath the bridge, then flew up into the sky, vanishing into the sunlight.